"You were [...] *of hiding here on Diamond Cay,"* Kara said.

"The reason I'm hiding, and the reason I told you there's no future for us, is because I'm wanted by the police."

Max felt his jaw drop. He had convinced himself that it was a bad family situation Kara had run from. He'd figured that maybe, at the very worst, there was still a legal husband that would have to be dealt with. He hadn't even considered the possibility that she was running from the police.

"Wanted for what?" he asked.

She waved her hands. "Who knows? Trespassing. Destruction of private property. Accessory to murder."

Max shot from his chair. "Well, which is it, Kara? There's a hell of a big difference between trespassing and murder."

"*Accessory to* murder."

"Sorry. You'll have to excuse me. I get a little out of sorts when I learn the woman I love might be wanted for murder. *Accessory to* murder," he amended.

Dear Reader,

Sophisticated but sensitive, savvy yet unabashedly sentimental—that's today's woman, today's romance reader—you! And Silhouette Special Editions are written expressly to reward your quest for substantial, emotionally involving love stories.

So take a leisurely stroll under the cover's lavender arch into a garden of romantic delights. Pick and choose among titles if you must—we hope you'll soon equate all six Special Editions each month with consistently gratifying romantic reading.

Watch for sparkling new stories from your Silhouette favorites—Nora Roberts, Tracy Sinclair, Ginna Gray, Lindsay McKenna, Curtiss Ann Matlock, among others—along with some exciting newcomers to Silhouette, such as Karen Keast and Patricia Coughlin. Be on the lookout, too, for the new Silhouette Classics, a distinctive collection of bestselling Special Editions and Silhouette Intimate Moments now brought back to the stands—two each month—by popular demand.

On behalf of all the authors and editors of Special Editions,
Warmest wishes,

Leslie Kazanjian
Senior Editor

PATRICIA COUGHLIN
Shady Lady

Silhouette Special Edition

Published by Silhouette Books New York

America's Publisher of Contemporary Romance

SILHOUETTE BOOKS
300 East 42nd St., New York, N.Y. 10017

Copyright © 1988 by Patricia Madden Coughlin

ISBN: 0-373-09438-8

First Silhouette Books printing February 1988

America's Publisher of Contemporary Romance

Printed in the U.S.A.

PATRICIA COUGHLIN,

also known to romance fans as Liz Grady, lives in Rhode Island with her husband and two sons. A former schoolteacher, she says she started writing after her second son was born, to fill her hours at home. Having always read romances, she decided to try penning her own. Though she was duly astounded by the difficulty of her new hobby, her hard work paid off, and she accomplished the rare feat of having her very first manuscript published. For now, writing has replaced quilting, embroidery and other pastimes, and with a dozen published novels under her belt, the author hopes to be happily writing romances for a long time to come.

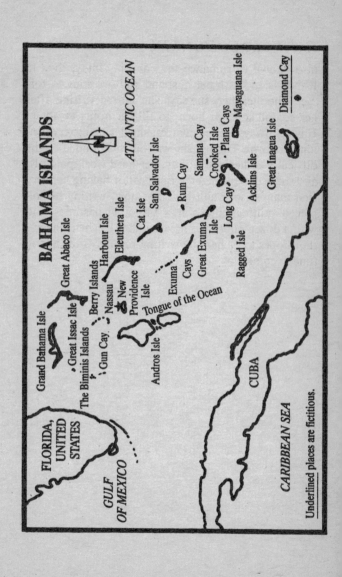

BAHAMA ISLANDS

FLORIDA, UNITED STATES

GULF OF MEXICO

Grand Bahama Isle

Great Issac Isle

The Biminis Islands

Gun Cay

Great Abaco Isle

Berry Islands

Harbour Isle

Nassau

New Providence Isle

Eleuthera Isle

Cat Isle

San Salvador Isle

ATLANTIC OCEAN

Andros Isle

Tongue of the Ocean

Exuma Cays

Great Exuma Isle

Rum Cay

Samana Cay

Crooked Isle

Long Cay

Plana Cays

Mayaguana Isle

Diamond Cay

Ragged Isle

Acklins Isle

Great Inagua Isle

CUBA

CARIBBEAN SEA

Underlined places are fictitious.

Prologue

The Nashua Greyhound bus terminal was always busiest early in the morning when a steady stream of commuters passed through on their way to Boston. It was a good time to get lost in the crowd. The young couple standing in the narrow wedge of space between the wall and a cigarette machine appeared to be attempting exactly that.

They were both young, the woman no more than twenty and the man perhaps several years older. She was tall and slender, with thick, dark hair that fell straight to the middle of her back. She was pretty enough without makeup to suggest that she'd be a beauty if she ever took the trouble to apply any. The man's hair was also dark, and long enough to curl over the turned up collar of the faded green army jacket he was wearing. Slung around his neck was a black-and-red plaid scarf, which he removed and gently looped around the woman's throat.

"There." John Haggerty smiled as he flipped the scarf end over end and gave it a tug to secure it on his sister's neck. "You'll need that for sure."

It took every ounce of acting ability Carolyn Haggerty possessed to force a sliver of a smile. "Is it really that cold in Chicago in March?"

"Sure. They don't call it the Windy City for nothing, you know." John's own smile had been weak, and now it drained from his face altogether, leaving him looking tired and older than his twenty-five years. "Besides, it might be a good idea to keep it tucked up around your chin when you're passing through the Boston terminal. Not like that!" he admonished with a chuckle as she draped the scarf across her face Mata Hari style. "For God's sake remember to keep a low profile and not do anything to call attention to yourself."

"I will," she promised, her facial muscles tightening almost imperceptibly. "If there's one thing I'm good at, it's slinking around and not calling attention to myself. After all, I've had almost a whole year of practice."

The shadows that drifted across her brother's face made Carolyn instantly regret the bitterness that had colored her last remark. This mess wasn't really his fault any more than it was hers. Or maybe it would be more accurate to say it was her fault as much as it was his. Either way, what was done was done and couldn't be undone no matter how much they both might wish it. It could only be "dealt with," as John, with his maddening practicality, insisted on putting it.

The static-riddled voice of the bus dispatcher, announcing that the 7:05 to Boston was now boarding, spared her any further thoughts of blame-placing. John lifted the heavy canvas bag that held all Carolyn's worldly goods and handed it to her. In that instant what had until then been only a plan, the subject of hushed discussions between the two of them, became reality, and her eyes filled with tears.

"John, I...I don't want to go."

"Damn it, Carolyn, this is a hell of a time to pull a stunt like this. You have to go. There's no other way."

"Maybe if we tried talking to the authorities...feeling them out anonymously..."

"No," snapped John.

Muttering under his breath, he jerked a handkerchief from his pocket and swiped at her eyes with it before stuffing it into her hand. Inside he was twisted up into so many knots that he didn't know if he'd be able to talk fast enough to get her on that damn bus. He felt guilty and bitter, angry at the way things were turning out, and frustrated by his inability to change them. He never should have let things go this far. He should have put a stop to Carolyn's involvement right at the start, the very first day she'd shown up at the office of the university's chapter of Students for a Democratic Society, insisting she wanted to help out. But who could have known things would turn out the way they had?

Him. At least he should have known. The cold truth of that still kept him awake nights. He had been on the inside, way inside, and he should have been able to see that things were about to explode. Unfortunately, he'd miscalculated. Badly. Once things started happening they'd raced out of control like a pyromaniac set loose with a box of matches. What was to have been a peaceful sit-in became an armed, violent occupation of the administration building. Carolyn, a virtual innocent, was implicated by her presence, slapped with the label "radical" and sought by more law enforcement personnel than he liked to think about.

The worst of it was that as a result she'd been swept into the underground along with him, migrating from safe-house to safe-house, coming into contact with others on the run. Now that the war was over that didn't mean only your average harmless draft dodger. It meant men and women who saw violence as the only means to overthrow a government they opposed and who had chosen an underground existence as a way of life. It also meant Dwight Billings, a fanatic if John had ever met one.

Lately Billings's interest in John's kid sister had been intensifying. A few nights before, despite all his warnings to Carolyn, he'd found the two of them alone again. Maybe it was innocent, and maybe she was smart enough not to be taken in by Billings's snakelike charm, but John wasn't going to bank on any maybes. The situation was too dangerous, for Carolyn and for John himself. That's why he'd finally made the decision to get her out, regardless of the risks involved, and that was also why, tears or no tears, she had to get on that bus.

"This is the only way," he said finally, firmly. "You have to trust me."

"I do. but—"

"No buts. Do you have the ID I gave you?"

"Yes. And I'd still like to know how you managed to—"

"Yeah, I know you would," he broke in, "and maybe someday I'll have time to tell you all about it. But not now. As soon as you get to Chicago I want you to call the man whose name and number I wrote down for you. He'll help you find a place to stay and a job."

A confused frown tugged at the edges of Carolyn's mouth. "But who is this guy? Is this just another safe-house like—"

"No." He cut her off with a quick shake of his head. "It will be safe all right, but very different from the places you've been staying lately. You don't have to worry. You can trust Victor, and I'll be in touch as soon as I can...Kara." When she wrinkled her nose at the unfamiliar name, he shrugged. "Better get used to it, honey. From now on you're Kara McFarland."

"I suppose it could be worse," she sighed. "At least Kara sounds a little like my real name."

"Exactly. I could have given you the other ID—the one made out to Divinia Lucanbush." The sound of her laughter lifted his spirits a little, and he threw his arm around her shoulders and squeezed. "That's more like it. You're going to be okay, pumpkin."

Pumpkin. Now, that name was familiar to her. It was a nickname he'd called her since they were kids. Once it had made her cringe, but now...now her eyes misted with longing for a part of her life gone forever. The tears made it difficult for her to see as John steered her through the crowded terminal. A safe distance away from the line of ticket-holders he halted, gathering her close for one last brief, nonattention-attracting hug. Then he pointed her in the direction of the bus and disappeared.

Chapter One

Something was wrong. Kara McFarland knew it the instant she rode up to her small bungalow on the northernmost point of Diamond Cay. As usual when she arrived home from work at this ungodly hour of 3:00 a.m. the only sound to be heard was the gentle roar of the surf rolling onto the private beach beyond the house, and the only light was the narrow beam from the headlight anchored to the front fender of her bike. Still, it wasn't anything she'd seen or heard that had put her on edge. It was more of a feeling, and to Kara that made it even more imperative that she pay attention to it. During the past thirteen or so years she had learned to rely on her feelings out of necessity. Most of the time they were all she had.

Climbing off the bike, she leaned it against one of the mango trees that bordered the wooden walk, leaving the headlight on. Ordinarily she would have switched it off and let the long years of habit guide her steps to the front door, which, like that of many island houses, faced the sea instead of the road. But not tonight. Walking even that short distance in the dark with these shivers dancing a warning along her spine would have been taking a chance, and Kara never took chances, not even small ones.

Unlocking the door, she stepped inside and began a cautious tour of the whole house, flicking on lights as she went. It didn't take long. The bungalow, originally intended as servants' quarters for the main house next door, consisted of a tiny kitchen, an almost equally tiny bedroom and a decent size living room-dining area made to look even larger by the patio doors that opened onto a private terrace. The size suited Kara fine. She favored a place she could keep spit-shined in the thirty or so minutes she saw fit to devote to housekeeping each week.

Satisfied that no one was lurking behind the rattan sofa or potted hibiscus, Kara released the breath she hadn't been aware she was holding and went back outside to put her bike away. Feelings weren't always on target, she knew, and this one had been a long shot. The dangerous, unexpected and out-of-the-ordinary just did not happen on Diamond Cay. Which is exactly why she chose to live on this small island on the southern outskirts of the Bahamas, a one-hundred-and-seventy-acre patch of earth lacking televisions and shopping malls and a great many other things most women born and bred in a city the size of Boston would consider necessities.

It wasn't that she was an anticivilization type. After leaving college in a hurry during her freshman year she'd spent almost twelve months living on a series of small farms throughout New England, plenty long enough to flush any idealistic back-to-nature impulses from her system. At thirty-one Kara had no quarrel with the conveniences a fast-paced society had to offer. Circumstances simply forced her to live without most of them.

Instead she was blessed with pleasures and comforts of a different sort. Such as having a deserted, pink-sand beach right outside her door and being able to spend all day sunning herself on it if she chose to. She enjoyed being able to swim year-round in the warm, crystal-blue waters of the Atlantic and being on a friendly, first-name basis with each and every one of the small island's other inhabitants. What Kara loved most about Diamond Cay, though, was that she was free here. And if she wanted to remain free, which she most assuredly did, she knew Diamond Cay was the safest place for her to be.

The entire island, including her bungalow and the graceful stucco house next door, was the property of Victor Hazard. A man still as driven at sixty as he must have been at twenty, Victor rarely took time off from his Chicago-based business empire to visit the island. Occasionally during the five years Kara had lived here he'd permitted friends to use the luxurious retreat originally built by his grandfather, always courteously informing Kara first so she wouldn't be alarmed to discover she had temporary neighbors.

The two houses stood alone on the island's northern point, surrounded by dense tropical foliage. There were several other modest bungalows closer to the island's center, but aside from that, everyone who resided on Diamond Cay lived and worked at the exclusive resort on the western coast. Even Anne Hazard, who several years ago had assumed the resort operation from her father, preferred living there to the isolation of the family home. Her choice pleased Kara. She and Anne had become good friends, but Kara still wouldn't have liked living so close to the bustle of people and excitement that seemed to constantly swirl around the other woman. Through the years she'd grown accustomed to spending time alone, and she liked it that way, despite an occasional night like tonight when it would be reassuring to have a neighbor within shouting distance.

Stowing her bike in the small alcove between the two houses, she stood for a moment in the circle of brightness shed by the outdoor floodlight and gazed at the Hazard place. Everything appeared to be as it should over there as well, and Kara finally turned to go inside, resolving to ignore the still itchy sensation between her shoulder blades.

It was warm for a late February night, and she changed from her jeans and sweater into a loose cotton nightshirt before strolling into the kitchen and pulling a half-full bottle of Chardonnay from the small refrigerator. She seldom drank socially and never while at work as manager of the Shady Lady, the least formal of the island's nightspots. But a glass of wine and a few minutes at the keyboard were exactly what she needed tonight in order to unwind enough to fall asleep.

That was another advantage of living way out here alone: there were no neighbors to complain that she was disturbing them when her topsy-turvy schedule had her running the blender or banging the keys at an hour when most people were asleep. Conversely, there was no one to bother her with normal activity noise when, after a particularly hectic night, she slept until past noon.

After some deliberation she chose a Scott Joplin tape from the impressive collection she'd acquired by mail and slid it into the cassette player, which had also been selected from one of the mail-order catalogues overflowing the magazine rack in the corner. The Shady Lady featured jazz and rhythm and blues, and after a long night of it Kara craved a musical change of pace. Besides, pitting her meager, self-taught talents against Joplin's ragtime mastery was sure to either wear her out or discourage her very quickly, and she'd soon be ready to call it a night.

Fishing out the proper sheet music from the stack beside her, she switched on the Casio keyboard and waited with hands poised for the first jubilant notes to fill the room. She would have preferred a real piano, even if it meant making space by chucking the round glass-topped table and eating off a tray, but so far the only one she'd seen in any catalogue would cost as much to have shipped to the island as it did to buy. The Casio was a sensible, economical alternative.

"The Maple Leaf Rag" began with a staccato burst of high notes, and this time Kara missed only one before she and Joplin merged, skating through the body of the piece and then surging together on the upbeat finale. When the music ended she laughed out loud with exhilaration. She was really getting better at this. Much better than she'd

ever been at that oil painting correspondence course. Or
the learn-at-home karate program. To progress at karate,
Kara had discovered after impulsively investing in the in-
struction books and tapes and the outfit, you really needed
an opponent. Squaring off against a kitchen chair just
hadn't worked in eliciting the right mind set. So she had
cheerfully thrown in the towel and given all the barely used
paraphernalia to Anne, who promptly organized a begin-
ners' class at the resort gym. Kara had always preferred
things she could accomplish by herself anyway.

"Leola," the second piece on the tape, started more
slowly but soon escalated to an intricate series of notes she
was having trouble mastering. She was absorbed in her effort, cheating a little by letting her gaze dart from the music to the keyboard, when a dark shadow suddenly fell
across both.

Kara screamed as she leaped from the seat. Whirling
around, she came face to face with a man she'd never seen
before. Her gaze jerked quickly from his unsnapped jeans
to his bare chest, then froze as it encountered a fierce
expression she thought best not to dissect too closely. She
was already frightened enough. So frightened it took her
a few seconds to register the fact that he was shouting at
her. At least it looked as if he was shouting. Between the
blood pounding in her head and the sound of Scott Joplin
jauntily playing on without her, she couldn't actually hear
a single word that gushed from the man's snarling lips.

For a moment she continued to stare at him in panic-
stricken silence, a second scream locked deep in her throat.
Unbidden, her gaze skittered from his face to the half-open
zipper and unsnapped front of his pants, and sweat broke
out on her back at the unavoidable thought of what they
might forebode. Hastily she forced her eyes back up to
meet his.

His lips were still moving, this time around something
that looked decidedly obscene. Kara was frantically de-
bating the merits of bolting when his hand shot toward the
stereo, his fingers jabbing wildly, pushing buttons and
spinning dials until he finally managed to subdue it. That

left only the ear-splitting whine of the keyboard, which Kara dealt with automatically. Then there was silence. That is, if you didn't count the raspy, shuddering breaths her intruder was having trouble bringing under control.

Unconsciously Kara wrapped her arms across her chest as her mind was assaulted by a host of possible explanations for his being there—all of them unsettling. And as always when she was confronting the unknown or unexpected, an icy sense of apprehension sliced through her, filling her with the fear that she'd finally run out of luck.

As he stood there panting, his chest heaving, she detected a hint of expectancy in his wild-eyed stare, as if he expected her to be the first one to speak.

"I'm sorry." She had to force the words out, willing herself to affect the sort of calm, unthreatening tone she would use with a wounded animal. "I...I didn't quite hear what you were saying."

"How could you?" he countered harshly. "What I said is, what the hell do you think you're doing?"

"Oh."

Something in his stance, his expression, the fact that he was a great deal bigger than she was, cautioned Kara against just coming out and ordering him out of her house. The island security jeep would eventually be by on routine patrol. Until she heard it approach she had no choice but to play along as calmly as she could and not do anything to rile him any more than he was already riled.

"I was playing the piano," she explained.

He was looking at her as if she were the crazy one, his eyes so wide that she could see flecks of amber in their jade depths. His hands remained clenched at his sides. She was no expert on body language, but that didn't strike her as a good sign.

"Well, not the piano exactly," she amended hurriedly. "It's like a piano, but it's actually an electronic keyboard."

"Lady, I don't give a damn if it's an electronic hummingbird. Do you have any idea what time it is?"

Her gaze quickly shifted to the clock behind him. "It's three fifty-seven."

"Almost four."

"That's correct."

"A.M.," he growled emphatically.

"Right again."

"Are you out of your mind?"

"Am I out of my mind?" she echoed, pondering the safest way to answer that.

"No sane person plays the piano at four in the morning—especially not when they stink at it as badly as you do."

"I do not stink at it," Kara countered with automatic indignation, then halted.

Of course. Like lightning it struck her that he wasn't insane, simply furious. About the volume of the music, apparently. If she hadn't been so frightened she would have understood that right away. She felt a strong wave of relief begin to wash away the tension knotted inside her. With his enraged expression cooled a bit, the man before her didn't look nearly as wild as he had at first. Also, now that she thought about it in context, his unsnapped pants and general dishevelment might simply indicate that he'd jumped out of bed in a hurry. A possibility that raised more questions in Kara's mind than it answered.

"Who are you?" she demanded, giving voice to the question that seemed most pertinent.

"None of your business."

She glared back at him with a mingling of impatience and disbelief. "None of my business? You're standing in my house, screaming at me about how loudly I choose to play my music, and you say it's none of my business who you are?" She suddenly remembered the unusual care she'd taken to lock the doors before sitting down to play. "How did you get in here, anyway?"

"The window," he replied just as she turned and saw the raised screen behind her.

"I don't believe it," she muttered, moving to slam it shut before any more bugs checked in. "That's breaking and entering."

The man shrugged. "I'd say it was more like self-defense. Drastic situations call for drastic measures. Did you expect me to lie awake the rest of the night hoping your fingers cramped?"

"You could have knocked."

"I did. Obviously you couldn't hear it over that racket."

Instinctively Kara ducked as he swung his arm, but he was only using it to gesture at the stereo speakers, leaving no question about which "racket" he was referring to. She quickly straightened, feeling silly and resentful. She didn't like his smirking sarcasm any better than she did his shouting.

"Only a tasteless...jerk," she informed him, "would refer to Scott Joplin's music as a racket."

"I wasn't referring to Joplin's. I was referring to yours."

She tucked her wounded pride behind a smug smile. "That's why I need so much practice."

"You won't get any argument from me on that score. Just see that you don't get it while I'm trying to sleep."

Feeling too irritated to be civil, Kara snapped, "Sorry, but it so happens I like to play at four in the morning. I do it often."

He shook his head and smiled, a slight angling of his lips that somehow managed to convey more menace than humor. "Not as long as I'm here you don't."

Something prompted Kara to sidle a cautious half-step closer to the door before responding. "Are you threatening me?"

"Of course not." His silky tone sharpened abruptly. "I'm threatening your electronic hummingbird. I'm going back to bed now, and if I hear one more tortured note out of that thing tonight, I'm going to come back here and silence it permanently—with a burial at sea."

"Back to bed where?" Kara asked as soon as he finished ranting. She was feeling a little braver—and a lot more curious—now that she knew he hadn't forced his way in here to wreak mayhem. When he ignored her question, she added, "In case you're not aware of it, this is a private island. Camping out anywhere on it is forbidden. You'll be arrested and tossed off as soon as the patrol jeep spots you."

His mouth quirked into a wry smile. "Thanks for your concern, but I'm not camping out."

"Then where—" Kara broke off to examine him through narrowed eyes. No, there was no way this man could be a guest at the resort. Even if he'd been wearing a shirt, Kara was certain there wouldn't be a designer logo on it, and besides, his hair was all wrong. She'd seen enough of the standard meticulously, expensively casual hairstyle common to super-rich males to recognize it anywhere. This man's disheveled mane of dark hair spoke more of disinterest than wealth.

He grinned at her bewildered expression. "As a matter of fact," he drawled, "I'm sleeping in a very comfortable bed right next door. Or at least I was until you suddenly felt inspired to light up the night with sound."

Next door? Kara's mind balked at the idea. Still, on the remote chance that he was a friend of Victor's...

"I'm sorry," she told him, experiencing her first twinge of remorse over the whole episode. "Usually there isn't anyone around here for me to disturb. I didn't realize anyone was staying next door."

He didn't seem to comprehend that that was his cue to explain how he happened to be there. Or else he'd really meant it when he said it was none of her business.

"Sometimes," she continued, when it became obvious he had no intention of explaining, "playing helps me unwind so I can sleep."

"Have you ever heard of warm milk?"

"Have you ever heard of earplugs?"

"Have you ever heard of being fined for disturbing the peace?"

"Not on Diamond Cay," Kara volleyed with a triumphant lilt. Enough pussyfooting. "So, are you a friend of Victor's?"

"Victor?"

"Hazard," she supplied, glancing at him suspiciously.

"Oh, you mean the guy who owns the island."

"As well as the house you're staying in—yes."

"No."

"Then exactly how did you get a key to his house?" she pressed, wondering if he really had permission to be there after all.

He paused, and for a few seconds Kara thought he wasn't going to answer that question, either. Finally, with a shrug, he muttered, "Let's just say I'm a friend of a friend of Hazard's."

That told her a lot. "Usually he lets me know in advance if someone will be staying over there," she explained. "It helps to avoid scenes such as this one."

She decided he must practice that careless shrug. No one was that good at it naturally.

"I guess you'll have to take that up with him," he said. "Believe me, I would have told you myself if I'd known it would avoid this."

"I am sorry about the music," she apologized again, with more sincerity this time. "It won't happen again while you're here." Then, with studied offhandedness, she inquired, "How long did you say you'll be staying?"

"I didn't."

"Oh. Well, then. At any rate, how long will you be staying?"

"I haven't decided."

Forthcoming he wasn't. If direct questions weren't going to yield any more information than a subtle approach had, she would simply have to come up with something else. Maybe he was more of a monkey-see-monkey-do sort of person. On impulse she extended her right hand to him.

"As long as we're going to be neighbors for a while, we might as well be friends. I'm Kara McFarland."

He took her hand with a faintly quizzical grimace, as if he'd never been called on to introduce himself before or as if telling her his name was a matter of national security, for heaven's sake. At least while he was vacillating he gave her hand the sort of firm, unsolicitous shake Kara liked from a man.

"My name's Max," he revealed eventually.

"Max...?" Kara countered in a leading manner.

He dropped her hand, giving her another odd, questioning look. "Just Max will do. And I think I should warn you that I came here to be alone, and I expect to be left that way."

His tone wasn't cold exactly, but it was sure a long way from warm. For no good reason Kara felt her cheeks coloring, as if she'd been rebuffed for coming on to him instead of making an attempt to be cordial. She folded her arms stiffly across her chest.

"Don't worry," she assured him, "if I were interested in neighborly coffee klatches, I wouldn't have moved way out here in the first place."

"Then we should get along perfectly."

"Perfectly."

He smiled as he turned to leave, and as much as it galled Kara to admit it, when he wasn't shouting or sneering, the man had a certain rough appeal. Not that she was interested. But if she had been, and if she hadn't discovered firsthand what a rude recluse he was, she might have been intrigued by his eyes—the greenest she'd ever seen—and by that pouty bottom lip that could unexpectedly and magically soften the harshly etched lines of his face. Then there was also the matter of his body. She'd had a nice, long, close-up look at it tonight, and it just happened to be the sort that always caught her eye—perfect. So it was probably just as well they weren't going to get too friendly. Perfect men always turned out to be so flawed.

"Good night," he said at the door.

On principle Kara didn't answer. She simply stood there with her arms still folded like a marine drill sergeant until he was gone. It *had* been a good night until he'd descended on her. Her movements were jerky with unvented anger as she checked to make sure all the right switches were turned off on the stereo and keyboard. Burial at sea, indeed. It would serve him right if she called his bluff. On the other hand, she quite literally owed her life to Victor Hazard, and there was no way she was going to embarrass him by being rude to a friend of a friend to whom he'd seen fit to extend his hospitality. Even if the man was a jerk.

Besides, she really ought to get some sleep. First thing in the morning she planned to pay a visit to Anne Hazard's office and find out a few things about Mr. Max whatever-his-name-was. Such as what he had to hide.

Chapter Two

Max's lungs felt as if he were breathing fire. And his back hurt. Almost as much as his legs did. Hell, he hurt all over, and he still had at least a mile to run before he made it back to the house. What a miserable way to start the day.

If he was still alive when he reached the house, he was definitely going to treat himself to a cigarette. Just one, and then he could handle the rest of the day cold turkey. Whoever said you shouldn't have even one when you were trying to quit had never dragged himself out of bed at dawn and tried to run five miles without so much as a cup of coffee for fuel. He deserved a cigarette. Maybe it would even make the shin splints more bearable.

How was it possible to get so out of shape so quickly? He didn't look out of shape, but the throbbing in his muscles was proof that he was, and it irritated him. Sure he knew he hadn't been eating or sleeping right for weeks now—well, months, actually—but he hadn't expected a little jog to make him feel as if he were being stretched on a rack. It had to be age. At the moment he felt twice his almost forty years. And sounded even worse, he thought, listening with disgust to his breath being ripped from his lungs with each step. From the sound of it, the very last thing he needed was a cigarette, even if he did want one more than he wanted his next gasp of hot air.

It occurred to Max as he drove himself forward, willing one foot to land in front of the other, that quitting smoking made a nice, neat metaphor for his reason for being here in the first place. It all had to do with control. Either you were in control of your life or you weren't. And if you weren't, then you bounced and danced every time someone jerked one of your strings. Max was tired of dancing. No matter what it took he was going to leave this damn island stronger and tougher than ever, and he was going to prove to himself and anyone else still interested that he was back in control.

The first step toward exerting control was not to give in to this craving for a cigarette. It would be tough, but he could hack it. After all, if he'd been able to keep from weakening and lighting one up after tangling with that witch next door at four this morning, getting through the rest of the day ought to be a breeze.

Ignoring the pain in his stiff muscles, Max quickened the pace a beat as the rambling white stucco house loomed into view up ahead. The sun was just rising over the tallest peak of the red tile roof, creating a palette of fiery colors that bled into each other, like a volcano erupting against the cobalt-blue sky. He had to hand it to Victor Hazard, he'd found the perfect location for a getaway spot.

The house itself was a beauty. Max had seen some ingeniously designed oceanfront homes back in California, but none that topped this. Louie, his business manager and the friend who had arranged for him to stay here, hadn't been exaggerating when he said this place redefined the word *private*. The only evidence that there was other life on the island was the cottage next door, and even that was strategically located so it faced the opposite direction, maximizing the privacy of each dwelling.

Inside the Hazard house were more rooms than Max had
felt energetic enough to explore when he'd arrived late last
night. They were arranged on several sprawling levels
connected by scattered, open staircases, with the walls
facing the water constructed almost entirely of glass. Outside, the same feeling of random spaciousness was echoed
in a maze of terraced patios and decks, the final one designed so that it was literally overhanging the blue-green
waters of the Atlantic ocean.

Maybe he'd eat breakfast out there, Max thought as he
dragged himself up the flagstone steps leading from the
beach to the house. Eating ought to keep his mind off
smoking for a while. He started moving a little faster in
anticipation, then slowed, grimacing as he remembered
that the closest thing to food he'd been able to find in the
entire place was a couple of six-packs of German beer in
the refrigerator. Last night he'd been too tired to care, but
right now he was feeling hungry enough to wish he hadn't
been quite so adamant about telling Louie he would take
care of everything himself. He'd shortsightedly thought
that he'd be better off without overly solicitous house-
hold help lurking around while he was trying to work.

Refusing to succumb to the urge to collapse on one of
the padded chaise longues he passed along the way, he
ambled into the kitchen and made another quick inspec-
tion of the cupboards, as if something might have grown
in them overnight. Nothing had. With mounting annoyance he continued to survey one bare shelf after another,
finding only the same extensive assortment of spices in
fancy glass jars that had been there last night. He slammed
the door of the final cupboard with a disgusted oath.
You'd think that whoever was gourmet enough to stock
crap like lemon salt and mint extract could have left behind a box of stale crackers.

With a resigned sigh he crossed to the refrigerator and
pulled out a beer. At least he was lucky enough to locate
the bottle opener in the first drawer he checked. Prying off
the cap, he swallowed half the contents of the bottle in one
gulp. It wasn't ham and eggs, but it beat an empty belly

any day. Later he would have to see about having some food delivered. Right now he was itching to get started. After grabbing a second beer, he detoured through the front hallway to collect his guitar and notebook and made his way back outside.

Settling into a chair on the deck, he arranged his beer and the open notebook on the low glass-topped table in front of him. The notebook was an old one he'd found buried in the bottom of a drawer when he was packing to come here. About seven years old to be exact, full of scribbled line fragments and musical charts, full of memories. Good memories. Memories from the days when his fingers drifting across the strings had always felt right, and the words to go with the feelings had always run from his brain faster than he could push the pencil across the paper to capture them.

He'd brought the notebook with him as a sort of talisman. In general he considered good-luck charms and omens about as reliable as the daily horoscope, but under the circumstances he wasn't about to deny help from any quarter whatsoever. Besides, having the notebook around made him feel good, and these days that alone was a minor miracle. It reminded him that when it came to writing songs, he'd been able to do it once—and do it damn well— and he could do it again. He simply had to relax and let it happen.

Idly he strummed the wire strings, not aiming for even the simplest melody, just waiting. God, it was getting hot already. Maybe he'd be more comfortable working inside. No. That was just an excuse to get up, to move, to put off the moment of truth a little while longer. And for no good reason. Writing music took time. He of all people should know that. There was no cause to panic just because there wasn't a damn note or line in his head. If he just sat here and didn't press, it would come.

He worked the strings with his fingers again, then broke off abruptly to reach for the fresh beer and took a swig. Of course beer on an empty stomach probably wasn't helping the creative process any. Immediately Max's lips twisted with grim self-deprecation. It probably wasn't hurting, either. After all, beer for breakfast had never hindered him back when writing music had been as natural and persistent as breathing. Back before he'd ceased being simply a musician and become a star, blessed and cursed with all that that entailed.

He took another drink before putting the bottle aside to thumb through the notebook, trying hard not to acknowledge the fine edge of frustration already slicing across his nerves, making his chest burn with the ingrained desire for a drag of warm, calming smoke. The pack of cigarettes was out of his shirt pocket before he remembered he'd quit, that he was only carrying them around to prove he didn't have to have one just because they were there. Vexed that he'd ever decided to give them up in the first place, he hurled the pack onto the table so forcefully that a few cigarettes scattered free, fanning temptingly across the surface of the glass.

Max closed his eyes, instantly filled with the restless urge to get up and walk away. Instead he forced his attention back to the well-loved and time-scarred instrument in his lap. Today even the familiar feel of it in his hands wasn't producing the same sense of tranquility it usually did. Desperation was beginning to creep in, making his fingers feel stiff and awkward as they cradled it. Maybe playing something would help him loosen up. Not something of his, he decided. He was never able to play his own stuff without feeling the inclination to refine and polish, even years after a song had proven a critical and financial success. No, instead he would play something he wished he'd written, something rowdy and not too complicated so his subconscious mind would be free to wander.

He plunged into "Bad Moon Rising" and realized instantly that it was the right choice. His fingers danced over the strings effortlessly. Midway through the chorus he leaned back, propped his foot up on the table and started singing along. His voice sounded as it always did to him, rusty, a little off-key and far too rough around the edges to be heard outside the privacy of the shower. Luckily for his career, millions of people disagreed. When he'd cut his first album several years ago critics hailed it as a voice that had been "lived in—and hard living at that." Max hadn't been able to argue with the assessment then, and he supposed it was even more true today.

Without pausing when the song ended, he moved into the opening riff of "Proud Mary" keeping it up-tempo. This was the music that had fueled his desire to be a songwriter, the sound he'd tried to absorb and make his own, and he still loved it. He was flying high by the time he ripped into Neil Young's "Saddle Up The Palomino," his voice strong as it rasped through the early-morning quiet. The pressure and frustration were beginning to recede. Soon, soon, if he stayed loose and stayed focused, the music would start to flow from inside him.

At first when Max noticed his ornery neighbor come whipping around the corner of her small house, he figured she was heading for the beach and he kept right on playing, taking care to direct his gaze downward so he wouldn't be forced to say hello. Then she turned and started up the steps to the deck where he was sitting, and he groaned inside. Hadn't he made it clear enough last night that he didn't want to be bothered?

Still playing, he raised his head to scowl at her as she approached. He came to the rapid conclusion that this wasn't to be a social call. Max wasn't sure what was eating her, but he could almost hear the bell sound for round two. For one thing she was marching, literally *marching* up those steps, her expression clearly indignant. It also looked as if she'd dragged on that yellow robe in a big hurry. One sleeve was bunched up around her elbow, and the tie was comically lopsided. There was nothing comical about her legs though, Max mused as his gaze took in the generous length of firm, tanned thigh the short robe left exposed.

Odd that he hadn't noticed legs that great last night. But then, last night he hadn't been in a mood to notice much about . . . what had she said her name was? Karen? Carol? Kara, that was it. Now he made a point of taking a good hard look from head to toe and was surprised to find that he liked what he saw. True, she didn't have either of the qualities he usually looked for first in a woman—blond hair and big boobs—but she looked nice just the same. She looked healthy and strong, as if she spent a lot of time outdoors, and not just lolling on the beach.

She also looked intelligent, although he couldn't define exactly why. For sure it didn't have anything to do with that very soft-looking mouth; or with the shiny dark hair that was long and tousled about her face and shoulders. She must have had her hair bound up somehow last night or he definitely would have remembered it. Maybe it was her eyes that gave an impression of perceptiveness. They were appealingly wide and colored a clear, liquid blue, he observed as she drew within ten or so feet. Max couldn't believe he hadn't noticed all this last night. Either he'd been even more tired than he'd thought or the sunlight was working miracles. This was a very pretty woman. Too bad she was obviously such a bitch.

Max deliberately held the last note he played, letting it twang into silence a full five seconds after she'd come to a halt directly in front of him. He gave an obligatory nod. "Good morning."

"I guess that all depends," she snapped. "Personally I'm one of those people who likes to sleep until the obscene hour of, oh, say six or seven a.m."

This wasn't the greeting Max had expected. Last night he'd caught her off guard, scared her really, in a way he'd sort of regretted afterward. But he'd thought that surely now, with him sitting in full sunlight, a guitar in his hands, she would have to recognize him. He expected that familiar, inevitable look of surprise to slowly light her face. She'd stammer and looked awed; he'd be as gracious and patient as possible before telling her he really had to get back to work. But none of that was happening. Instead of stammering, she was bitching at him as if she had no idea who he was. It was a situation that left Max not knowing quite how to react.

Finally he lifted one shoulder just enough to convey his total indifference to her sleeping habits and asked softly, "Who's stopping you?"

"Oh, please, spare me the innocent routine. I know exactly what you're up to."

"You do, huh?"

"Of course. An idiot could figure it out."

"I guess that makes you as qualified as anybody to explain it, so why don't you go ahead?"

She lifted her chin, which gave the impression that she was looking down her nose at him, and smiled as if to say that she was civilized enough to ignore his pettiness. To Max the look was as provoking as a red flag waved at a bull, making him wonder just how petty he was going to have to get to send her running.

"You're paying me back for disturbing your sleep last night," she announced. "*Unknowingly* disturbing your sleep, I might add, which is more than you can say for this blatant, childish act of revenge."

Max combed his fingers through his hair and squinted at her. "You think I'm sitting here playing just to get back at you for last night?"

"Isn't it rather obvious?"

"Must be," he conceded with a dry inflection. The fact that she'd been the furthest thing from his mind when he sat down to play didn't stop him from deriving a small amount of nasty satisfaction from having evened the score without even trying. "Not a very fun way to be jolted awake, is it?"

She rolled her big blue eyes, folding her arms across her chest in a way that caused Max to upgrade his initial appraisal of her breasts.

"I thought I'd already acknowledged that last night," she said, "at the same time that I apologized. Obviously that wasn't good enough for you. So, now that you've enjoyed your little moment of retaliation, do you suppose we could call a real truce?"

"Why not?" Max was for anything that would let him get back to work quickly.

"Good. I promise not to turn on the keyboard after midnight, and you agree to keep it down until at least, shall we say, nine a.m.?"

"Yeah, sure." Max started to nod automatically, eager to be rid of her. Then he realized what he was agreeing to, and his eyes narrowed in angry disbelief. "What do you mean nine a.m.? I plan to have already put in a couple of hours work by that time."

She eyed the guitar in his hands with a mingling of amusement and skepticism that rankled Max more than it should have.

"Work?" she queried.

He stared back at her. "That's right."

"No," she contradicted, shaking her head with a maddening little smile. "I'm afraid that's wrong. You see, I work late nights, and I really need to get some sleep in the morning. Now, I realize that you're here as Victor's guest, but I'm sure he would appreciate your cooperation as much as I would."

"Can it, lady," Max growled. "You're not going to manipulate me into doing what you want by appealing to my sense of decency. I don't have one."

"Then maybe I can appeal to your common sense," she shot back, her voice rising, "or don't you have any of that, either? It's not even seven o'clock in the morning yet. Normal people don't start banging away on a guitar before they've even had breakfast."

Max nodded at the empty beer bottles on the table. "I've had breakfast."

"So I see," she responded, her lips curving with distaste as she followed the direction of his gaze. "Maybe that explains this eccentric compulsion of yours to start the day with a Hank Williams impression."

"Hank Williams?" Max echoed, her stupid mistake and derisive tone pushing him to the limits of his patience.

She smiled, a bogus smile if he'd ever seen one, and regarded him with eyes that were impossibly wide.

"Isn't that who you were pretending to be?"

She was baiting him, Max realized, intentionally baiting him. And then everything began to fall into place. Of course. It all fit, her playing the piano at an hour sure to make him come running in protest, then pretending not to recognize him. She probably figured that was real innovative and sure to intrigue him. When it didn't work she grabbed the first flimsy excuse she could to come trotting over here for another encounter.

You would think he'd been on the receiving end of enough outrageous come-ons not to be taken in by an aging groupie, even a pretty one. But it looked as if that was exactly what had happened. She must have found out he'd be staying here—somehow her kind always did—then planned this elaborate charade. Not that he had any ironclad objection to groupies. They served a purpose from time to time.

Like maybe right now, Max thought with a flash of inspiration brought on by another long look at her legs. Maybe giving his new neighbor what she was after was just what he needed to work off some of his own edginess. A small voice inside attempted to remind him that he'd already tried that remedy for easing his frustration before leaving L.A.—numerous times with numerous partners. It hadn't worked. Max choked off the small inner voice. True, to encourage her in any way would be to invite future interruptions, guaranteed to become a chronic pain in the butt with her living right next door. That's why he was going to have to spell it out for her afterward that this was a one-shot deal. And do it in a no-nonsense way sure to keep her and her long legs on her own side of the fence for the rest of his stay.

He lifted the edges of his mouth to unfurl a slow smile. "Hank Williams. Now, how did you know that's who I was pretending to be?"

She shrugged impatiently. "Lucky guess."

"Oh, I don't believe that." Max put the guitar aside and stood, rolling his shoulders in a lazy stretch. "I'll bet you're a big country music fan."

"Actually it gives me a headache."

Laughing softly, he stepped closer to her. "How about country singers? Do they make your head ache, too?"

"I don't know," she responded, giving him a strange look. "I don't know any country singers."

"Really? I would have guessed that you know lots of them . . . real well, too."

He was close enough now to touch her, and he did, letting his fingers stroke her cheek. She flinched and tilted her head out of reach. Another step would bring his body close enough to brush against hers. As he took that step Max shifted a little to the right, positioning himself between her and the steps.

"Look, Max," she said, darting backward until the deck railing brought her up short, "I really only came over here to ask you to stop playing so loudly."

"And I'm willing to do exactly that."

She nodded, her expression a study in wariness and uncertainty. Max had to hand it to her, she was handling her role perfectly.

"Well, good," she said. "Thank you. I'll be going then."

Max casually snagged her arms as she tried to move around him. "What's the hurry?"

"N-nothing. I'm just not really awake enough for a discussion of music."

"Of course not. It was thoughtless of me to wake you up in the first place. Bed is exactly where a woman like you belongs at this time of the morning." He'd been easily overpowering her subtle, obligatory attempt to free herself from his grasp. Now he slid his fingers down the soft skin of her inner arm to clasp her hand, the movement slow and skillful. "Why don't you come inside with me, Kara, and we'll talk it over?"

He smiled at her with confidence. It was a smile that never failed, a smile that said it was time to cut the crap and get down to what was uppermost on both their minds. Instead of melting into a responsive little smile of her own, however, Kara ripped her hand free and scooted past him. Max was too startled to try to stop her until she was

halfway down the steps. Then she turned back to face him
with such an outraged expression that something cautioned him to stay right where he was.

"I'm not going to chase you," he warned, his tone
matter-of-fact, almost uninterested.

"Good, because I don't want you anywhere near me."

Max countered with a harsh laugh of disbelief. "Really?
Then what the hell did you come over here for?"

"I told you—to ask you to keep the noise down."

"Oh, yes. Right." He laughed again. "Listen, honey, I
don't know what kind of game you're playing, but I'm already tired of it."

She shook her head slowly. "You're unbelievable."

"Don't you think that kind of compliment is a little
premature?"

"No, what I think is that you're crazy."

"I'm also through sparring with you." Turning away, he
reached for his guitar, at the same time arrowing a dismissive glance back over his shoulder. "That's your cue to
leave, baby. And this time try staying away."

"Gladly," she shot back. "As long as you abide by the
terms of our agreement."

"That's going to be tough to do, seeing as how we don't
have one."

Max settled back into his chair and flipped through the
notebook while surreptitiously watching her reaction to his
announcement. Flustered. Good. And apparently at a loss
for words. Even better.

Eventually she gave the belt on her robe a businesslike
little tug and cleared her throat. "You realize, of course,
that this whole thing is absolutely ridiculous. I'm sure that
once you've had a chance to think it over, you'll decide..."

While she was still speaking Max let his fingers and voice
find the place where he'd been interrupted, his movements slow and deliberate.

"...you'll decide to be reasonable about this." She was
shouting now, so Max had no trouble hearing every blis-

tering word over the rough grating of his own voice. "If not, I'll have no choice but to involve Victor."

She paused after that, eyeing him expectantly as if the mere invoking of his host's name was enough to snap him into an accommodating frame of mind. It should be, Max knew. But somehow the desire to win this crazy power struggle with her overshadowed all desire to be a well-mannered guest.

As she continued to watch him play in silence, Max saw all lingering traces of uncertainty and bewilderment gradually leave her face. She didn't even look angry anymore. She looked . . . resolute, he decided. He could read the determination in the upward thrust of her chin and the flash of fire in her eyes. He found himself intrigued to see what her next move would be.

"All right," she said finally. "I'll call Victor. Are you satisfied?"

The sight of her hair swirling around her shoulders as she spun and raced down the steps made Max think of shimmering brown silk splintered with gold. He grinned at his poetic musing. Splintered with gold. There ought to be a song in that someplace.

Once she was out of sight he abandoned what he'd been playing and experimented with a few random chords, determined to shake off thoughts of what had just happened—or rather, almost happened—and get back to work. It wasn't easy. His gaze kept drifting in the direction she'd taken as if she might suddenly reappear and announce she'd changed her mind about wanting him near her. Not that he wanted her to. He had too much at stake here to waste time with a woman who had done nothing more than come up with a slight variation on a very old theme. If he was lucky, her next ploy would be the silent treatment.

He'd give a lot, though, just to be able to listen in on her conversation with Hazard. She was bound to put a very interesting slant on the story. That is, if she even made good on her threat to call him. More than likely it was just an idle threat to cover up her embarrassment at being shot down.

And for that the woman had only herself to blame. He'd certainly been willing enough until she started scampering away from him as if his touch were acid. Talk about overplaying your part. She was probably the type who liked to play games during sex, too—another reason he should be thankful they hadn't gotten started. He'd already played all those games.

Irritated by his inability to concentrate, Max turned his head to look out over the water and at the same time realized that his idle picking had miraculously turned up something that sounded pretty good. Usually it was the words that came to him first, but he wasn't going to quibble. He played the notes again, several times, growing more excited as he varied the tempo until it sounded just right. Satisfied at last, he took a breath deep enough to make his lungs ache. Now all he had to do was to come up with some words to go with it.

That was all.

His mouth quirked. That was a tough enough task when he wasn't preoccupied. Now, with his thoughts still tangled from his clash with Kara, it was going to be about as easy as shoveling horse manure into a strong wind. Splintered with gold. Sappy as it was, that seemed to be the only original thought he was able to come up with today. Those three words kept drifting through his mind, refusing to make room for others, until he finally tried half singing, half humming them to the fragment of a tune he'd discovered. They didn't work, no matter how he shaded the inflection or altered the tempo.

Irked anew, Max focused his attention on his hands and kept it there. Still, all he kept seeing was the sunlit movement of Kara's hair as she whirled to go. And he kept hearing that clipped, condescending tone she'd used for her parting shot. Was he satisfied? she asked.

Was she crazy?

Thanks to her, he was sitting here right now feeling far from satisfied.

The string of words had barely formed inside his head when Max felt a familiar acceleration of his pulse. Far from satisfied. He quickly shifted his fingers on the strings to try them with the music, but years of experience already told him he'd found what he was looking for. A hook. A place to begin. *Far from satisfied.*

Westwind, as the resort on Diamond Cay was named, was appropriately located on the island's western shore, about a ten-minute bike ride from Kara's bungalow. Today, with temper spurring her on, she made it in under seven. As she crested the final hill and looked down on the resort, it seemed to sparkle in the sun, all serene pink stucco and dewy green grass. There was no high-rise hotel at Westwind, only a picturesque string of minivillas overlooking a harbor basin with slips for a dozen yachts.

There was also no fence surrounding the impeccably manicured grounds, and not even so much as a discreet little sign posted at the end of the drive warning that you were about to enter one of the most posh and pricey vacation spots in the world. Actually there was no need for either. Everyone who lived on Diamond Cay was somehow involved with the resort, the island's only commercial venture, and resort guests were welcome to roam the small island freely. Few, however, ever found any reason to stray far from the tiny oasis of luxury that was Westwind.

Without relying on advertising of any sort, Westwind drew its clientele from the small, closed circles of the super rich. People came here for relaxation, to be pampered in the health spa and catered to by the staff of the five-star restaurant, and they were never disappointed. As manager of the Shady Lady, the less formal of the resort's two nightspots, Kara had grown adept at overseeing some of that pampering and catering. From time to time she was even called upon to bite her tongue and endure the antics of a particularly rude guest. But that was business. She had no intention of making such allowances for the ill-mannered lout who had moved in next door.

Coasting to a halt in the central courtyard, she stowed her bike in the rack discreetly positioned behind a flowering hedge. The resort's administrative offices were located on the upper level of an arcade-style building, which also housed the health spa, hair salon and several small boutiques. Kara bounded up the outdoor staircase, along the balcony bordered by flower-filled planters and into Anne Hazard's office.

She wasn't sure Anne would be there; her active management style meant she spent more time out of the office than in. But Kara felt confident that Anne's secretary, Ben Harris, would be able to answer her questions about Max. At first Kara had been skeptical when Anne hired Ben, whose blond good looks fueled the fantasies of more than a few resort employees and guests. But he had proven to be extremely efficient, exactly what his somewhat freewheeling boss needed to project an organized image.

That's why Kara knew the instant she saw Ben's desk piled high with papers and envelopes that he wasn't around. Belatedly she remembered that he was on vacation for two weeks. Obviously whomever Anne had pressed into service as his replacement wasn't nearly as capable—or as punctual.

Still, the door had been unlocked, which meant someone was here. Crossing to Anne's private office, Kara rapped lightly on the door, smiling with surprise when it was quickly opened by Anne herself.

Anne Hazard was one of those rare individuals upon whom fate had smiled most heartily. Born with access to the best of everything—schools, travel and career opportunities—she was also blessed with the beauty and brains to make the most of them. Tall and willowy and naturally, vibrantly blond, Anne had more cause to be snooty than anyone Kara had ever met. That she wasn't in the least made Anne one of her favorite people, the closest thing to a best friend Kara had ever had.

"Kara, hello."

Anne's smile was easy, her greeting unhurried, in spite of the fact that she was obviously in the middle of a meeting with the three men gathered around her desk. Dark business suits were such an anomaly on Diamond Cay that Kara knew immediately that the meeting was important.

"I'm sorry, Anne," she said, "I didn't realize you were in the middle of something. I'll come back later."

"No, wait," Anne returned, halting her attempt to turn and leave. "I'm glad you stopped by. I was going to call you later. There's something I have to discuss with you right away."

Kara felt a small glimmer of satisfaction. Evidently Anne already knew why she was here. After excusing herself from the meeting for a few minutes, Anne closed her office door and pressed her back to it, wearing a grin worthy of a kid playing hookey.

"Max the obnoxious," Kara murmured with anticipation, her own smile growing a little wider, a little more amused.

Anne's grin gave way to a look of confusion. "Max who?"

"I wish I knew. Isn't that what you wanted to discuss with me?"

"No. The truth is, I don't have anything to discuss. I just needed a little breather from those guys in there. Architects working on the expansion plans," she volunteered before Kara could ask. "Don't ever let anyone tell you that architects are the least bit personable. We're talking industrial-strength serious here. So who's Max?"

"That's what I'm here to find out. Does this mean the expansion is definite?"

"Looks that way. Dad has already hired this trio to come up with something brilliant."

"Have they?"

"That depends. Do you consider concrete tinted to look like pink beach sand brilliant?"

"Not very."

"Then they haven't come up with it yet. Forget them. Tell me about Max."

"There isn't much to tell," Kara explained with a shrug. "He just showed up last night out of nowhere—I'm speaking literally—and announced that he's staying next door. Indefinitely. He claims to be a friend of a friend of your father's.''

Anne looked surprised. "Dad didn't mention to me that someone would be using the house. Did he call you?''

Kara shook her head. "No."

"That's strange."

"That's what I told Max."

"And what did he say?''

"Something charming along the lines of 'That's not my problem' and 'I want to be left alone.''

For about two seconds Anne looked incredulous; then she gave a hoot of laughter. "I suppose I should be worried about a stranger in Dad's house, but this is too much. I want to hear everything.'' She moved to the coffee urn set on a table in a corner of the office and waved a cup in Kara's direction. "Are you indulging or is this another health kick week?''

Kara wrinkled her nose at the reference to her perpetual battle to convince herself she really liked carrot juice and Brussels spouts better than coffee and candy bars.

"Why not?'' she said. "A little caffeine can't possibly make me any more frenzied than I am already.''

Anne arched one finely shaped brow. "That bad?''

"Worse."

"Oh, I can't wait.'' She handed Kara a cup of coffee, then perched on the corner of the desk with her own, her expression gleeful. "Shoot. And don't leave anything out.''

Kara didn't. By the time she finished describing her two bouts with Max, complete with enthusiastic imitations of his steely glare and raspy singing, Anne was laughing too hard to dare take a sip of her coffee.

"Then what the hell *did* you come over here for?'' she chortled, echoing Kara's words. "This guy really said that to you?''

"Uh-huh. That may have also been when he called me *baby* in that sort of sneering drawl he uses. I think he rehearses it.''

"He sounds charming—like an escapee from a singles' bar."

"Easy for you to be witty," retorted Kara, even though she was having difficulty keeping her own expression sober. "You're not living within wailing distance of him."

"True." Anne slipped off the desk and walked over to pat Kara on the back. "But look on the bright side . . ."

"Does anything I've said lead you to believe there is one?" interjected Kara.

"Sure. I intend to check out his story about being a friend of a friend of my father's, but if it's true, the odds are he's a businessman of some sort."

"That's the bright side? I want to get some sleep, Anne, not discuss the trade deficit."

"I realize that, and the fact that he's in business means you'll soon be able to. How long can he possibly take off from work? A week, two tops, and he'll be gone. In the meantime I'll see that he gets the message about respecting your right to a little peace and quiet in the mornings."

Kara was still pondering the basis for Anne's theory. "I don't know, Anne," she said, "Max just doesn't look like a businessman."

Kara had thought her tone neutral, but something in it obviously piqued her friend's interest. Anne parked herself back on the desk, folded her arms and regarded Kara with a knowing smile.

"Oh, really? How does he look?"

Chapter Three

Kara hesitated. She tilted her head from side to side, giving Anne's question serious consideration. She chewed her bottom lip.

"He looks good," she admitted finally. "Not handsome exactly, but...compelling." She sighed, searching for words to capture an appeal she didn't fully understand. "His face is ordinary, yet extraordinary. Does that make any sense?"

"Perfect sense," Anne pronounced. "It also tells me that annoyance isn't the only thing you feel for the mysterious Max. Maybe when I'm talking to Dad I should pump him for a few more details—you know, last name, country of origin, marital status...."

"Don't bother. Like you said, in a week or so he'll be long gone."

"Yes, but you sure could have a lot of fun in the meantime. Think about it, Kara. This is a tropical island, for heaven's sake, most people's idea of a sensual paradise—not a nunnery."

"I get the point. Again," Kara groaned. This was territory she and Anne had been over before. "I've already told you that when a man comes along who interests me, I'll have no objections—moral or otherwise—to getting involved. However briefly. But this definitely is not the man."

"If you say so," Anne conceded, looking unconvinced. "But if my father happens to volunteer any interesting tidbits, I'll let you know right away."

Kara laughed, fully expecting to hear an earful of "tidbits" as soon as Anne could get a call through to Chicago. "Thanks, Anne. I really hate to bother you and Victor about this, but I'll feel better knowing his story is legit."

"No problem. I'm just surprised Dad didn't let one of us know beforehand that this guy was coming." A frown suddenly furrowed her smooth brow. "Unless..."

Anne trailed off and began rummaging through the mountain of paper on Ben's desk, eventually holding an envelope aloft with a sheepish look.

"From Dad," she explained as she ripped it open and read out loud.

"Dear Anne,
This is to let you know that a friend of Lou Basinger will be arriving sometime this week and staying at the house for a while. I told Lou to tell him to contact you if he needs anything. I know you'll extend to him our full hospitality. Also, please let Kara know he's coming. About the bill for those dock repairs..."

Anne glanced up from the letter. "The rest is business. I'm sorry, Kara. If I'd seen this when it came in, I could have saved you a scare last night." She looked around dejectedly. "Without Ben here this place seems to be falling apart around me. I told his replacement to sort the mail daily and bring me anything that looked even vaguely important, but she's inexperienced and..." She trailed off with a shrug.

"And good help is hard to find," Kara finished for her.

"Especially at the upper-management level, it would seem," added Anne with a self-deprecatory grimace that Kara deemed completely undeserved.

True, Anne might eschew handling details, but she more than compensated for it with her ability to deal with people. She ran Westwind with a combination of hard work and fairness that made for happy guests and satisfied employees.

"Don't worry about it, Anne," Kara told her. "Now that I know this guy's telling the truth and that he's not a mad rapist, the whole thing seems a little funny."

"Let's hope you still feel that way at six o'clock tomorrow morning."

Kara groaned. "Please, don't remind me. I'm hoping he at least takes a long enough lunch break this afternoon for me to get in a nap. Otherwise I'll be sleepwalking at work tonight."

The sight of the mess on Ben's desk caught Kara's eye as she made a move to leave, sending a prickly message to her conscience.

"Would you like me to give you a hand sorting through all that?" she offered, trying not to think about the perfect day waiting for her outside.

Anne shook her head. "Thanks, but I think I ought to do it myself, just to be sure there isn't anything else buried in there that should have been taken care of last week. Now, if you had offered to sit in on a meeting with three—"

"Sorry," Kara cut her off with a laugh. "Even friendship has bounds. Have fun, and don't let them sell you any pink concrete."

She closed the door on Anne's chuckle and headed for the stairs leading to the rear of the building where the laundry was located. As long as she was here, she might as well pick up her dry cleaning and drop it off at the club. Riding her bike to and from work meant wearing jeans and changing into something properly fancy when she got there, but most nights Kara preferred that to depending on security for transportation. To make life easier she kept most of her dressy clothes in her office at the club. At home "dressy" usually meant pulling a T-shirt on over her bathing suit.

She was halfway down the stairs before the realization jelled that she really didn't know any more about Max now than she had earlier. Except that he wasn't the brazen interloper she'd been half hoping he'd turn out to be. How satisfying it would have been to watch him being hauled away in the back of the security jeep.

So he had Victor's permission to be here. Big deal. That didn't justify the way he'd behaved toward her. Especially this morning, leering at her the way he had, implying that she'd gone over there for something other than registering a righteous complaint. Of course afterward, when she'd caught a glimpse of herself in the bedroom mirror, she'd been forced to admit that bolting out wearing only a flimsy cotton robe—a very short, flimsy cotton robe—hadn't been the most prudent way to respond to his daybreak quest for revenge.

If in fact that's what it had been. Stifling a yawn, Kara reluctantly entertained a suspicion she'd been too angry to consider before now. Max's reaction when she'd first confronted him this morning had been hesitant, even a bit bewildered. Not quite what you'd expect from a man who had climbed out of bed with retaliation in mind.

And later, while she'd been dressing, the sounds wafting over from his place had been quieter than those that had blasted her awake. Not better, just quieter—tentative, even. Personally she was having enough trouble reading music, never mind trying to write it, but now that she thought about it, it had sounded as if that's what Max had been making a fumbling attempt to do. That could explain why he'd referred to his guitar playing as work.

By the time Kara had collected her clothes and walked the short distance to the club, she had just about convinced herself that Max had come to Diamond Cay to try his hand at songwriting. It was probably a lifelong dream of his, she mused—and a secret one at that, judging from his obsession with privacy. In which case he should be pitied, not harassed. Based on what she'd heard so far, he would have been better off going snorkeling.

Maybe Anne was right about his being a vacationing businessman, even if he didn't look like one. A quick glance at a recent *Newsweek* was proof that times had changed since the days when Kara had lived in a big city and jockeyed for subway space with the wing-tip set. She surmised they no longer all looked like bankers. Maybe Max worked in some offbeat line, like commodities. Of course she had no idea if commodities could be considered an offbeat part of the business world, but it seemed plausible that a man who traded hogs for a living would be adventuresome enough to let his hair grow over his collar. And as long as Max was loath to reveal so much as his last name, she would just think what she pleased about him.

Kara couldn't suppress a small, slightly smug smile as she shouldered open the club door with its stained-glass rendering of the Shady Lady's namesake, a 1920s knockout, her black felt hat tipped low over one eye. Poor Max. All things considered, maybe she ought to make an effort to show him a little kindness. Not only might it influence him to let her sleep mornings, but he deserved it. Hogs and country music made such a depressing combination.

"Looks like someone's day got off to a great start," observed a deep voice as she strolled into the club still smiling broadly at the product of her fanciful imagination.

Kara's eyes hadn't yet made the adjustment from sunlight to the shadowy interior, but she had no trouble matching an image with the voice coming from behind the bar. Jack Hogan—tall, dark wavy hair, linebacker shoulders, a gentle smile. As the newest addition to the bartending staff, Jack pulled more than his share of daytime setup duty. He arrived early to slice fruit for drinks and prepare mixes while those with more seniority basked in the sun.

"To tell you the truth," confided Kara, draping the plastic-sheathed clothes she was carrying over the padded leather back of one barstool while she climbed onto another, "my day actually got off to a horrible start."

Without needing to be asked, Jack set a tall glass of ice water with a slice of lemon in front of her. "Then why the big smile?"

"Oh, hogs and country music," she responded breezily.

"If that's the punch line, I can't wait to hear the joke."

"Impossible. I might be able to arrange for you to meet it, though."

Kara anticipated the look of confusion that settled over Jack's familiar features.

"You've lost me," he admitted.

"I just meant that there is no joke," she explained with a laugh. "There's only this . . . this character who's going to be staying next door to me for a while."

Immediately worry lines appeared at the corners of Jack's blue eyes, prompting Kara to groan inside. She must not be thinking straight or surely she would have remembered his tendency to be overprotective and would have chosen her words more carefully.

Jack put aside the glass he was drying and flipped the linen towel over his shoulder.

"What sort of character?" he asked, his usually laconic tone suddenly curt. "And what's he doing staying out there? Is he bothering you?"

His last question caused Kara to smile ruefully. "Much as it pains me to admit it, I think I'm the one bothering him."

"What's that supposed to mean?"

"Only that I woke him up at about three o'clock this morning with a duet—me on the keyboard, Scott Joplin on the stereo. Then, when he returned the favor at dawn, I exploded."

"He was playing your keyboard at dawn?"

"No, Jack, he was playing a guitar, his guitar. But he was obviously doing it just to get back at me. At least that's why I thought he was doing it at the time. Now I'm not so sure. Anyway, I went over and told him exactly how childish and vindictive he was being.''

Jack's grin retained a hint of caution. ''What did he say to that?''

Kara quickly censored most of what Max had said. ''He said he liked to work early in the morning.''

''So why wasn't he working instead of playing a guitar?''

''I think he thinks that is work. I have a hunch Max is a frustrated songwriter.''

''Let me guess. Country songs.''

''Sounded that way to me.''

''About hogs?''

Kara's shoulders lifted with laughter. ''Not exactly. At first everything he played just sounded loud, and I was still half asleep anyway, but when I got closer I definitely heard him wailing something about a horse.''

''And all this took place at dawn?''

''Barely.''

''No wonder you look so awful.''

''I do not.''

Despite her quick protest, Kara instinctively glanced up to check her reflection in the mirror above the bar. What she saw was an animated face, framed by wavy wisps of hair that had slipped from her barrette during the ride here. If there were shadows under her heavily-lashed dark-blue eyes, they were minuscule, and at least there weren't any of the lines or sagging she'd once thought synonymous with age thirty-two. All in all, it wasn't a bad face. Perhaps not the classically beautiful one she would have chosen if God had asked up front, but she was happy with it and confident that even on a bad day it was a long way from ''awful.''

''Why do I listen to you?'' she muttered, bringing her gaze back to meet Jack's amused one.

''Force of habit,'' he shot back. ''Besides, even if you don't look awful on three hours' sleep, I'll bet you feel that way.''

"I won't argue with that," Kara conceded, sliding to her feet and reaching for the clothes beside her. "That's why as soon as I get rid of these I'm going home to take a nap. See you later."

"What if your neighbor's still feeling creative?" Jack called after her as she moved toward her office.

Kara paused to shoot him a look that was close to cocky. "No problem. I've come up with a whole new way to handle him."

"How? With a baseball bat?"

"Of course not. I've decided to kill him with kindness."

"And if that doesn't work?"

She sighed. "Do you have a baseball bat I can borrow?"

No matter how doomed Jack might consider her plan to deal with Max, Kara was determined to make it work. She just wasn't quite sure how to get started. She spent most of the afternoon considering various possibilities while she tried in vain to doze on her favorite chaise longue. Evidently he didn't break for lunch. Moving inside the house muffled the music somewhat, but it didn't help her come up with any workable ideas. Somehow she had to get across to Max the message that she regretted the unfortunate start to their... friendship? Wrong word. Relationship? Worse. Their whatever. And also that she intended to behave only graciously toward him in the future. However, she definitely did not want that message to be misconstrued as had happened this morning.

That ruled out anything that even smacked of flirting. The direct approach appeared to be the safest in that regard, except Kara was afraid that, given his attitude problem, they would only end up going head to head again, and that would put her back at square one.

It wasn't until six-thirty the following morning that she had a brainstorm, brought on, no doubt, by desperation. The grating, fragmented sound of his strumming even penetrated the pillow she clutched over her ears. It wasn't so much that his playing was so loud, she thought with teeth clenched, it was just so...irritatingly twangy, a nerve-shattering rerun of the day before.

She could picture vividly the way he'd looked when she'd stormed over there, his jaw darkened by three days' worth of stubble, a sweat-dampened T-shirt clinging to a chest she knew to be perfection, a pair of empty beer bottles on the table in front of him.

It was the memory of the beer bottles that did it. It seemed reasonable to assume that anyone reduced to drinking beer for breakfast, for whatever reason, could use a good home-cooked meal. Besides, it was a time-honored truism that the way to a man's heart was through his stomach. And Kara wasn't even aiming for anything as crucial to Max as his heart. She simply wanted to bribe him into allowing her a few extra hours of sleep each morning.

Once she'd decided on food as a weapon, she spent a good part of the day refining her battle plan. Chocolate chip cookies had worked once when she'd been desperate to wheedle Jack into covering an extra shift, but somehow they struck her as being too cutesy for this situation. What was called for here was something thoughtful but not fawning. She finally decided to simply bring him half of whatever she made for herself for dinner, then proceeded to comb her recipe file for something spectacular that also happened to call for ingredients she had on hand. Spinach lasagna won by default. Maybe it didn't quite rate as spectacular, but she had noodles and cheese, and there was frozen spinach as well as her last remaining quart of homemade tomato sauce in the freezer.

By late afternoon the lasagna had finished baking and was ready to go. All that remained for Kara to do was dry her suddenly sweaty palms, walk over and give it to him. At that moment the short distance between their two houses might as well have been the Swiss Alps, she was so nervous about crossing it.

What if he refused her offering? Worse, what if he was twisted enough to jump to the conclusion that she was offering something more personal than a home-cooked meal? Kara quickly shrugged off the cloud of pessimism

and forced herself to answer a more important question.
What if she had to survive another day on less than four
hours of sleep?

Before leaving, she took time to brush her hair, sweeping it away from her face on the sides and anchoring it with
tortoise-shell combs. As she put down the brush she
frowned at her reflection in the bathroom mirror. Her hair
was fine, but the loose-fitting white shirt she'd had on all
day looked somewhat rumpled. Unfastening the buttons
as she hurried into the bedroom, she grabbed a yellow tank
top from her drawer and pulled it on, smoothing it over the
hips of her cutoff denims. A second later she had shed the
cutoffs as well and replaced them with a pair of pleated
navy-blue cotton shorts. With the yellow top tucked inside the shorts, and sandals on her feet instead of sneakers, she was finally satisfied with her appearance. And
disgusted with herself.

What was she thinking of, primping for a man she knew
nothing about, a man who had given her no reason to believe he could be tolerated, let alone trusted? The answer
was obvious. She wasn't thinking. It was a dangerous
lapse, one Kara knew a woman in her position couldn't
afford to make.

Grimly she faced up to the fact that Anne's suspicions
about her interest in Max were more on target than she
would like to believe. Maybe it was a case of wanting what
you couldn't have, but at least part of the reason he'd been
on her mind almost nonstop since they met was plain old-
fashioned attraction.

It took very little effort to recall the way she'd felt yesterday morning when he touched her, trailing his fingers
over her shin with slow precision. She'd felt alarmed, yes,
but it had been overlaid with another, more elusive sensation. It was as if his touch had created hot spots all along
her arm that lingered long after she'd retreated in a fury.

Hot spots. An apt description, Kara told herself, slipping on a pair of oversized sunglasses, adjusting them as
carefully as if they were a suit of armor. Hot as in fire, the

stuff that burns if you get too close. It was something to keep in mind whenever she was dealing with Max.

Unfortunately, by the time she walked next door, all thought of caution had been pushed from her mind by her efforts to think of something witty and nonchalant to say when she handed him the dish of lasagna. Naturally, he had chosen this time to take a break, forcing her to knock on the door instead of just casually bumping into him on the patio. Her stomach muscles clenched as she waited for him to appear, and every nerve transmitter in her body was flashing a message to flee. A message Kara would have heeded in an instant if she weren't convinced that Max would arrive at the door just in time to catch her.

She hadn't come up with anything suitably witty by the time he showed up, so she simply held out the dish and forced her tight lips into a semblance of a smile.

"Hi. I brought you a peace offering."

Standing in the unlit kitchen, with the screen door between them, he appeared as a dark shadow, and even bigger and grimmer than she remembered. *Menacing* was the word that sprang to Kara's mind. As he pushed the door open she was filled with a crazy urge to toss him the hot casserole dish and run.

Resting his shoulder against the jamb, he propped the door open with one bent knee and locked gazes with her. Even his eyes were more than she remembered. More green, more intense. Kara was mesmerized, and he still hadn't so much as smiled.

"A piece of what?" he asked softly. There was none of the animosity or irritation Kara had feared would be in his rough voice, but there was plenty of amused challenge.

Kara refused to wilt. She willed away the blush threatening to heat her cheeks and stretched her smile to the limit. "Spinach lasagna."

Max's eyes narrowed as his gaze dropped to the covered casserole. "Did you say *spinach*?"

"Right," she confirmed, grateful the conversation was moving along in a somewhat normal fashion. "You use it in place of the hamburger."

He looked at her strangely. "Why?"

"It's better for you."

"Great," muttered Max, shaking his head with dismay Kara surmised was feigned. "A vegetarian. I might as well have stayed in California."

"Oh, I'm not a vegetarian anymore," she explained, following with a slightly wistful sigh. "Not that I was ever a very good one. Now I do my best to stick to healthy foods and stay away from the real bad stuff, like sugar, salt, caffeine. Unfortunately, bacon burgers and chocolate bars keep getting in my way."

She'd been so busy rambling that she didn't notice the change in his expression until she stopped to catch her breath. Even though he'd been behaving reasonably neighborly for the past several minutes, Kara was very aware of the reserved, almost wary look that had persisted in his eyes. Suddenly it was gone. Even his stance was more relaxed, and the look on his face now, Kara realized with a little leap in her pulse, could only be described as captivated.

"Chocolate bars just pop up out of nowhere, huh?" he queried, his smile undermining the forbidding effect of his darkly whiskered cheeks and jaw.

"If they don't, I go looking for them," admitted Kara. "Then I atone for my sins with spinach lasagna."

His gaze dropped to the casserole dish still in her hands, and his smile tightened almost imperceptibly. Kara almost thought she'd imagined the change until he lifted his head and she noticed the glint of distrust back in his eyes.

"I guess this is when I'm supposed to invite you in to share it with me," he ventured, his tone subtly mocking.

"You can ask if you like," Kara countered, "but the answer will be no. I have to work tonight, so I already ate dinner." That was a lie, but she'd starve to death before she'd give him any cause to think this was some sort of setup. "Do you think you could take this?" she asked, pushing the casserole toward him. "My fingers are getting a little warm."

"Oh...sure." He straightened and took it from her hands, awkwardly heeding her warning to use the pot-holders because it was hot. Instead of retreating inside with it, however, he lingered with the door still half open. "Where do you work?"

The question was sudden and stilted, as if he'd been desperate for something to say. Did he think a halfhearted pretense of interest would make up for his rudeness a moment ago? Kara suppressed the urge to get back at him by snapping that it was none of his business.

"The Shady Lady. It's a club," she explained quickly, noting the rapid, slightly amazed lifting of his dark brows. She was used to fielding remarks about the club's name, which had been chosen before her arrival. Unfortunately, she couldn't share with anyone how ironically significant a name it was.

"We feature a little jazz, a little rhythm and blues," she continued. Belatedly it occurred to her that none of that would probably appeal to a man who sang about horses. "Music aside, though, even the setting is gorgeous. It's located right on the harbor, with a wide veranda for dancing or just for sitting. And there's even a light menu—sandwiches, cheese and crackers, that sort of thing. And drinks, of course—everything from beer to the kind that come with the paper umbrellas on top."

She was rambling again, instinctively driven to fill this unnatural void that seemed destined to exist between them. She gave a slight wave of her hand, attempting to appear casual and looking fidgety instead. "Stop by some night if you get bored out here alone and I'll buy you a drink."

"I don't think so."

His smile was gone. That full, sulky-looking mouth once more tipped down at the edges, beneath eyes that were relentlessly sober.

"Suit yourself," Kara returned, shrugging. She started to go, then turned back and paused. She couldn't resist. "And you're welcome for the lasagna."

She was rewarded by a dull red band appearing high on his cheekbones.

"Thank you." He spoke the words as if gratitude were a foreign language. "I... it looks..." He glanced down, then quickly back up with a hint of his earlier good humor. "Interesting."

Kara barely nodded before taking off.

Interesting.

The word seared her brain as if branded there. *Interesting.* She'd wasted almost an entire day, changed her clothes, marshalled her courage and endured his abrasiveness, all for an *interesting.* And the way things had gone, she probably hadn't bought herself so much as five extra minutes of sleep.

Chapter Four

The guitar music with its insidious twang insinuated it-self into Kara's subconscious even before she was awake. She slowly peeled her eyes open and squinted at the clock on the bedside table. 6:00 a.m. The man was a sadist. And evidently not susceptible to bribery. Either that or she hadn't hit on the right bribe yet. She had been exaggerating slightly when she told Max that country music gave her a headache, but she was far from being a fan. That's why it shocked her that she was able to identify the song he was playing. "Your Cheatin' Heart." If there was a worse way to start the day, Kara had never experienced it.

Cursing fate for dropping Max into her life, she burrowed her head under the pillow. She needed sleep—at least another three hours of it. Last night the club had been sheer madness. All this week saxophonist Earle Biddle was playing. Although never a commercial success, Earle was legendary among those who loved jazz, and the crowd at the club had been wall to wall and enthusiastic. Kara hadn't gotten home until three-thirty this morning, and then she'd fallen into bed convinced an earthquake couldn't wake her before noon. Wrong again, it seemed.

After a brief attempt to sleep in spite of the noise next door, she surrendered. Tossing and turning was only adding to her bad mood. She staggered to the kitchen and gazed out at the ocean while sipping a glass of orange juice, wondering how long it would take her to rally enough energy for her morning swim. Probably about a week, she calculated miserably. There seemed to be a buffer between her and the rest of the world, dulling her senses, making her feel as if she were doing everything in slow motion.

In an effort to shake off the feeling, she forced herself through the motions of rinsing out her glass and making her bed, eventually deciding she might as well swim after all, since she had no idea what other people—other normal people, at least—did at this hour of the morning. She changed into a bathing suit and grabbed a towel from the linen closet before heading down to the beach.

From his position on the deck Max watched her appear with something akin to relief. His throat was getting sore from singing so loudly. If he'd had an amplifier with him, he'd have used it, obvious or not. This might be a childish way to get a woman's attention, but it was the only surefire route he could think of, aside from approaching Kara directly. And he wasn't sure how to handle that.

He was no longer convinced that Kara was a groupie, but he also wasn't convinced that she wasn't. It was a situation that left him not knowing quite how to play his hand. Waking her up with a song she was sure to hate would at least elicit a predictable response: anger. After he'd given her a chance to blow off some steam, he would appear to have a change of heart, feign a little remorse and see what happened next. It was the closest he'd come to actively pursuing a woman in years.

The instant Kara came into view Max had lowered his head while continuing to chart her progress out of the corner of his eyes. He bided his time, and just as she drew close enough to see clearly, he looked up suddenly, as if noticing her for the first time. If only the critic who'd said he couldn't act well enough to be cast in home movies could see him now. Stilling his fingers on the strings, he steeled himself for her opening blast and was caught totally off guard when she gave him a cheerful wave and continued on her way, veering off onto the path leading down to the beach.

She didn't look angry, he noted in amazement. Hell, she didn't even look annoyed. Had all that complaining about needing her sleep been an act after all? Or was *this* the act? Frustration made him want to run after her and ask what the hell she thought she was doing. Except technically speaking, she wasn't doing anything...except driving him crazy.

He forced himself to stay put and settled for watching her back as she walked away. It was no effort at all. She had a fantastic back, its contours as sleekly feminine as the rest of her. She was wearing a one-piece bathing suit that was sexier than any bikini Max had ever seen. It was the color of ripe raspberries and shiny, cut to someplace south of her waist in the back and high enough on the sides to inspire in him all sorts of erotic fantasies about her long legs. Max stared at the graceful curve of her bare shoulders, the gentle sway of her hips, the slight, fascinating movement of her fanny inside that hot raspberry suit, and he felt the attraction that last night had been only a flicker flare into something much hotter and more urgent.

It would be easy to write off what he was feeling as lust. Max would actually prefer it that way. But he'd felt lust often enough to recognize it immediately, and he was still honest enough with himself to admit that this wasn't it. Oh, lust was part of what he was feeling, to be sure. But there was more. Kara McFarland intrigued him. Even more miraculous was the fact that she inspired him. He sensed something about her that would be pure magic captured in a song. She was a mystery, a fascinating contradiction. One moment she appeared vulnerable enough to make even a hard case like him soften toward her. At those times she displayed an almost childlike spontaneity

and openness, like when she'd confessed her failure as a
vegetarian, and later when she invited him to visit her at
work. Then the next moment she was all lofty, feminine
self-confidence, and his defenses sprang back into place.
Thank God.

Max had spent last evening telling himself that most
likely his complex impression of her was simply an illusion, or worse, an artful facade. But while that possibility
irked Max as a man, it didn't matter to the writer in him.
That part of him cared only about his perception of Kara
and how he was able to turn that perception into words
and notes, into magic. And so far his perception of her was
as a woman who was fragile but strong, as if she'd weathered her own kind of storm. Emotionally Max could identify with that, having weathered more than a few himself.

He bent his head over the guitar in his lap and listened
to his fingers work. Filtering through his mind were dozens of words and phrases that might help him translate the
uniqueness of one woman into sound. For the time being
the woman herself ceased to exist, along with the beach
and the cloudless blue sky overhead and everything else
outside of the music and the moment. The melody grew,
and along with it came the words. They were different
from anything he'd written before, more complicated, less
direct, but they were right. Max could feel it. He also felt
a subtle stirring of the confidence he'd thought he'd lost
somewhere along the way. Almost immediately he was totally engrossed in his thoughts, in his work. So absorbed
he forgot his plan to watch for Kara to start back so he
could accidently bump into her on the path.

His head was still lowered almost an hour later when
Kara passed him on her way back to her place. She moved
as slowly as she could without crawling, hoping he would
glance up and say something, telling herself she was only
seeking an opportunity to enlarge on her plan to be the
perfect neighbor. Any opening would do. Even if he
groused at her for straying too close to his domain, she
would counter with a pleasant apology. It was frustrating

trying to be nice to somebody who hardly noticed that you were alive.

She'd be darned if she'd ask him how he had liked the lasagna. Even a hobo knew enough to express thanks for a handout. Max hadn't seen fit to so much as return her wave as she hurried past on her way to the beach. He'd simply leveled her another of those looks that suggested her mere existence was an intrusion on his privacy. Well, he could just look that way all he chose. She was here before he came, and she'd be here after he left. If that glorious day ever arrived. Until then she would ignore him when she could and continue her hopeful policy of being sweet to him when she couldn't. Even if it killed her.

As the day dragged on, Kara was disturbed to discover it was easier to be civil to Max than it was to ignore him. She was constantly aware of his presence nearby. Not that she stooped to watching him through the window... exactly. She did try it, just once and briefly, only to discover that the view to his deck was obscured by an overgrown flowering hibiscus. But watching him wasn't really necessary. She seemed to have developed some sort of inner radar that kept her subliminally tuned to him even while she was busy doing other things. She told herself it was self-defense and worried that it wasn't that at all.

She weeded the small garden outside her front door, aware of each short break he took. The music would fade, and next Kara would hear the screen door slam. She could imagine the rest: the sound of the refrigerator door opening, the clatter of a beer bottle cap hitting the counter. She pictured him tipping his head back to drink with long, thirsty gulps. Instinctively she knew that Max wasn't a sipper of anything.

While she ate an early lunch he worked steadily. Kara told herself she should turn on the stereo to drown him out, but she made no move from her salad to do it. Either he was getting better or she was getting used to his sound, because it wasn't grating on her nerves nearly as much as it had at first.

She was stretched out on a chaise longue on the patio reading a thriller when the music suddenly stopped once more. She kept reading, gradually becoming aware that this break was lasting longer than any of his others. She found herself darting glances between the mayhem unfolding on the pages in front of her and the deserted deck a few hundred feet away, with the deck steadily winning the battle for her full attention. Finally she discerned a shadow moving on the other side of the thick foliage separating the two yards, and a few seconds later Max sauntered into view at the start of the path to the beach. Kara peered over the top of her book at him, confident that even if he turned around, her sunglasses would conceal the fact that she was watching.

He didn't turn, though, didn't glance over his shoulder to see if she might be around, didn't give the slightest sign that he was aware there was other life on the island besides himself. He just walked, his stride relaxed and easy, almost lazy. Watching him, Kara somehow knew it would be that way even if there were a million pairs of eyes trained on him. When he drew close to the water he dropped to the firmly packed sand and did a quick series of push-ups. Kara was too distracted by the supple play of muscles in his arms and long, powerful legs to keep count, but she knew the number was high. Unnoticed, the thriller fell shut in her lap. By the time he levered back to his feet, sweat glistened on his smooth skin and formed dark patches on his light-gray T-shirt, and Kara was impressed.

She anticipated him pulling off his socks and sneakers and his T-shirt—especially the T-shirt—and plunging into the water. Instead, though, he bent in a few preliminary stretching exercises before breaking into a jog and heading off down the beach.

Mainlanders, Kara thought wryly. Who else would go jogging at midday? Even without humidity, eighty degrees felt uncomfortably hot, and there wasn't a cloud in sight to diffuse the sun directly overhead. Shaking her head as he disappeared in the distance, she searched for her place in the book and tried to read, but her gaze kept slipping up to scan the horizon in the direction Max had taken. From the length of time that passed before he reappeared she calculated that he'd run a good three miles. She wasn't surprised that the first thing he did when he reached his starting point was quickly strip off everything but his faded blue bathing suit, tossing the rest next to the towel he'd dropped earlier, and take a running dive into an incoming wave.

After all her patience and anticipation, the glimpse Kara finally got of his bare back was disappointingly fleeting. It was, however, long enough to confirm that her first impression was right. His shoulders were nicely broad for someone as lean as he was. Watching as time after time he swam out past where the waves were breaking and attempted to ride one all the way back to shore made Kara feel somewhat guilty over her latent voyeuristic tendencies. Somewhat. Not enough to make her stop. It also made her feel like walking down and telling him what he was doing wrong.

Max was an excellent swimmer and obviously a great deal stronger than she was, but the tide here at the island's northern point was contrary. Huge rock formations farther out caused it to fork and drop right out from under you even as it rushed you toward shore. It had taken Kara weeks of practice to master the ability to predict where the wave would split and position her start accordingly. A good neighbor, she prodded herself, would share such hard-earned knowledge with a newcomer.

Before she could get to her feet, however, Max was out of the water. Kara sank back in her seat, uncertain whether the small twinge she felt was one of disappointment or relief. He did a haphazard job of drying off, then flipped the towel down on a patch of dry sand and collapsed on it. From a distance, with his face half buried in his folded arms and damp waves of dark hair tumbling over his forehead, he looked younger than he did at closer range. Up close, flecks of silver near his temples hinted that his age was closer to forty than thirty, and there were finely etched lines and creases that seemed to warn that those beautiful, wary green eyes had seen it all.

Once more Kara found her curiosity aroused by thoughts of what Max might do when he wasn't struggling to write music on a tiny island in the middle of the Atlantic. Try as she might, she couldn't picture him in any type of business attire seated behind a desk. She was still working on it a few minutes later, unable to come up with any theory that could top hog trading, when it occurred to her that he hadn't moved in quite a while. He must have fallen asleep, she thought with an absurd sense of glee. Like a shot she was off the chaise and heading for her own bed, whispering a silent prayer that he would wear himself out with a run about this time every day for the rest of his vacation.

Even when she was dead tired Kara couldn't sleep for longer than an hour or so during the day, but somehow that was enough to leave her feeling human again. Without stopping to wonder why, the first thing she did upon awakening from her short nap was stroll outside to the patio and glance at the beach below. She fully expected to see only a man-sized depression in the sand where Max had been lying and was startled to find him still stretched out on his towel, evidently still asleep. The only changes in his appearance were that his head was now facing the opposite way and the skin on his back and legs had turned a shade Kara had once heard a lifeguard at Westwind describe as "tourist crimson."

Max wasn't what she would call pale, but he certainly wasn't as tan as she would expect someone from sunny California to be . . . if that's actually where he was from. Who knew? He could be as adept at dealing red herrings as he was at avoiding questions.

Even Anne had been stonewalled where Max was concerned. She'd dropped by the club last night to hear Earle's second set and to tell Kara that her father didn't know much more about his taciturn houseguest than they did. He simply had his good friend Lou Basinger's word that Max could be trusted. Anne had also relayed a message from Victor instructing Kara to get in touch with him immediately if she felt otherwise.

Kara did her best to assure Anne that she was relatively comfortable living next door to Max for the time being. Certainly she didn't distrust him enough to ask Victor to rescind his invitation. And today, after finally getting some much-needed sleep, she was inclined to feel even more magnanimous toward him. Maybe she would go so far as to walk down and wake him before he had to be peeled off the hot sand.

And give him another opportunity to stare at her as if she were some mutant life form? challenged a voice deep inside her. No. He'd made it clear that he wanted to be left alone, and until he gave some hint that he'd changed his mind, that's exactly what she would do. With a last glance at his sprawled form she turned and headed for the shower. For Max's sake she hoped Victor had left behind a better supply of first-aid supplies than he had food.

After showering, Kara pulled on clean shorts and a sleeveless top and automatically reached for the hair dryer. With a sudden change of mind she pushed it back into the drawer. Usually she showered later in the day, then had to rush to dry her long, thick hair before leaving for work, but today she was enough ahead of schedule to let the sun dry it while she read another few chapters in her book. Besides, she couldn't resist checking to see whether Max had finally woken and headed for the shade. He hadn't, Kara observed a moment later, suffering a swift stab of...guilt? Compassion?

A mixture of the two, she decided as she hurried back inside for a beach towel. The worst of the damage had already been done to him by the midday rays, and she suspected Max must be even more tired than she was for him to sleep for so long beneath a fiery sun. Rather than wake him—as she no doubt should have had the courage to do an hour ago—she gently covered him with the towel. He stirred and made a disgruntled noise, but he didn't open his eyes, and Kara left him safely tucked beneath a field of bright-pink terry-cloth orchids.

She couldn't predict exactly how Max would react when he finally came to and discovered she had covered him with one of her towels, but she had no reason to believe he would be anything but angry. He might claim that she had no right to interfere with the third-degree sunburn he would probably insist he was trying to get, or he might berate her for not having had the brains to cover him up sooner. Either way, Kara expected to be on the receiving end of some abrasive comments.

That's why she felt suddenly disoriented when he appeared at her door several hours later wearing what could only be interpreted as a friendly smile. She nearly stuttered her greeting, and she knew she was gaping, totally amazed that a simple muscle contraction like a smile could alter his face so drastically. Then she realized it wasn't only the smile that was responsible for making him look more amiable and less ferocious; he had shaved as well. Gone was the multiday black stubble that had shadowed his strong jaw and hidden, she discovered, a quite appealing cleft in the center of his chin. His hair was also neatly combed for the first time since she'd known him, and it appeared that he'd put an extra modicum of care into dressing. True, he was barefoot, but he had gone so far as to tuck in his black T-shirt and add a somewhat worn leather belt at the waist of his faded jeans.

"Am I wrong?" he asked.

"No, you're just fine," she replied. Kara's soft, strangely dreamy tone sounded in her ears like a fire alarm, shattering her mood of wonderment. Flustered, she jerked her gaze up to meet his.

"I mean . . ." she began in a desperate attempt to correct any salivating impression she might have just given him, then realized she had no idea what he was talking about and shrugged. "I'm sorry, what did you say?"

"I just asked if I was wrong—about the towel being yours."

He lifted his hand, and for the first time she noticed he was holding the pink and white towel from that afternoon.

"No...I mean yes, it is my towel."

His mouth, with its full, soft-looking bottom lip, slanted into another smile. Kara's stomach seesawed crazily.

"I figured it had to be," he told her. "I'm beginning to feel like we're the only two people left in the world."

"I guess if you're not used to it, the isolation can get to you," Kara murmured agreeably.

"I wasn't complaining."

Kara had just about recovered her equilibrium, and he managed to set her spinning again with no apparent effort. *He wasn't complaining.* Three little words uttered in a scarred baritone, and she was tingling as if she'd just won the Irish Sweepstakes. But it wasn't only what he'd said, it was the way he'd looked at her when he said it, a heated look that pronounced her the only woman in the entire universe he *wanted* to be with. Which was absurd. He hardly knew her, and what he knew he didn't seem to care for much. Kara wasn't such a gullible, love-starved romantic that she'd forgotten the parameters of reality. But for a few seconds, at least, that was how his look had made her feel.

Abruptly she became aware that he was still holding the towel out to her, and automatically she took it from him, struggling to subdue the mad desire to reach up and touch the dark hair that looked fluffy from a recent washing.

"You're welcome...for the towel," he added pointedly when Kara blinked in confusion.

She quickly realized he was mimicking her sarcastic gibe of last evening and smiled a grudging acknowledgment. "Thanks for returning it."

"Thank you for supplying it."

Her eyes narrowed with concern. "How's your back?"

"It only hurts when I move...or try to breathe," he added with a wry smile. "Believe it or not, I usually do know enough to come in out of the sun. I only planned to lie there until I dried off. I guess I was more tired than I thought."

"Must be all those early mornings," Kara commented. The slight trace of satisfaction in her voice didn't escape Max's notice.

He laughed. "Point taken. I promise that starting tomorrow you won't hear a note out of me until after nine."

"Or a wail?"

"Or a wail. Okay?"

"Okay," Kara agreed quietly.

She felt as if she should do something besides stand there staring at him with a drugged smile—say something, at least—but she wasn't sure what. He didn't seem too sure of what to say next, either. Then, just before the silence grew awkward, he lifted his other hand.

"I brought your dish back, too," he said as if suddenly remembering it. "The lasagna was..."

"Interesting?" she teased before he had a chance to complete the thought.

"Better than I expected."

"Well, that's a step up from interesting...I think. Anyway, thanks for bringing the dish back."

"Thanks again for the meal." He chuckled, shaking his head. "You know how I feel? Like we're trapped in that old kids' story, 'After You, Alphonse.' Only instead of saying 'after you' all the time, we can't stop saying thankyou to each other."

"At least we're not shouting," Kara pointed out.

"True. Which brings me to the other thing I came to give you: an apology. I've been acting like a real bastard since I got here, and it's..." He hesitated, and it seemed as if he had to make a real effort to shrug off the bitterness Kara saw lurking at the edge of his expression. "Let's just say my rotten mood had nothing to do with you, although you ended up bearing the brunt of it. I am sorry, Kara."

It was the very first time she'd heard his gravelly voice caress her name, and Kara couldn't tell if it was that or the fact that he'd just apologized—twice—that had her so rattled.

"Don't worry about it," she somehow found the presence of mind to respond. "We all have bad days."

"Days? Try months." The harshness that edged his short chuckle was gone as swiftly as the cynicism that flickered briefly in his eyes. "Anyway, I didn't come over here just to apologize. I plan to make it up to you."

He silenced her quick murmur of protest with an equally quick finger pressed to her slightly parted lips. It worked. The feel of his callused fingertip left Kara hardly able to think, much less argue.

"I want to invite you to dinner," he explained. "Nothing fancy, just a couple of steaks on the grill, maybe a salad. What do you say?"

She knew what she wanted to say. Every fiber of her being wanted to shout yes, every fiber, that is, except the hard core of caution that had been years in the making. Pulling back, saying no, avoiding risk—it was all a way of life for her, especially in a situation as fraught with uncertainties as this one.

"I appreciate the invitation," she said, the regret in her voice genuine, "but I'm afraid I can't accept tonight. I have to work."

"I figured that. That's why I came over early. You've still got three hours before the time you left for work last night—that's plenty of time to grill a steak."

He was right, she thought, frantically trying to piece together a story about how she always went in early on Wednesdays to...to sweep the floor? Count the swizzle sticks? It didn't matter. A glance at Max's expression was enough to tell Kara she'd taken too much time coming up with her excuse. Skepticism had already twisted his smile and wrinkled his brow.

"C'mon, Kara," he urged, his tone low, cajoling, too irresistible to be legal. "I need you."

Kara's eyes blinked wide open.

"The truth is," he continued before she had a chance to embarrass herself by jumping to any conclusions about what he needed her for, "I couldn't cook a steak or make a salad if the survival of the whole human race depended on it. I'm afraid it's either you or more beer."

Something in his unabashedly vulnerable appeal made it impossible for Kara to do anything but smile.

"Some invitation," she grumbled, knowing he had her poised on the edge of acceptance. Max knew it, too. The light of certainty sparkled in his eyes.

"It was sincere," he insisted. "I may not be able to cook, but I'm great at following orders."

"Then you're in luck," Kara heard herself toss back with a mixture of horror and anticipation. "Because I happen to be great at giving them."

Something crackled in the air between them, simmering just below the surface, woven beneath and through their slightly flirtatious verbal sparring. Kara was well aware of it—heck, she was even contributing to it—but she didn't fully understand it. For all their smiling and flippancy, what was happening here was something much more reckless than the banter she occasionally engaged in with a friendly male customer. She only knew it was exciting and dangerous and that she couldn't afford to let it get out of hand.

"Then what are we waiting for?"

Max made a motion with his hand as if he expected her to go with him right then and there, without thinking each potential disaster through beforehand, without even some time alone to gather her defenses. Kara panicked.

"I . . . I have to change first," she blurted.

She felt the drift of Max's gaze over her body as if it were a blow torch.

"You look fine just the way you are," he told her in a tone that was gruff and sexy.

"But I can't go to work dressed this way," she lied. "If I change now, I won't have to worry about it later. I'll be able to relax and enjoy dinner."

The look he gave her made Kara think that he had seen her take off for work last night dressed much as she was now, but he didn't argue. Shoving his hands half into the front pockets of his jeans, he said, "Okay, change. I'll wait."

Wait here? The words raced to the tip of Kara's tongue. She locked them behind a quick smile. She needed a few minutes alone to think, to mull over her reaction to this new, improved Max. And she wouldn't be able to do that with him waiting on the patio practically right outside her bedroom window.

"I have a better idea," she countered in a bright, used-car salesman sort of tone. "I'll change, and you go light the grill. It'll save time."

Again Max surprised her by not arguing. As soon as he'd sauntered off, Kara raced to her closet. She flicked past the hangers holding jeans and cotton pants; they were all too casual now that she'd told him she would be dressing for work. Unfortunately, almost everything she would actually wear to work was already there. She hesitated briefly at a clingy silk tunic outfit, then moved on with a roll of her eyes. Too obvious. A short black dress with a plunging back and slit side didn't even rate a pause. Too everything.

She was about to give up and go as she was, even though it would mean swallowing her pride and confessing her little white lie, when she came to a white cotton sundress. Unadorned except for the tiny, bright flowers embroidered along the wide band at the bodice, it also had a skirt full enough to enable her to pedal a bicycle. Kara had bought the dress on impulse, then realized it fell in between her needs and had never had occasion to wear it. Until tonight.

She quickly changed into the dress, choosing a pair of comfortable low-heeled white sandals to go with it. It took her only a few minutes to apply some mascara, brush her hair and secure it on the sides with gold combs. She added a pair of small gold earrings shaped like shells and a locket on a fine chain, telling herself over and over that she wasn't doing anything she wouldn't do if she were dressing for work. Except maybe for the cologne, a light flowery scent, which she sprayed behind her ears and knees. For some reason it seemed crucial to Kara that she keep this impromptu barbecue in perspective. She might not be able to control her racing pulse, but she could certainly control her thoughts . . . she hoped. She had to keep in mind the fact that, ornery or friendly, Max was still a stranger, and strangers were always risky business.

On impulse she grabbed a bottle of mineral water and a fresh lemon from the refrigerator and slowly, casually, walked next door. She followed the maze of steps and angled decks to the terrace adjacent to the house. A low wall built from the island's unusual pinkish-tan stone bordered the terrace. Baskets and clay pots overflowing with orange, pink and yellow blooms were everywhere, their healthy splendor a testimony to the careful tending they received from the resort's gardeners. At this time of day the setting sun glazed the red tile roof and bathed everything below with a soft pink glow. Even Max, Kara thought, glancing at the reddish-brown color of his arms as she approached from behind.

Max was seated in one of the white wrought-iron chairs surrounding a matching glass-topped table. He had an open notebook in front of him and a pencil clamped between his teeth. Kara shifted her gaze from his relaxed posture to the gas grill built into the cooking center in one corner of the terrace, and her lips curved in a suspicious smile.

"Grill all set?" she asked by way of announcing her arrival.

Max stood, removing the pencil to smile at her. "Not exactly."

It wasn't an embarrassed smile, Kara noted, not even a sheepish one.

"I did try," he went on. "I think it's broken."

Kara placed the lemon and the bottled water on the table. "I know it's traditional to bring wine," she explained when he glanced at them quizzically, "but I don't drink before work."

"Good policy," Max observed dryly. "One I probably ought to adopt."

"What's the problem with the grill?" she asked, moving to it and lifting the lid.

"I'm not sure. I pushed the button marked start—several times, actually—but nothing happened. Do you know how to cook on a stove inside?"

Kara started to smile, then realized the hopeful-sounding question was serious. "Yes, but steak never tastes as good that way. Are you sure you turned the gas on before you pressed the starter?"

"Gas?"

Kara groaned and bent down to turn the knob that controlled the flow of gas from the in-ground tank to the grill. Standing up once more, she hit the starter and instantly heard the soft whooshing sound that signaled it had lit. Just to be sure, she passed her hand over the top and felt the heat rising. Within a moment or so the lava rocks inside were tinged with red.

"How about that!" Max exclaimed. There was honest admiration in his voice, even a hint of humor, but again no trace of the discomfiture Kara would expect any man to feel at being unable to perform such a simple, traditionally male task as lighting a grill.

"Tell me," she began curiously, "how does a man who claims to be from California, that bastion of outdoor living, survive without knowing how to start a grill? And as long as we're on the subject, why doesn't he have a tan?"

"I am tan," he protested, extending his arms as proof. "It's just hidden underneath the sunburn."

"Way underneath," mocked Kara.

Max shrugged. "So I haven't spent much time outdoors the past few months. I still pay my state taxes. As for the grill, I guess there's just always been someone else around to do that kind of thing."

Someone else. The words filtered through Kara's mind at slow speed. A thought that hadn't really occurred to her before did now, full-blown and unsettling.

"Someone like a wife?" she queried lightly, fiddling with the controls on the grill to avoid direct eye contact.

"No," Max returned after a pause. "I haven't had one of those around for a while."

Kara wondered about the reason for his hesitation. She turned to meet his gaze levelly. "A while? Like three days maybe?"

Max's laughter sent a pair of gulls who'd landed on the deck railing below arcing skyward with a violent flapping of wings.

"Three days? Do I honestly look that domesticated to you?" He laughed again, only slightly less uproariously at her awkward shrug. "Actually, it's been more like ten years, Kara. And it feels like several lifetimes. Now, is it my turn to ask you a question yet?"

His laughter had faded, leaving behind, Kara noted with distress, a look of sober determination. "I . . . I'm sorry," she said. "That was rude of me."

"Uh-uh." He shook his head. "It's only rude if you don't give me equal time."

Without warning he lifted his hand and slid it effortlessly beneath the heavy curtain of her hair to curl his fingers around her neck. Kara suddenly felt a warm rush of anticipation. When he didn't make a move to get any closer, however, she realized that he was only holding her that way so she couldn't turn away from whatever questions were coming. Still, the foolish ripples of pleasure persisted. How was it possible, she wondered, to tremble from fear and excitement at the same time?

"What I want to know," Max began, his deep voice soft, "is how long you're going to keep this up?"

Her expression flickered from wary to confused. "Keep what up?"

"Pretending," he shot back, and the bottom fell out of Kara's world.

Her mind reeled. Who was he? A cop? A private detective, some sort of bounty hunter? Or just someone who had recognized her by chance and now planned to turn it to his own advantage somehow? Was that the reason for his sudden change of heart toward her?

"How long are you going to continue this farce?" he pressed in the same relentless tone. "This little game we're playing?"

Kara tried to look away, but his fingers tightened on her neck forbiddingly. Each word he spoke was a long-dreaded dagger, slashing away at all the glib explanations she had practiced to use at a moment such as this, leaving her standing there in shivering silence.

"Come on, Kara," Max urged impatiently, once more squeezing her neck in a no-nonsense way that sent goose bumps dancing the length of her arms. "How long are you going to go on pretending you don't know who I am?"

Chapter Five

Despite the horrifying sense that her whole world was about to come crashing down around her, Kara retained enough presence of mind to realize that something about Max's question was all wrong. *How long are you going to go on pretending you don't know who I am?* Instead, shouldn't he be asking how long she was going to go on pretending to be someone she wasn't?

She quickly dismissed the possibility that they had known each other before, back when Kara McFarland was still Carolyn Haggerty, and that Max was simply waiting for her to acknowledge it. For one thing, if that was the case, why would he have held off for three days before confronting her? For another, Kara was absolutely certain she had never met or even set eyes on Max before the other night, not in this or any other lifetime. There was just no way she would have forgotten a man like him.

Drawing a deep breath, she struggled to bring her panic under control enough to make sense of what he'd said. At the same time she warned herself to be prepared to face the worst possible scenario: that Max knew who she was, as well as why she was hiding, and that he'd come here for the express purpose of hauling her back to the States to face some long overdue consequences. She was so consumed with her own thoughts that it took a few moments for her to register the subtle but unmistakable change in the way Max was looking at her.

Before his expression had been resolute, almost challenging, as if daring her to admit the truth. Now his narrowed eyes and the slightly softer line of his mouth reflected a degree of uncertainty. Was there a chance, even a slim one, that she might be able to bluff her way—

"You really don't know who I am, do you?" Max asked, interrupting her desperate thought. His tone was incredulous.

Kara tipped her head back defiantly, determined not to show him how thoroughly confused and anxious he'd made her.

"Or care," she returned with as cool and dismissive a glance as it was possible to give a man who was holding you immobile by the back of your neck.

"Hot damn." The words were a whisper, almost inaudible. Slowly Max released his grip on her. A smile tinged with disbelief and delight gradually took command of his wide mouth.

Kara wasn't sure what had just transpired or why, but she felt a wave of relief so strong that she almost laughed out loud. Along with it came a surge in her curiosity.

"*Should* I know who you are?" she asked him.

"No," he answered quickly. "I thought maybe you did, but I...I must have been mistaken."

"Why don't I believe that?"

"I have a more interesting question: why did you almost jump out of your skin a few minutes ago?"

"I don't know what you're talking about."

"I'm talking about the cold sweat you broke into when I brought up the subject of pretending. Now, maybe I'm a fool, but I buy the fact that you don't know me from

Adam. Which makes me wonder why that question made you so nervous.''

Kara smoothed a stray wisp of hair from her forehead while she grappled for the best way to respond. If she flat out denied that she'd been in a panic a few seconds ago, Max would know she was lying. On the other hand, telling him the truth was also out of the question.

"It was silly, really," she said finally, deciding that in this case a slightly evasive offense might be the best defense. "It's just that the way you grabbed me, and the serious look on your face..."

"I'm sorry if I upset you," Max said when she trailed off with a small shrug. In spite of the apology, he still looked skeptical about her explanation.

"That's all right, you just took me by surprise. And then for just a moment I was afraid—I mean, I thought that you might actually be someone I knew a long time ago."

Max shook his head. "I definitely would have remembered you."

The sudden warmth in his gaze as he echoed her own feelings made Kara's breath catch. "Yes, well, it looks like we both made a mistake. What do you say we forget about the past and about asking questions and concentrate on dinner?"

The thoughtful expression on Max's face as he considered her proposal assured Kara that he understood she wasn't simply being polite but she was tactfully setting a fresh ground rule for their friendship. Friendship alone was a big risk for her, but at least now she felt certain that Max hadn't come to Diamond Cay to put an end to her precarious freedom. Even so, she would never be able to relax around him if she had to be constantly dodging questions. And respect for privacy was no more than he'd already asked—or rather, demanded—of her. Finally Max nodded his assent, and Kara's relief was complete.

"Agreed," he said. "Want to come inside and find out if I'm any better with a salad than I am with a grill?"

Laughing, she followed him into the spacious, brightly tiled kitchen. Somehow it didn't come as any surprise to her that he was no more adept at rinsing lettuce or slicing tomatoes than he was at lighting a gas grill. Actually, contrary to his earlier claim, the only thing Max demonstrated a clear talent for was *giving* orders. He didn't give them with arrogance exactly, although Kara knew firsthand that he could be plenty arrogant if he chose to be. His delivery was more subtle. He simply announced that he hated radishes or didn't eat cucumbers with skin on them as if confident that someone—Kara, in this case—would see to it that none appeared on his plate.

It was obvious he was a man accustomed to having others listen when he spoke and heed what he said. And quickly. She'd assumed that he had money; he wouldn't have friends in common with Victor if he didn't. But money alone didn't account for his casual air of dominance. Kara had met enough wealthy people at Westwind to learn that and to recognize that Max's attitude was a reflection of both money and power. She almost regretted their agreement not to pry into each other's lives.

At first she also worried that the agreement might put a strain on their conversation, especially once they no longer had the distraction of cooking to occupy them. Instead, by the time the table was set and the steak barbecued to perfection, they were talking and laughing together easily. Kara would never admit it to him, but Max possessed a quality that more than made up for his shortcomings in the kitchen. He might not know a baster from a spatula, but he knew plenty about women.

He made her feel special, as if she were the most fascinating person alive. When she spoke he listened, really listened, and focused his gaze on her so exclusively that Kara could easily believe the entire universe started and ended with her. Although they never touched on any subject that would rate as too personal, an unmistakable awareness permeated each word, each glance, creating an aura of unspoken intimacy.

They ate dinner outside on the terrace, where the shimmering pink light of the setting sun enhanced the tropical beauty of the island. A mild breeze caressed their skin and caused the flowers surrounding them to bow and dance to the distant music of the surf. It would have been a sensually stirring scene even if Kara had been alone, as she usually was at this time of day. Sharing it with Max made it even more pleasurable, and undeniably romantic. She was spellbound, amazed and amused that she could find even the mundane act of chewing fascinating if Max was the one doing it.

Swallowing her last bite of steak, Kara reached for her glass and took a sip of mineral water, thinking that it might as well have been wine after all.

"Pretty smile," Max observed, pushing his own plate away. "Any special reason for it?"

She hesitated, then recklessly admitted the truth. "My prudence in bringing a bottle of water instead of wine. I think it backfired, because I feel slightly..."

"Drunk?"

"Light-headed."

"Must be all those minerals or something."

"Or something."

Still holding her in the path of his hypnotic smile, Max idly lifted his right hand to his chest. The smile shattered as suddenly as if zapped by lightning.

"Damn," he muttered. At Kara's quizzical frown, he added, "Looking for my cigarettes."

"Did you run out?"

"Quit."

Kara nodded, solemnly and with complete understanding. "I once tried to quit Hershey bars cold turkey."

With a laugh Max dropped his hand away from his empty shirt pocket.

"C'mon," he said, getting to his feet and circling the table to pull her chair out. "If I sit here, I'll go crazy remembering when every meal used to end with a cigarette for dessert. Dessert," he repeated, groaning. "I forgot all about it. I don't even have a candy bar to offer you."

"Then we'll suffer together," she countered teasingly. Glancing up at him over her shoulder, she bent to start stacking the used dishes. "I have just enough time to help you clean up before I have to leave for work. You wash, and I'll dry. You can't smoke if your hands are wet.''

"No way." Reaching around her with both arms, Max gently loosened her fingers from the plate she was holding. Kara was too conscious of his sudden closeness to protest. His chest felt hard against her back, and the clean soap-and-water scent of him filled her head.

Still standing behind her, Max slid his hands up her arms to rest lightly on her shoulders. "If I only have a little time left with you, I don't want to spend it playing house. At least, not in the kitchen," he qualified, his tone growing husky as he turned her to face him.

Kara wasn't sure where to focus her attention. She was reluctant to meet Max's gaze, certain that at this moment it was hot enough to scorch. Staring at the hard, muscled expanse of his chest just inches away, however, didn't feel all that much safer. It wasn't that she hadn't sensed the evening gradually building toward this moment. She had. Part of her had even been looking forward to it. But now that it was upon her she was filled with apprehension. Was she really prepared to confront this moment, with all its potential ramifications, head on?

Even more pressing than the question of where to look was the problem of where to put her body. Max hadn't backed away as he'd turned her, and so Kara felt herself angling backward to avoid caressing his chest with more than her gaze. As it was she was close enough to feel heat radiating from his lean frame, the same way it did from a stone that had baked in the sun all day.

When the silence seemed to have grown more ominous than anything she could possibly say, she forced herself to meet his gaze. His green eyes were as dark as a rain forest and glittering with faint amusement.

"Are you afraid of me, Kara?" he asked softly.

"Of course not. I was just thinking about all these dishes. Are you sure—"

"Very. Leave them for—"

"The maid?" she supplied pointedly when he broke off with a sudden frown.

"For later. Maybe galley duty will distract me from wanting a smoke after you go."

Kara drew a deep breath. "And what about now?"

She was like a child playing by the edge of a dangerous river, unable to keep from dangling a toe in just to see what would happen.

"For now I have you," Max countered, just as with some primal sense she had known he would. His voice was as deep and beckoning as any river Kara could imagine.

He reached for her, shifting position as he did, so that his back rested against the stone pillar at the end of the wall. Bracing his feet wide apart, he pulled her into the heated strength of his body and said roughly, "Distract me, Kara."

He lowered his head, and his mouth moved against hers, the pressure hard and firm. Kara's eyes were wide open; her fingers splayed against his chest in a feeble attempt to keep his body at a safe distance. Their noses bumped awkwardly, and she instinctively moved to pull away.

"No, please," Max breathed, bringing his mouth close to her ear. "Don't fight me, Kara. All I want is a kiss. Just a kiss," he whispered, drifting back across her cheek until his lips once more brushed hers.

There was strength in the way he was holding her, but no force. Kara sensed that if she really tried to break away he wouldn't stop her, and so she wasn't compelled to try. Her hands relaxed slightly on his chest, although her lips remained tightly sealed. She could feel a smile forming on his.

"Better," he allowed hoarsely. "Now try opening your mouth for me."

Cautiously Kara complied, and Max groaned as he took her in a kiss that was swift and fierce, as if afraid she might change her mind if she had a chance to think. He had no way of knowing that Kara *was* thinking, that she was much too well-disciplined to stop thinking, especially at such an unpredictable moment as this.

What she was thinking was that she should heed the warning being flashed by her well-honed system of defenses. And she would, she told herself. But first, just once, she wanted to be kissed by the full, sulky mouth that had been driving her to distraction all evening. Just once. Surely if she recognized up front the inherent danger in being swept off her feet by a man she knew almost nothing about, then there couldn't be any harm in sharing just one kiss. Just one.

The problem was that she had difficulty determining if she and Max were engaged in one long kiss of many colors or a string of small ones that melted sweetly together. At first his tongue had been a rough intruder, hungry and demanding. Once he sensed her acquiescence, however, Max was in no hurry. Cradling her head in his hands, he explored the smooth, silky chamber of her mouth. He circled her tongue with his and playfully traced the straight line of her teeth. Kara let him pull her arms around his neck. Her breasts were crushed against his chest as she went up on her toes, curling her fingers around his corded nape, relishing the taut smoothness of his skin there.

His fingers spread across her back, trailing down along her spine to caress the slight curve of her hips through the thin cotton dress. He sucked in a quick, harsh breath, and then without warning his tongue quickened once more, plunging hard and deep, demanding her body's most primitive responses. At the same time he cupped her bottom in his hands and urged her deeper into the vee of his open thighs. Prickly heat exploded inside Kara, as if there were a giant sparkler where her belly should be, burning out of control. She quivered uncontrollably as he pressed her hips closer still to his, reacting to his heat and hardness like a match to friction.

Kara had been kissed and held by men before, had been the recipient of more lengthy, more intimate caresses. But never before had she felt this way. This feeling coursing through her was new and intricate and confusing. The intensity of her response to Max was what had driven her to return his kiss and caresses with a reckless abandon, and now that very intensity was the force reining her to a halt. She was still thinking clearly enough to know that the greatest danger here lay inside herself. To surrender to passion was to let down your guard utterly and completely, and that was something Kara couldn't afford to do on impulse.

Gently but unmistakably she moved to create distance between her body and his, silently indicating that she wished to be released. Max complied only as far as easing his hold fractionally and dragging his mouth from hers to scatter kisses in the sensitive shallow beneath her ear and along the column of her throat.

"Max, please," she murmured, "I really have to..."

The slow, damp kiss he was bestowing in the hollow of her throat climaxed with the lazy dragging of his tongue along the slant of her collarbone. The contact was wet and gritty and the most unexpectedly erotic thing anyone had ever done to Kara.

"...go to work now," she finished in a ragged tone, trying to conceal the tremor he'd sent rushing through her.

Max lifted his head to gaze down at her with a sexy, crooked smile that threatened to reignite the smoldering sparkler inside her. "Call in sick."

Kara wasn't certain whether the words were a plea or a command. For her the most shocking thing was that, either way, she longed to heed them. That knowledge only added to the conviction that she had to get away.

"I can't," she replied quickly before the hungry look he was giving her did any more damage to her resolve.

Max's eyes crinkled at the corners as his smile deepened into a gently mocking grin.

"Chicken," he goaded.

"That's not it."

"No? Shall I wait up for you, then?"

Kara was assailed by the recollection of the way he'd looked the last time she'd seen him at that time of night, shirtless and rumpled from sleep and tempting in spite of his rudeness. If he smiled at her in that condition, the effect would be devastating.

"No," she said, hoping her voice didn't betray the quickness of her breathing. "I'm sure I'll be very late. I guess I'll just see you tomorrow."

"Tomorrow," he echoed quietly.

His hands were still framing her hips. Now he took his time removing them, underscoring his reluctance with an almost wistful frown. Again Kara marveled at how effortlessly he managed to make her feel desirable. Skill or pure instinct, it was potent stuff.

The afterglow from his attention lingered all the way to the Shady Lady. Kara replayed in her mind the hours they'd spent together, analyzing some of his remarks, savoring others, wishing she could take back a few of her own more awkward ones. It was like being a teenager again. She felt uncertain and giddy, as if she were poised on the brink of some wondrous new discovery. All in all, it was a ridiculous way for a thirty-two-year-old woman to feel, she admonished herself as she hurriedly changed into a sleek, strapless red dress in her office at the club. Ridiculous and delicious.

If only it were possible for her to lower her defenses and simply enjoy the feeling for a little while. Quickly, without having to glance in the mirror, she wound her hair into a loose coil at the back of her neck, thinking that, unfortunately, it had been a long time since her life had been that simple. Like everything else she did, the situation with Max was fraught with complications. True, she was no longer concerned that he might be a direct threat to her freedom, but there were other risks. To ignore them would be foolhardy. The fact that she'd been tempted to do exactly that at the mere suggestion by Max that she take the night off troubled Kara.

Her life on Diamond Cay might not show much evidence of it, but there was inside her a streak of recklessness she'd thought she'd outgrown. As a child and later, during high school, it had prompted her to undertake small acts of rebellion that usually failed to cause more than a minor stir in her parents' very busy lives. She knew it was that same reckless streak that had led her into a relationship with Dwight Billings when she was a freshman in college. The results of that error in judgment had been disastrous, exacting a price she might well go on paying forever.

She'd long ago stopped blaming herself for all that had happened back then, attributing it to the inexperience of youth. Obviously, though, she hadn't grown as wise and levelheaded as she had lulled herself into believing. Not if one little... all right, she corrected herself, sighing, one monumental kiss from Max could tempt her to throw caution to the wind this way.

She had applied her makeup before putting on her dress, so all that remained was to run a sheer red gloss stick over her lips before joining the exuberant crowd waiting for Earle to take the stage. As she did she couldn't help but notice that the glow on her face was more radiant than anything Elizabeth Arden had ever put in a bottle. Even worse, she looked as if she might giggle at any second. Tossing her lipstick back into her makeup case, Kara turned toward the door. Thank heavens the lights in the club were dim. Now, if she could get through the night without dancing on any tabletops, maybe no one would notice her regression into adolescent giddiness. And maybe—please God, she thought—it would pass soon.

Kara spent most of the evening on her feet overseeing another busy night. Making sure she was available but as unobtrusive as possible, she moved among the crowded tables, arranging for a complimentary bottle of champagne for a couple celebrating their anniversary, lingering to chat for a while with a group who visited the island often. By the time most of the customers had left, she was exhausted and feeling quite proud of herself. She'd managed to behave perfectly normally in spite of the fact that her thoughts were on Max most of the time. After saying good-night to the last couple to leave, she hoisted herself onto the corner barstool with a grateful sigh. The sigh was cut short when she saw Jack bearing down on her with a glass of ice water and a smug expression. Evidently her pat on the back over the fact that no one had noticed her giddy mood had been a bit premature.

"All right," he said, slapping a cocktail napkin on the bar before setting down the glass, "let's have it."

"Have what?" Kara countered obligingly.

"Whatever *it* is. Whatever has put wings on your feet and stars in your eyes."

"Don't be ridiculous."

"I'm not. Ridiculous is you referring to a daiquiri as fizzle with a swizzle and a cherry on top."

"I didn't do that." She bit her lip, troubled by the vague stirring of her memory. "Did I?"

"Twice. You also hugged that old bat Mrs. Issacson and told her you were glad to see her."

"That's business."

"That's bull. Kara, this is me you're talking to, remember? I know you, and I know you're too honest—not to mention stubborn—to say that to Issacson after what she called you the last time she was here."

"Hussy," Kara murmured, remembering.

"*Brazen* hussy—let's get it straight. After all, you were trying to make her husband."

"Trying to make him stop hanging over the deck railing, you mean. Next time I'll let him fall." She took a sip of water, recalling the absurd scene that had taken place when the Issacsons were here a few months ago. A smile started to curve her lips, only to fade abruptly. "Ouch. My smile aches," she grumbled in response to Jack's questioning look.

"Can't say I'm surprised," he remarked dryly. "It's been on duty pretty nonstop tonight."

She took another sip. "I actually hugged Mrs. Issacson?"

"Well, squeezed might be a better description."

Kara groaned. "I must have been delirious."

"My thoughts exactly. Which brings us full circle. What's going on, honey?"

Kara lifted the glass to her lips again and held it there until Jack reached over and relieved her of it. She was too tired to talk about this with him of all people.

"Drowning yourself isn't going to help," he told her. "I want an answer."

Planting her elbow on the bar, Kara rested her chin in her palm and closed her eyes. "I'm too tired to make one up. Can't you just guess?"

"No. If I had to guess, I'd say you're acting like you're in love."

She shook her head without compunction. She didn't have any hands-on experience with love, but she knew that what she was feeling was too soon and too purely hormonal to be it.

"Yeah, I knew that was a long shot," muttered Jack. "I haven't seen you hanging around here with anyone, and you're all alone out there on the point—except for the character next door, of course."

It wasn't necessary for Kara to open her eyes. She could feel Jack's eyebrows lift, hear the wheels spinning in his head.

"Good night," she said, starting to slip off the stool.

Jack's arm shot forward to hook hers, locking her in place. "Not so fast."

"Jack, I'm dead on my feet."

"You can sleep late in the morning."

"No, I can't. I told you Max starts playing at six." To mention their new truce would only weaken her protest.

"So you did," Jack agreed. "Now I want to hear what else old *Max* has been up to out there."

His not too subtle emphasis on Max's name strengthened Kara's hunch that he was going to be a pain about this. Old habits died hard.

"Nothing. He hasn't been up to anything. He plays, he runs, he swims, we had dinner, he—"

"Stop. Hold it right there," he ordered, releasing her to throw his hands up in the air. "You call having dinner with the guy nothing?"

"Yes. For Pete's sake, Jack, it was only dinner. A barbecued steak at that, not pheasant under glass."

"All part of your grand scheme to kill him with kindness, I suppose?"

Kara's nod had a startled quality she was sure didn't escape Jack's sharp eye. She'd forgotten all about her plan. What had happened between Max and her tonight had been genuine and spontaneous. And futile, she reminded herself.

"Yes," she marshalled her wits enough to lie. "It was part of my plan. I lent him a towel, and he invited me to dinner. I accepted in the hope that being cordial might inspire him to do the same."

Jack's expression was only skeptical. "Cordial?"

"Right."

"Kara, cordial is 'Hi, how are you?' A barbecue is downright friendly, and sharing towels... Why the hell doesn't he use his own towels, anyway?"

"Because he forgot to bring one down to the beach." Another lie. "Aren't you supposed to hang a bright light over my head for this?"

"This is not an inquisition."

"Could've fooled the suspect—oops, I mean me."

"Cute, Kara. Is it so outlandish for me to be curious when I see you acting this way?"

"What way? So I'm happy." It was Kara's turn to throw her hands in the air. "I'm always happy."

"Happy, yes. This is something different. This is..."

Kara met the shrewd blue eyes that were resting on her with gentle concern and let a smile form even though it hurt. "Delirious? Wacky? Spaced out?"

Jack chuckled along with her. "All of the above. And I'm not complaining. I love seeing you like this. I just want to make sure that you're okay. That you're not going to get hurt."

"I won't, believe me. Odds are Max won't be here long enough to hurt me. Story of my life," she added flippantly.

Jack stabbed his fingers into his hair with an anguished look that instantly made Kara feel guilty. She should have known how he'd take such a remark. "Look, Kara, I've said it before, if you're not happy here—"

"I'm happy. I am," she stressed when he peered at her doubtfully. "Isn't that what started this whole discussion in the first place? I wasn't bemoaning the fact that Max will be leaving eventually. In fact, I'm glad he is."

"I thought you liked him," Jack countered, looking baffled.

"I do," admitted Kara. "But I'd like him even more if I knew for sure how soon he'd be leaving Diamond Cay."

Jack closed his eyes briefly, reached for a bottle of whisky and poured a shot glass full. After he'd swallowed it in one gulp, he said, "Now I'm ready to hear the reasoning behind that last statement."

"It's really simple," Kara began, already suspecting that explaining her philosophy on sexual involvement to Jack wasn't going to be at all simple. "Living on the island permanently while most of the eligible males around come and go presents a few problems."

"And a few challenges?"

"I've noticed how neatly you handle those challenges," she observed with a wry smile. In the short time he'd been here, Jack had become friendly with a number of the young women who worked at Westwind and also found time to entertain several unattached female guests. And why wouldn't he be in demand? Kara thought almost wistfully. He was attractive and charming and wasn't saddled with her fear of letting people get too close.

"Jack, you've adapted to this life-style a lot more quickly than I did," she continued. "When I first moved here I was too busy learning how to manage the club to have much of a social life. Finally, after I'd been here about a year, I met a man, and we became—" she fumbled for a word that would be accurate without being graphic "—involved."

Jack nodded, appearing a trifle amused by her awkwardness in discussing this matter with him.

"Anyway, Peter—that was his name—Peter was here with a friend. They were both in real estate and had stopped to take a few days off after scouting some property here in the islands. I guess that was what lulled me into thinking there could be more to it than there really was. I figured he'd be coming down often to check on his investments and that we could see each other. It would be almost normal, I thought."

Kara stared at a spot somewhere over Jack's shoulder as she spoke. Probing these old memories was . . . not painful exactly, at least not as painful as it once was. More like uncomfortable. And embarrassing. It must have showed on her face because Jack shifted his feet awkwardly.

"Kara, if you'd rather not drag up all this—"

"No, it's all right," she cut in. "I just want you to understand why Max won't be able to hurt me, why I'll never be that gullible or leave myself open to that kind of heartache again. To be brief, so we can both get home and get to bed, Peter left, promising he was going to write, call, miss me desperately—all that good stuff—and then nothing."

"Nothing?" Jack looked quietly furious. "He never got in touch with you?"

"Well, not yet, anyway," she replied lightly. "And it's been four years. His friend has been back since, and I casually asked him about Peter, certain he was going to say he'd died tragically and no one had thought to notify me. He hadn't, of course."

"Bastard."

"The biggest," agreed Kara. "Although in a way he did me a favor. He made me face reality. There's no future for me with a guy who's only here for a week or so. And that's best all the way around."

She had no intention of staying up the rest of the night attempting to explain to him why that was best, so she continued in a rush. "Now that I've accepted that fact, I'm free to simply enjoy a man who interests me for the short time that he's here with no strings attached. In other words, my expectations no longer exceed the reality of the situation. The problem with Max is that I'm not sure how short his stay will be. If Victor's house is at his disposal, and he has unlimited means, which I suspect he does, he could end up being here quite a while. And that could get sticky—emotionally, I mean."

Jack was looking at her as if she had lapsed into Swahili midway through her explanation. "In other words, what you're talking about here is casual sex?"

He made it sound as if she were talking about drawing and quartering someone. "No, I'm talking about unencumbered sex—and with an expert on the subject, I might add."

"And how many men would you say you've enjoyed this sort of unencumbered sex with since you've—how did you put it? Oh, yes, since you've faced reality."

His nonchalant wiping of the bar as he spoke didn't fool Kara. "I'd like to say dozens," she told him, "but the truth is, none. Just because I've made the mental decision to have a fling if the situation is right doesn't mean I've actually met a man who interests me that way yet."

"But this Max character interests you that way?"

"Yes," she admitted. "And stop calling him a character."

"Sorry, it was your word." He tossed the wet cloth aside. "Would you really have a—a fling with a guy you know nothing about."

"Of course not." Jack's relieved look was fleeting. "If I knew nothing about him, I wouldn't know if he planned to stay. And if he stayed, I wouldn't want to have a fling with him."

"But if he was leaving soon, you would?"

"Right."

"Kara, this is insane."

This time she was off the stool before he could stop her. "Thank you for your opinion, Jack, and I promise I will give it my full consideration. Then do exactly as I please," she concluded as she turned to leave.

"Go ahead," he shouted after her. "And I promise I'll be watching you like a hawk to see to it you don't do anything rash."

Kara whirled back to face him in exasperation. If she weren't so tired, she'd really let him have it. As it was she settled for an indignant "You have no right," the effect of which was greatly diminished by the yawn that followed closely.

"I have every right to look out for you, pumpkin," Jack corrected, unable to suppress an affectionate smile for all that Kara knew he was attempting to look stern and authoritative. "Every right in the world. It's a big brother's prerogative."

Chapter Six

Kara had been overjoyed when her brother first announced his plans to join her here on Diamond Cay. Now she fretted that it might be a mistake, however temporary the arrangement was supposed to be. Not her mistake, she reflected testily. Victor's.

When John—or rather, Jack, as she still sometimes forgot to call him—first sent her to Chicago to see Victor thirteen years ago, Kara had found it difficult to believe that the two men even knew each other, much less that they were friends. Through the years since, however, she'd seen irrefutable evidence that they were precisely that. Not that she understood the bond between them even now. Victor was rich, successful, law abiding. And Jack . . . well, Jack was none of those things.

The only things she could see that the two men had in common were a passion for major league baseball and an infuriating reticence. At different times she'd questioned each of them about how they became friends and heard basically the same short story. They met at a Peace Corps fund-raiser in Washington sometime during the two years Jack had been a volunteer and had hit it off. No amount of hinting or tactful prodding by her had ever elicited an explanation of how such a casual friendship could survive all that had transpired since or why someone of Victor's stature would be willing to speak with, let alone do favors for, a man who was wanted by the FBI.

Kara had been walking along the beach; now she plopped down in the sand a short distance from the house and stared at the ocean. The morning sun had already risen well up in a sky that was almost too perfectly blue to be real. The incoming tide claimed another narrow strip of dry sand with each cresting wave, and the late risers of the island's bird population swooped low over the water in search of breakfast. Kara hardly saw any of it.

Instead she saw the New England university campus as it had looked on a warm spring day almost fourteen years ago. She saw herself, part of a group of restless, chanting young people surging up the wide brick steps of the administration building, bent on occupying the dean's office until the world bowed to their naive demands. Or rather she saw a younger version of herself—younger and more eager and innocent. Back then Kara would have bristled at the use of the word *innocent* in reference to herself, but she realized now that that was exactly what she had been.

Resting her forehead on her bent knees, she closed her eyes, not wanting to see the rest of that infamous day she was doomed to relive thousands of times in her mind. Unfortunately, it wasn't as easy to shut off the feelings invoked by the memory as it was the images. She no longer shook uncontrollably from residual panic, but it was there nonetheless, still potent enough to make her palms sweat and her stomach knot. Most of her recollection of that day was a blur, penetrated by scattered, horrifyingly clear fragments of memory. What always confused her most about what had happened was how quickly events had gone from being normal—boring, even—to violently out of control.

She remembered clearly sitting by an open window with a girl she knew slightly from English class, sharing a candy bar and whispering about how they half wished the dean would hurry up and send in the police so they'd be spared spending the night on the floor. Barely a half hour later she was screaming with horror after hearing the explosion of the gun in Dwight's hand and seeing an elderly security guard's back slam against the wall from the bullet's impact. She remembered crying so hard that she threw up in the dean's wastebasket.

Kara's mouth compressed into a tight, thin line. Thoughtful and tidy even on the brink of disaster—that was her. She wasn't sure how much later it was that Jack found her and dragged her down a narrow staircase to the outside, where she could finally breathe again because the air smelled of lilacs instead of tear gas. The next thing she remembered was waking up in a strange bed in a strange room, waking up to a whole new life, as it turned out. And cut off from her old one as surely and completely as if she'd been hurtled to another planet with no way to get home.

The only oasis of familiarity in that precarious new world had been Jack. Some time later it had occurred to Kara that the reason that hadn't been more of a hardship was because, in a way, that's how it had always been. Growing up, the two of them had been closer than most brothers and sisters, despite the six-year difference in their ages. Kara had once glumly asked Jack if he thought they were close by default, because it was either each other or nothing. Realistic as always, he had responded by asking her what difference it made. When Kara pictured her father from her childhood it was always coming or going through the front door—usually going—with his black medical bag in hand. If possible her mother had spent even more time away from home than her father had, rehearsing or appearing in plays with the local repertory theatre group, from which she apparently derived more pride and satisfaction than she did from either of her children.

Only Jack had always been there, faithfully writing to her from college and later from his Peace Corps station in Africa, sending her presents on her birthday and at Christmas—real, honest-to-goodness presents that clearly had been chosen with her in mind, not extravagant checks presented with an offhand "Pick yourself out something nice." Especially during the past thirteen years his presence in her life had been crucial. Months went by when she didn't see or hear from him, but she lived with the daily certainty that if she needed him, Jack would be there. That was why she would do anything, make any sacrifice, to ensure his safety.

Kara had never told Jack so, but if not for him she probably would have surfaced and faced whatever punishment awaited her for her role in the botched demonstration years ago. The biggest reason she held back was fear that once the authorities had her in hand they would use her to force Jack to turn himself in. And Kara suspected, although Jack grimly refused to discuss his activities past or present, that for him the consequences would be much more serious. Once, years ago, when she'd been feeling particularly angry and frustrated, she'd declared that if Victor was a real friend he would intercede on his behalf. Jack had sullenly dismissed that as a possibility, and Kara had finally accepted the fact that if his situation was something even Victor couldn't pull enough strings to fix, it was pretty bad.

Not that Jack seemed to want the situation resolved. True, he always got that anguished look in his eyes whenever they discussed the limitations she was forced to live with. And several times he'd come out with a wistful "Someday..." but always he stopped himself short and backed away from whatever it was he'd been about to say. Kara had the feeling that, aside from his concern for her, Jack enjoyed the unsettled, shadowy condition of his life. And although he never spouted off about it around her, his conversation was peppered with enough offhand references to places such as Managua and Bogotá to convince her that his ties to radical politics were as strong as ever.

She'd been secretly nurturing the hope that his stay here
on Diamond Cay might change that. She did her best no
to pressure him about it, mostly because she knew a hard
sell approach would never work. It seemed possible, how
ever, that here, far away from the influence of whoever
and whatever kept him living on the edge of danger, Jack
would have time to think things over and maybe decide i
was worth taking whatever steps were necessary to ensure
a safer, more normal future. For both of them. Now tha
she'd had time to work through her resentment of las
night, Kara had to admit that she still hoped that and wa
still glad he was here. Even though at the moment he wa
threatening to be a royal pain in the rear.

As if this situation with Max weren't already complicated enough, now she also had to worry about Jack worrying about her. Kara knew from experience that i
wouldn't do any good to tell Jack the truth, which was that
she could take care of herself. No matter how dazzled she'd
been by Max last evening, when push came to shove she
was no starry-eyed, impressionable teenager who could be
swept off course by a sexy smile and a pair of broad
shoulders. She'd been strong and resourceful enough to
build a life for herself here, and that should tell Jack
something. Granted, it was a life of caution and control,
but there were worse fates. For the most part Kara wa
content. And until she was absolutely certain that Max
would be a pleasant interlude in her contented life and no
a threat to it, she was going to keep her distance.

At least she was going to keep her distance emotionally.
Physically was another matter, and one she didn't really
have any control over, Kara reminded herself as Max ambled into view on her left. At the first sight of him Kara felt
something similar to the strangely light-headed sensation
she'd experienced last night. Light-bodied, she thought
with distracted amusement. It was as if gravity had released her and any minute she might soar as high as the
silver-winged gulls overhead. Her instantaneous response
to him forced her to acknowledge that on some level, beneath her thoughts of the past and her concern for her

brother, she'd been sitting here waiting, hoping, wishing that Max would show up.

Now she was wishing she'd remembered to put on her sunglasses so he wouldn't be able to read in her eyes her fascination with the long, lazy stride that carried him ever closer. He was wearing only a bathing suit, the same ancient blue one as yesterday. It was worn and faded, and, although slightly baggy, it seemed to fit his lean hips as comfortably as his skin did. Already the sunburn on his arms and shoulders had turned to rich bronze. If he stayed another week, he would be darker than she was. Yes, a week, Kara mused. That would be just about perfect. A week would allow plenty of time for a graceful affair but not enough for her to become emotionally entangled. Somehow she had to find out how long Max was planning to stay here. And soon.

"Good morning," he said as he drew near enough to drop to the sand beside her.

His gravelly voice was all it took to send an already familiar spark of excitement flickering through Kara. Hard on its heels came a more dangerous rush of heat as his gaze traveled over her with lazy attention to detail, lingering on her slightly breathless smile, the curve of her breasts beneath her oversized yellow T-shirt, and the shapely, golden-brown length of her legs below. By the time he lifted his gaze to meet hers, Kara's mouth was so dry that she had to swallow hard to keep from croaking like a frog when she returned his greeting. She was only partially successful.

"I didn't expect to see you up and about this early," he remarked, amusement lifting the corners of his entrancing mouth.

"I couldn't sleep." The truth was out before Kara had time to consider how he might interpret such an admission. She hastily added, "I had a lot on my mind this morning."

Max nodded, his suddenly solemn expression somehow managing to convey more dry humor that his smile had. "Me, too."

The softly rasped words unfurled ribbons of intimacy that seemed to lace together the reasons each of them had had trouble sleeping into one tidy package labeled Each Other.

"It had nothing to do with...you know, you or last night or anything. I mean," Kara hastened to add, "with our bargain. You were very quiet this morning. Thank you."

"You're welcome."

Jerking her gaze away from his deadpan expression, she stared off to her right, as if suddenly mesmerized by the absolutely deserted stretch of beach, which was all that lay in that direction. Great, she thought with disgust. First croaking hello and now babbling like an idiot. So far she was doing a bang-up job of staying cool.

Since her disastrous affair with Peter she'd seldom been alone with a man this way. She was a whiz at dining and dancing, but lack of experience in the less structured aspects of the mating game was definitely starting to show. If she couldn't control what rolled off her tongue, how in the world was she going to control this attraction that set her heart to beating faster whenever Max was near? She'd thought it was strong before, but it was worse with him stretched out beside her in the sunlight, his green gaze steady on her, the soft-looking black hair on his chest a temptation her fingertips could barely resist.

"Last night," he began in a voice so low-pitched that it made the skin on the back of Kara's neck prickle, "had everything to do with why I couldn't sleep. Would you like to hear about it?"

Kara took a deep breath, stunned that a man—any man—was able to scramble her senses so easily, but determined not to let it continue. By the time she turned to face Max a split second later, she had manufactured a smile she hoped was carefree and confident enough to hide the tumultuous feelings inside.

"Not especially," she replied. "I think we could probably come up with a safer topic of conversation."

"Possibly. But there are a lot of things I'd rather feel than safe. How about you?"

Max tossed the question off teasingly, assuming Kara would field it in the same spirit. Instead, it was as if a cloud suddenly passed in front of just that part of the sun that shone on her, sending shadows drifting across her face.

"No," she said quietly after a stricken pause. "I can't think of anything that feels better than being absolutely safe."

A dozen provocative comebacks about how he could teach her something that felt better sprang to the tip of Max's tongue. He bit them all back, certain from her pensive expression that whatever chord he'd just touched ran too deep inside Kara to be treated as fodder for a suggestive joke. Her sorrow at that moment was almost palpable. Looking at her, Max was reminded of a lost child, and an unfamiliar protectiveness swelled inside him. He was ill-equipped to deal with the feeling, especially knowing as he did that Kara was still far too apprehensive around him to open up to him. She sure looked as if she needed to unload on someone, though. Sweeping aside a half-formed wish that he could be that someone, Max concentrated instead on coming up with some way to make this moment pass easily for her by swinging the mood back in a lighter direction.

Almost immediately he remembered the float beside him and was glad he'd heeded the impulse to bring it along. He'd carried it folded under his arm, dropping it by his side when he sat down. Now he reached for it, flipping it open with a flourish and letting it settle like a stiff blue plastic blanket over Kara's lap.

"All right, then," he said, "no more about my trouble sleeping...for the time being. Instead, see if you can guess what this is."

The look on her face told him she hadn't noticed it until that moment. Her surprise quickly gave way to a matter-of-fact shrug. "It's a float."

"You're quick," Max countered in a drawl of exaggerated admiration. "Think you can blow it up?"

"Sure."

"Good girl." He lifted it by the plastic air hole and of
fered it to her.

Kara's hands remained braced behind her as she peered
at him from beneath scantly raised eyebrows. "You asked
if I *could* blow it up, not if I would."

"My mistake. *Will* you blow it up? Please," he added.

It startled Max to discover that the word *please* used as
something other than a mechanical part of a verbal order
felt unfamiliar on his tongue. Unfamiliar and good. "I'd
do it myself," he continued, "except I don't think my cig
arette-ravaged lungs have enough air. I wouldn't want to
embarrass myself."

With a skeptical grin Kara reached for the float and
brought the plug to her mouth. Max watched the way her
slender fingers positioned it carefully between her parted
lips. Looking soft and slightly moist, her lips settled deli
cately into place, and her eyes closed as she exhaled the
first deep breath. Lord, what he would give at this mo
ment to be a $5.98 plastic toy. Just the thought of it made
it necessary for Max to shift his position in the sand,
bending one knee strategically. A bathing suit wasn't the
safest choice of clothing to wear for fantasizing in public,
especially when you were as easily aroused as he seemed to
be lately. Regretfully, Max forced his mind onto a differ
ent path.

Taking advantage of Kara's preoccupation with the
float, he studied her face, wondering how long it had been
since he'd met a woman so absolutely unconcerned about
having him see her without makeup. It didn't matter that
her face was half hidden by the dark, shiny curtain of her
hair. Already its finely carved features and wide range of
animation were imprinted on his brain, more easily sum
moned and held before him than the faces of people he'd
known far longer and better. Max was sure of that fact
because he'd tested it over and over during the long hours
before sleep had come last night. He'd lain awake teasing
himself with her memory and anticipating seeing her this
morning. Just seeing her. After the way she'd bolted last

night he'd reconciled himself to the fact that things with Kara were not going to move at the pace he was accustomed to.

He still hadn't been expecting the awkwardness with which she'd greeted his appearance this morning. He'd immediately turned to flirting with her to loosen her up because that's what came most naturally to him, and for a few seconds there it appeared to have worked. But she definitely had not been flirting when she made that comment about feeling safe. Inadvertently he'd stirred something deep and troubling inside her, and he would pay a hefty sum to find out what it was.

Ordinarily if he wanted to know something this badly, he would simply ignore what she'd said last night about asking each other questions and come right out and ask anyway. The privileges bestowed and allowances made for celebrities had long ago made deep inroads into whatever manners his mother had managed to teach him. But something other than politeness held him back. Sensitivity, maybe.

The notion sent a smile of self-mockery shooting to Max's lips. Sensitivity had never been part of Max Ellis's image, public or private. So either he was developing some at this late date or else the woman beside him was remarkably transparent. Either way, the fact remained that she didn't like to talk about herself. Max suspected that if he asked too much too soon, the stone wall she threw up to hold him at bay would be permanent and impenetrable. He didn't know why that thought was so painful to him, only that it was.

After a dozen or so breaths the float was about midway between flat and full, and Kara's cheeks were flushed from exertion. Max was about to suggest a break when she paused on her own, clamping her finger over the air hole so none leaked out.

"So tell me, Max," she said between heavy breaths, "do you really think this will make it any easier for you to ride a wave all the way to shore?"

Max winced when he caught the laughter sparkling in her eyes. "You mean you saw me out there yesterday?"

Kara nodded. "I saw all right."

"And here I was worried about embarrassing myself in front of you by getting winded. Give me this damn thing." He yanked the float from her with a disgruntled sound and started to blow into it furiously. He had it full almost to bursting before she'd completely stopped chuckling.

"There. I did it." He was doing his best not to gasp for air as if he'd just run a four-minute mile, but the smile simmering on Kara's lips told him she wasn't fooled. Probably because his face was purple, Max thought with disgust.

"You mean you did half of it," she corrected.

"It sure felt like more than half," he groused.

"But it wasn't."

"Great. I risked respiratory arrest and still didn't prove my manhood to you."

"Sorry."

"Don't be. I'll just have to keep trying." The retort harbored an undercurrent of sensuality, but Max purposely kept his smile easy and unthreatening, and this time there was almost no trace of awkwardness in the smile Kara flashed back.

"Of course," she ventured, "the fact that we each did half of the work presents a problem. Who gets to use it first?"

"Whoever's tallest?" Max shrugged off the venomous look with which she greeted that suggestion. "No? Okay, how about strongest? I've got it," he declared, standing and firing the float toward the water. The wind was with him, and it sailed a good thirty feet before crashing in the white foam close to the shore. "We'll race. First one to the float gets first crack at it. One, two..."

"That's not fair," exclaimed Kara as he reached down and hauled her to her feet. "I still have on my T-sh—"

"Three."

Max broke into a run, gambling that she was too stubborn to hand him an easy victory. Sure enough, she came pounding the sand right behind him. Purposely he slowed his gait. He had no intention of beating her *or* letting her win. He allowed her to gain on him, letting her pull a step ahead and timing it so that her hand landed on the float a half a heartbeat before his. They were both laughing, standing knee high in the warm, swirling water, tugging on opposite ends of the float. By pulling first one way and then the other, Max easily kept her using most of her energy in a struggle for balance. He could just as easily have ended the battle with one swift yank if he wanted to. That wasn't what he wanted.

"Hold it!" he shouted finally.

She laughed up at him, her brilliant blue eyes flashing with excitement. Her smile was exuberant and utterly relaxed. Max's heart threatened to rise right out of his chest.

"Give up?" she demanded teasingly.

"Never. How about a compromise?"

"Sure. As long as I go first."

"Witch. What I had in mind was sharing it."

Her eyes widened. "Together?"

"That's usually what sharing means."

"We'll never—"

"Know unless we try. Climb aboard."

She hesitated. Max could almost see the battle taking place inside her, her desire to go on having fun warring against what he was beginning to suspect was a very cautious nature. Finally, with an almost defiant toss of her head, she took her right hand off the float to execute a comical salute.

"Aren't I supposed to say 'Aye-Aye' or something before climbing aboard?" she joked.

"A simple 'Yes, sir' will do just fine."

"Don't hold your breath."

"What little breath I have left, you mean."

Pausing as she was about to swing one leg over the float, she glanced up at him with mock concern. "Do you really think it's safe for you to try this without an oxygen tank?"

"A lot safer than it is for you to make fun of me when I have enough ocean handy to drown you in. Now up."

God, he loved the sound of her laughter. It wafted through his head like sunshine, illuminating nooks and crannies of tenderness that had been dark for so long he'd forgotten they were there. As they were talking he had gradually inched farther out until they stood about waist deep in the water. Now he held the float steady while she climbed on, her lithe movements indicating she was at home in the water. Once she was straddling the float she followed his directions and slid all the way to one end, leaving the other free for him.

"Do you really think this will work?" she asked him.

"Sure." Actually Max had no idea, but he fervently hoped it didn't. He hadn't blown his lungs out just to sit three feet away from her. With a lot less care than she had taken, he jumped on.

"You know, Max, I think you should try to center your weight—"

The rest of her advice was lost in a yelp as the unbalanced float turned belly up, sending them both flying in a spinning pinwheel of arms and legs. Kara came up sputtering. Her thin cotton T-shirt was nearly transparent when wet, and it was plastered to her body like saran wrap, revealing a pretty skimpy-looking bikini and the taut condition of her nipples. Definitely a sight worth taking a dunk for, in Max's estimation.

"Center your weight!" she wailed. "Didn't you hear me say to center your weight?"

"I thought I was centered," Max lied. "Don't worry. I think I've got the hang of it now. Let's try again."

It took three more attempts, alternating who went first, before Max gauged that Kara was frustrated enough not to balk at the suggestion that they try moving closer together. A lot closer. Climbing on first, he settled himself dead center and held out a hand to help her up. She stood her ground, staring at the float as if it were a caldron of boiling water she'd just been invited to jump into.

"Why don't you try getting on with your back to me?" Max suggested. "That way we'll be paddling in the same direction."

Kara's expression brightened, confirming Max's hunch that she would be more comfortable with that idea than she had been with the prospect of straddling it facing him. This time he really did center his weight as she slid on, slowly backing in close to him, and like magic they remained upright.

"It worked!" she exclaimed.

"Yeah. Fancy that." Max was doubly thankful he'd suggested sitting this way. Not only did her rounded bottom feel like heaven nestled between his spread thighs, her position also prevented her from seeing the satisfied smile he couldn't seem to quell.

"The next step," he told her, plunging his hands into the water and making a few tentative strokes, "is to see if we can stay on while we're moving. Take it slow," he cautioned as she began paddling along with him. "Let's get some kind of rhythm going here."

"Oh, no," she moaned. "If you pick the rhythm, it will probably be a country shuffle."

"Are you making fun of my music, woman?"

"Music? I wondered what you called it."

"Careful. We're rapidly approaching the point where the water is over your head."

"Then I take it all back," she countered with haste, turning just enough to glance at him over her shoulder. "I hope you know that I'm only kidding. Actually your sound has been sort of growing on me."

"I thought country music gave you a headache."

"It does. But most of what you've been playing isn't really country, is it? It's more like . . . I don't know how to classify it, really."

Max chuckled at the familiar lament. "Well, don't feel lonesome, baby."

"What's that supposed to mean?"

"Nothing," he replied quickly, remembering that she had no idea who he was or how during the past ten years hundreds of critics had expressed the same bewilderment she just had when trying to stick him into an established musical pigeonhole. "I just think that a lot of people who

share your distaste for what's called country music might
like it if they listened with an open mind.''

"Could be. Maybe someday you'll become a famous
country superstar and succeed in converting the masses."

The humorous lilt in her voice told Max that she probably figured he had about as much chance of that coming
to pass as he had of becoming the next pope. "Yeah. Well.
Stranger things have happened."

The guilt Max felt over keeping her in the dark about his
identity was like a paper cut on his conscience, tiny but
irksome. It wouldn't be fair to Kara to let things go much
further without enlightening her, but just for a little while
longer he wanted to enjoy the novelty of not being Max
Ellis, Grammy Award-winning songwriter turned movie
star. Part blessing and part curse, his larger-than-life image was a weight he'd expected to carry with him every day
for the rest of his life. Meeting Kara was tantamount to
being plunked down in the middle of Fantasy Island. She
had no preconceived notions about him, leaving him free
to impress her or fail in the attempt all on his own. It was
crazy, given his history, but impressing Kara seemed to
Max to be the biggest challenge he'd ever faced. He felt
eager and uncertain at the same time, not to mention
slightly intoxicated in spite of the fact that he hadn't had
a beer since the one he'd had with dinner last night.

At least part of his intoxication Max attributed directly
to the sweet scent of Kara's neck. He risked being deep-
sixed by her in order to lean closer and inhale deeply.
Maybe quitting smoking had enhanced his senses. If so, it
was worth it. Because either Kara had found the perfect
perfume or her skin naturally smelled better than that of
any woman he'd ever known. It was a simple smell, fresh
and clean, reminding him of the early-spring flowers he
picked from his grandfather's garden when he was a kid.

Kara giggled softly as he unconsciously acted on the urge
to nuzzle the side of her throat. "Max! What are you
doing?"

"Smelling you."

"I don't smell," she shot back with feigned indignation.

"Yes, you do. You smell terrific. Almost as good as you taste, in fact." With his tongue he acknowledged the goose bumps that had just erupted along the curve of her shoulder. "What's it called?"

"My perfume? Spring."

"Spring." Max savored the word. All the women he knew wore perfume named after guys who designed overpriced clothes.

"At least that's the name on the bottle. Jack keeps telling me a more accurate name would be Eau de Unsophisticate. And I keep telling him that I refuse to take that as an insult."

Max paddled on automatically, seized by an insane urge to strangle a man he didn't even know. He waited long enough for the first premonition of disaster to pass before asking.

"Who's Jack?"

Kara only hesitated for a few seconds, but that was plenty long enough for Max to speculate about a potential problem he hadn't bothered to consider before now, not even last night when she'd tentatively broached the subject of his own marital status. Did Kara have a husband? A traveling salesman, maybe? Or maybe just a lover? Lord, when was the last time he'd worried about the competition?

Of course, he could always tell her who he was. That was almost guaranteed to keep him in the game, even if she was involved elsewhere. But something in Max was repelled by that prospect. Not only did he want to know if Kara could be interested in him when he wasn't wearing his aura of success, he was also afraid the fact that he'd been on the cover of *People* magazine might make a difference to her. And he didn't want to have to face that yet.

In the short time he'd known her, Kara had taken on true fantasy proportions in his mind. Her life was everything his wasn't—private, self-contained, serene. He thought of her as an honest, totally unaffected woman.

Maybe the last one in the entire world, and maybe his last chance to find a small part of himself that hadn't been packaged and postered and sold to the highest bidder. It was crazy, but he was even starting to have these strong feelings that fate had sent him here to Diamond Cay.

"Jack is a bartender at the club," Kara finally revealed.

"Oh, yeah? What else does Jack tend?"

"What?"

"Is he someone important in your life?" His chest was pressed to her back, and he could feel tension gathering there in the seconds before she answered.

"Not in the way I imagine you mean. Jack's not my boyfriend, if that's what you're asking."

Wryness shaped Max's smile over her casual use of such an innocent word as *boyfriend*. Then the urgency of uncertainty reasserted itself, and his smile faded. "Then who is your man?"

"What makes you so sure I have one?"

"Experience. A woman like you just doesn't run around free."

"I doubt you've ever met a woman like me." Instead of sounding vain as it should have, the comment sounded heavy with self-mockery.

Max lifted his hands from the water to gather her close. "I'm just beginning to realize that." He bent his head and stroked her satin shoulder with his jaw. "I didn't mean to badger you, honey. I just wanted to know what I was getting into. If you tell me there's no one special in your life, Kara, I'll believe you."

"Max, do you really think I'd be out here with you like this if there were anyone special?"

The question held a hint of exasperation, revealing a simple, no-nonsense attitude about a faithfulness that Max had thought extinct.

"No," he replied truthfully and without a flicker of hesitation. "No, I know you wouldn't be."

Tugging her back so she was leaning against him, he buried his face in the sweet-scented crook of her neck, using his lips and teeth and tongue in a gentle assault that opened the floodgates on the desire he'd been holding in check. With his palms flat on her rib cage, he pulled her closer still.

"Oh, Kara," he murmured between tastes of her honeyed flesh, "it feels so good to hold you, to touch you this way."

She made a small helpless sound, and gradually he felt the resistance leave her body. The float drifted unassisted as his hands moved over her, taking time to learn each subtle nuance of shape and texture. He framed her narrow waist with his palms, then stroked downward over the womanly curves of her hips and belly. The thin barrier of her T-shirt made the contact all the more tantalizing. She was like a fire smoldering beneath the layer of cool dampness, and Max tortured himself with the headiness of anticipation for long moments before thrusting his hands beneath the wet fabric to claim her directly.

He wanted her more than smoldering, he wanted her hot and hungry and panting for him, but he knew that such a response couldn't be rushed or demanded from Kara. The need to be patient shaped his every movement, each touch and caress, giving Max the sensation that he was doing this for the very first time. An absurd notion, but as powerful an aphrodisiac as he'd ever experienced.

Slowly he trailed his fingers over her bare skin, marveling at her responsiveness, registering each tremor of excitement, each delicate spasm of tightly clenched muscles. Hooking his thumbs inside her bikini top, he pushed it up, spilling the full bounty of her breasts. He heard Kara's breath catch and knew she wanted to be touched by him there almost as much as he wanted to touch her. Still, he held back, intensifying the electrical current arcing between them. Languorously he brushed the ultrasoft spot beneath her breasts with his fingertips, teasing himself and her by taking their plump weight on the backs of his hands and lifting them gently. Finally, with a harsh groan, he shifted so his wrists were crisscrossing her chest and captured her fullness with both hands.

He was prepared for Kara's sudden tensing. Bringing his mouth close to her ear, he whispered a soft, husky plea for her to trust him, promising that nothing would happen that she didn't want to happen. He meant every word of it. Her nipples were hard points of fire throbbing in the center of his palms, driving him crazy, but he forced himself to keep his hold on her loose until he once more felt her tension melt into acquiescence.

Her breathing became short and shallow, and each breath pushed her breasts deep into his cupped hands, snapping yet another of the slender threads tethering Max's passion. With his mouth still bestowing moist kisses on the velvet expanse of her throat and shoulders, he traced light circles until his fingertips closed on the tightly puckered tips. Kara's breath whooshed from her lungs with a soft cry that blended with Max's hoarse sound of delight. He scraped the sides of his thumbs back and forth across the sensitive buds, flicking gently, taking his greatest pleasure from the excitement he could feel coursing through the slender body now straining of its own accord to get closer to his.

Instinctively his legs tightened around Kara's hips, pressing his arousal against her and setting off another shock wave of desire in his loins. His hands left her breasts, one pulling free of her shirt to clasp her chin and turn her face up to his; the other plunging downward, caressing her flat belly beneath the water before finding its way inside the low-cut bottom of her bikini. Kara trembled violently as his mouth captured hers in a searing kiss at the same instant that his fingers became entangled in the soft nest of curls between her thighs. The double assault must have overloaded all her defense circuits, Max noted through the red haze of his own slightly primitive mood. After the merest flicker of resistance she crumbled, quivering, against him, throwing her head back to receive the rough, rhythmic thrust of his tongue, her eyes closed in passionate surrender. There was no doubt that she was caught up in the magic of this moment as thoroughly as he was.

Chapter Seven

As gently as though she were made of glass, Max probed the secret silken recesses of Kara's body. She was hot, wet inside and out, and she quickened against his hand, elevating the need in him to a level of urgency he hadn't known existed. His tongue invaded her mouth deeply, with aggressive strokes that were a fevered counterpoint to the slow, easy seduction his fingers were waging underwater. He felt her thighs clamp together and knew instinctively that the action was intended to lock him in, not out. As he continued to explore her, each touch deeper and more intimate than the last, her hips began to shift restlessly, sending warm water sloshing over their legs.

"Oh, yes, honey," he breathed into her open mouth. "Move with me, show me how it feels best. I want to make it good for you."

Kara moaned, her hands reaching back to grip his shoulders. Sensing her unsteadiness, Max wrapped his other arm securely around her middle. His touch grew bolder still. With his thumb he strummed the spot he'd discovered could make her shiver with pleasure. He could feel the inferno inside her flaring higher. Her head turned from side to side, entwining both of them in the wet satin streamers of her hair, and her fingernails bit into his shoulders.

When his fingers dipped lower, sliding deep inside her, Kara lifted her hips in response, causing the float to lurch heavily to the right. They would have capsized if the tide hadn't been steadily carrying them closer to shore ever since they'd ceased paddling, enabling Max to brace one foot on the firm ocean bottom to keep them upright. He smiled at the small yelp of surprise Kara gave as he quickly shifted both hands to steady her, thinking she sounded half surprised and half bereft at the loss of his touch. And no wonder. She was hardly at a point to be brought up short this way.

Sliding off the float, he scooped her up in his arms and cradled her against his chest. "I think maybe we ought to continue this on steadier ground."

"I think maybe we ought to have waited until we were on steady ground to start it."

Max took encouragement from the fact that she wasn't protesting that they had started in the first place.

"Can I help it if you arouse me past all reason?" he demanded with playful gruffness.

"I hope not."

The reply was soft, and as soon as she'd uttered it Kara shyly averted her eyes. But not before Max saw the smoky, eager look that burned in them. He quickly decided not to walk all the way up to the house and risk having that look tainted by second thoughts. Stopping just beyond the reach of the surf, where the sand was still hard-packed, he went down on one knee and carefully lowered Kara to the ground. Without pausing he followed her down, stretching his body on top of hers and seeking her mouth with his own.

The kiss they shared was long and sensual. Combined with the slow, grinding movements of Max's hips, it quickly brought Kara back to the same height of trembling anticipation she'd been at before the forces of nature had so cruelly interrupted. She wrapped her arms around him and slid her fingers over his back, worshipping each ridge of bone and muscle. He felt heavenly, big and strong and masculine. She loved the heated imprint of his body on hers, the slight roughness with which he'd twined his hand in her hair to hold her still for his kiss, the sweet, skillful way his mouth was making love to hers. When his free hand began shoving at her wet shirt, she wiggled to help.

"I thought about this after you left last night," he breathed as his palm settled over her bare breast. He lifted his head just enough to stare down into her eyes. His callused fingertips began to pluck the raised crest, making her breathless with need. "Hell, it's all I've been able to think about. I couldn't stop fantasizing about how you would feel when I touched you this way...and how you would taste."

Kara knew what was going to happen next, and a small part of her tried unsuccessfully to formulate a coherent protest. It was no use. There was, she discovered, a force inside herself much stronger than common sense, a force she'd never confronted before this. It demanded to take control, and Kara was helpless to do anything but abdicate to it. Right now she was willing to trade the rest of her cautious, well-ordered life for this one reckless moment of passion in Max's strong arms.

Breathlessly she watched as Max peeled her shirt higher, baring her breasts to the ocean breeze and to the dark, hungry gaze he slowly lowered from her face to drink in the sight of her. More than anything she wanted to please him, and the harsh grunt of approval that slipped past his lips told her more than words could have that she had.

She arched up to meet him as he lowered his head. When his mouth closed over the throbbing, aching peak of one breast, Kara had to bite her lip to keep from screaming with pleasure. The sensation of his rough tongue on her sensitive flesh was exquisite. Her head tossed from side to side in the sand, and her fingers threaded through his thick hair to urge him closer. His tongue was hot and wet and sinfully agile. He licked her until she was glistening and then swung his head around to treat her other breast to the same tortuous pleasure.

"Oh, Kara," he murmured, the words taking shape against her soft, lush curves. "What are you doing to me?"

His voice was hoarse with desire, one more caress of her heightened senses. Kara hardly thought about what it was he'd said until he lifted his head once more. With his gaze holding hers immobile, he caught a stray lock of her hair between his fingers and carried it to his lips. In the midst of such unleashed passion the gesture was heart-wrenchingly tender, and what Kara saw reflected in Max's eyes at that instant stunned her.

It was as if the wind had suddenly lifted a veil covering his soul and she just happened to be in the right place to glimpse what lay beneath his airs of casual indifference and confident sexuality. What she saw was naked longing of a sort quite different from the purely sexual hunger she'd expected to find there. Desire she could have handled. Lust even. But this was a hunger that what she had to offer could never even begin to ease, an emptiness she couldn't hope to fill.

Was Max even aware of the need he kept carefully hidden? she wondered. And even if he was, was it right for her to let something begin between them when she knew up front how quickly it had to end? She'd been so busy worrying about herself that she hadn't given a thought to Max's feelings or to the possibility of his becoming emotionally involved. Now she did, and reluctantly she faced the truth. It wasn't right.

She couldn't let this happen.

Dragging her hands around to the front of his shoulders, she pushed against them just as he slanted his head and began lowering his mouth determinedly.

"Max, wait."

"I can't," he countered, his voice marked by the husky playfulness peculiar to lovers. He easily crushed her hands beneath his descending shoulders.

"Max, please, I..." She jerked her head aside as his lips brushed hers, shoving harder to get his attention.

His hands rose to frame her face, turning it up to his. His smile held a trace of impatience. "Don't, Kara. Not this first time. I'm much too hungry to be teased."

"I'm not teasing," she declared, waging a miserable battle against her own desire even as she tried to evade his seeking lips. "I mean it, Max. I want you to stop. Now."

He drew back at her final sharp command and stared at her in silent disbelief. It cost Kara every ounce of her willpower not to weaken and do whatever it took to stem the hurt and bewilderment that slowly seeped into his gaze.

"Why?" he demanded between clenched teeth.

"Because..."

She hesitated, shaking her head in weary confusion. She couldn't tell him the truth. Maybe if she had some time to gather her wits she could contrive some plausible explanation, but she was lucky she could breathe with him lying on top of her, let alone think straight. Not that she could imagine any lie that could possibly make palatable the fact that she'd let things go this far before calling a halt.

"I can't explain it," she confessed finally, her very tone a plea for understanding. "But you have to believe me, Max, it's better this way for both of us."

"Better?" Max's lips twisted in a nasty parody of a smile. Cold resentment pushed the last trace of confusion from his dark eyes. "For you, maybe. Me—I've got a big problem, sweetheart."

He thrust his hips against her, hard, then reached for her hand. It took a second for Kara to realize what he intended, and by then it was too late. His fingers were an unbreakable vise around her wrist, dragging her hand between their bodies and pressing it against the steely shaft straining at the front of his damp bathing suit.

"There's only one thing that's going to make me feel better," he growled, clearly furious. Furious enough to

force her? Kara wondered with sudden panic. Then he was
wrenching her hand away from him and rolling to his feet
in one smooth motion.

"But you don't have to worry," he snarled, evidently
reading her fear accurately. "I make it a point never to
screw a teasing little bitch, no matter how much she needs
it—or asked for it."

After he stalked off, Kara listlessly rearranged her
clothing, then sat huddled on the beach, waiting until she
was sure he was back at his house before starting back
herself. Her tears didn't come until she was in the shower.
She adjusted the scalding hot spray until it bit into her flesh
like tiny needles, but still she couldn't wash away the sorrow and guilt she was feeling. It was as if she'd just
brought about the greatest tragedy of her life.

She tried telling herself there was no reason to feel so
shattered. By rights what she should be feeling was angry
at Max for the way he'd reacted. But she wasn't. How
could she be when she'd seen so clearly that his bitter
lashing out had been a desperate cover for the pain and
confusion she'd inflicted? She hadn't just *allowed* him to
kiss and touch her so intimately; she'd encouraged him.
He'd had every right to expect that she would complete the
act of love with him, and every right to be frustrated and
furious when she called such an abrupt, unexplained halt.
Understanding all that didn't lessen her own pain and embarrassment, however. Or her conviction that she'd only
done what she had to do.

She couldn't forget the look that had been on Max's face
when he'd tenderly kissed a lock of her hair. Despite his
size and strength, Kara had sensed a fragility about him in
that fleeting glimpse. Of course she knew just how Max
would react if she tried to explain that impression to him
or convince him that she'd said no only to avoid hurting
him even worse later on. He would snicker when she announced that there was absolutely no way she could become seriously involved and would probably demand to
know who the hell was asking her to. Any mention of how
she could never offer him what she was certain he needed

would provoke a similarly snide response. Then, when she was all done with her feeble explanations, he would doubtlessly break into that smug, macho expression he was so good at and tell her he could handle himself just fine without her help, thank you.

But Kara knew, without understanding how she knew, that in their case that just wasn't so. Some sixth sense told her that the hair-trigger attraction between Max's hormones and hers was only the tip of the iceberg. Beneath all that sizzling sensuality lay the potential for something deep and mysterious and very hard to handle. Something which, under the circumstances, was better left unexplored. Even if it did leave her feeling as if there were a crater where her heart should be.

The odd, hollow sensation remained with her throughout the day and followed her to work that evening. Tonight even the club's sleek black and white decor, which she'd been instrumental in designing, depressed her. Methodically she ran through her nightly checklist, making sure that everything from the black-and-white tile floor to the white marble tabletops was gleaming and that the single red rose in each table's slim black vase was fresh.

It was too much to hope that Jack wouldn't notice the dramatic downswing in her mood since the night before. Thankfully, when Kara fended off his first question on the subject with a shaky "Please, not now, not here" he obligingly desisted, limiting himself to enthusiastic but unsuccessful attempts to cheer her up. Usually Kara enjoyed the long nights she put in at the club, but tonight she couldn't wait to get out.

She was sitting at the end of the bar with her back to the door when something akin to an electrical charge ruffled all the tiny hairs on her body. Earle Biddle was in the middle of a rowdy second set, but beneath the smooth, rapid currents of his music Kara's ears seemed to hum, and she knew without turning her head that Max had just walked into the Shady Lady. The effect his mere presence had on her was appalling. Almost as unsettling was the question of how he would handle being in the same room with her

after what had happened on the beach. Had he come her
to rub her nose in his supposed indifference to her? O
perhaps to flaunt the fact that other women would wel
come the advances she had spurned?

Drawing in a deep breath that did nothing but acceler
ate her fluttering heartbeat, Kara finally turned her stoo
around to peer in the direction of the entrance. Sur
enough, Max was standing just inside the door. He looke
rakish in black slacks and a loose white cotton shirt ope
at the neck, the cuffs rolled back halfway to his elbow
Already the sight of him was achingly familiar, having th
same warming effect on her as hearing a snatch of an ol
favorite song often did. Kara fought to keep her feeling
from showing on her face as Max lowered his head, and fo
the first time she noticed the woman by his side, a woma
with the blondest hair and greatest body Kara had eve
seen.

It certainly didn't take him long to rebound, sh
thought, jealousy washing over her like alcohol poured o
an open wound. So much for her fragile, half-formed hop
that he'd come to make amends. And just as well, she tol
herself firmly. If Max found a playmate to entertain hin
for the remainder of his stay, she wouldn't have to worr
about her resolve weakening. The blonde placed her crim
son-tipped fingers on Max's arm, and Kara spun back t
take a long gulp of her ice water. Slamming the glass dow
on the bar, she glanced up to the welcome sight of Jack'
smile. All of a sudden she'd changed her mind about talk
ing. She was going to need a confederate to make i
through this night.

"Jack, do you know who just walked in?"

"Sure. Doesn't everybody?"

"Jack, this is serious," she hissed impatiently, surrep
titiously hitching her thumb in the general direction of th
door. "That's Max over there."

"That's right."

She wanted to shake him. Big Bird would make a mor
satisfying confidant. "Jack, I'm talking about Max
Max," she repeated emphatically, doing everything bu

pound her fist on the bar to make him understand how earthshaking a matter this was to her.

"Right, Max," he repeated. "Max Ellis."

Her expression clouded. "Ellis?" She glanced over her shoulder at Max, who was now standing at the center of a small group of eagerly smiling women, then back at Jack. "You mean you recognize him?"

He gave her the sort of brotherly look that silently questioned her mental competence to cross the street alone.

"You mean you don't?" Before she could answer, understanding sparked in his eyes. "Oh, God, Kara, you mean *that* Max is *your* Max? The character who's staying next door? And you really don't have any idea who he is?"

"Yes, yes and yes." She pressed her hands together and rested her forehead on her fingertips, her eyes closed. Suspicion was an icy finger trailing along her spine. "Oh, I feel like such a fool. He's somebody, isn't he, Jack?"

"He's somebody all right. And you're even more of a hermit than I thought. Don't you ever watch movies? Or read *People* Magazine?" There was affection and sympathy layered beneath his teasing, but Kara was too tightly wound to pick up on it.

"Occasionally," she snapped. "Now, do you think you could quit rubbing it in long enough to tell me who the hell Max Ellis is, for heaven's sake?"

"Sure. Judging from what I've read about Ellis, the word *character* wasn't entirely off the mark in describing him. *Complicated* might be another good choice." Glancing at her impatient frown, he continued hurriedly. "Why don't I just skip over the part about his being a war hero and a Golden Gloves boxer and get right to the good stuff: a handful of Grammy Awards for being the most innovative country-rock musician in years, magazine covers— some nonsense about the sexiest man alive—movies..."

"Movies. A movie star." She shook her head with belated insight. Evidently the hum she'd detected when he walked in hadn't been imagined. "You know, I'm sure I never saw a picture of him, but that name... Max Ellis. I know I've heard it before, or read it somewhere." Burying her face in her hands she muttered, "Grammy Awards."

All the derisive comments she had made about his music ran through her head. Finally, with a heavy sigh, she lifted her gaze to Jack's. The start of a wry smile tugged at her lips. "I knew there was something out of the ordinary about that man."

"Yeah, I think it's called star quality."

"And here I thought he was being obnoxious."

Jack shrugged, grinning. "He probably is."

"No," Kara protested with revealing quickness. "I mean, he's really very sweet and down to earth when you get to know him."

"And did you? Get to know him, that is?"

"Not exactly," she returned, making a not-that-it's-any-of-your-business face at him. "I sort of panicked in the crunch."

He gave a hoot of laughter. "Says a lot for the guy's technique. The sexiest man alive strikes out."

"It wasn't Max's fault," Kara explained testily. "It was me. I was afraid he'd get too serious and complicate my life. Pretty outrageous, huh? The man's a genuine sex symbol superstar, and I'm worried about breaking his heart."

"He could do a hell of a lot worse, pumpkin," Jack declared, reaching over to give her hair a playful tug.

Frowning, Kara brushed aside the strands he freed from the loose knot at the nape of her neck, too preoccupied to complain. "He could also do a hell of a lot better, and no doubt has. You can see for yourself how women react to him," she said, indicating the scene continuing behind her. "I can't believe I'm such a rotten judge of character. I should have guessed that he was somebody famous, instead of a hog trader."

"I'd say that's more a reflection on him than you. After all, he's the superstar. Maybe he should fire his press agent?"

"Why? It appears I'm the only one in this whole place—maybe in the whole world, for all I know—who didn't recognize him. I just feel so foolish," she continued distractedly. "There were so many obvious little hints that I didn't pick up on...or else totally misinterpreted. For one thing, there was that incredulous look he gave me the first night when I demanded he introduce himself. And then his reaction when I went traipsing over there the next morning in my robe. I can only imagine what he thought I was after."

What she imagined brought heat to Kara's cheeks. She glanced forlornly at Jack. "I'll bet he thinks I'm an idiot."

"Why don't you ask him?"

"Because I don't want to know badly enough to fight my way through that mob of adoring fans," she countered tartly. Cutting off Jack's attempt to speak, she added with complete honesty, "Besides, I don't ever want to have to face him again, I'm so embarrassed."

"You shouldn't be," admonished a soft voice directly behind her.

Max. So that's what Jack had been trying to tell her. Max's deep, gritty tone incited a small riot inside Kara. Her stomach seesawed and her pulse raced and she was certain every giddy bit of the inner turmoil was reflected in her eyes when she turned to face him. He was alone, obviously having dispatched the gathering that now settled for gazing at him from their respective tables.

"Do you mind if I join you?" he asked with a scant nod at the empty stool to her right.

"No. Not at all. But I can't sit long," she added anxiously. "I have to check on the..." She trailed off, losing her train of thought in the clear green depths of his eyes.

"Customers," Jack supplied from behind the bar. Humor permeated his voice. "Don't worry, I'll keep an eye on things for you so you can relax. Jack Hogan," he said, extending his hand to Max.

Remembering their conversation on the beach, Kara noted with amusement the calculating interest that lurked behind Max's friendly smile as he shook Jack's hand. She wondered what conclusions each of them was drawing from this man-to-man assessment.

"How you doing, Jack? Max Ellis."

"*I* knew that," Jack returned emphatically, grinning in spite of the glare Kara arrowed his way. "Can I get you a drink?"

"A beer, please," replied Max. "Draft's fine. And a…" He glanced quizzically at the half full glass in front of Kara.

"I'm all set. Thanks, anyway," she told him.

Neither of them said anything during the brief time it took Jack to return with the frosted mug of beer. Max lifted it to take a long gulp, and Kara couldn't resist a peek sideways at him while he was distracted. She wasn't sure if it was the clothes or the fact that she now knew who he was, but he looked sexier than ever to her. In every way he overwhelmed her senses. He smelled of something subtle and woodsy, and even under the club's dim lights his hair gleamed like polished ebony. The slightest brush of his shoulder against hers was electrifying.

She issued a silent prayer of thanks that she hadn't let her bad mood diminish the care she'd taken in dressing for this evening. The narrow black silk slacks she was wearing enhanced her long legs, and with all objectivity she had to describe the accompanying top as a knockout. Although it was blousey in shape, the supersheer black fabric clung flatteringly. A strategic scatter of fist-sized gold lamé flowers adorned the front, as well as the sleeves, which tapered to her wrists, and the neckline, which plunged to her waist in the back. The total effect might not be up to Hollywood's standards, but it definitely was one of glamour and sophistication. No one looking at her would guess that her palms were damp enough to grow mold.

Kara smoothed her pants leg and adjusted the slender belt of gold braid at her waist. She was a coil of nervous energy waiting to see what would happen next. Nowhere in his manner or his tone had she detected a trace of Max's earlier anger, but there was always the possibility that he'd keep it under wraps until he had her alone. He was an actor, after all.

Finally, setting the mug down, he broke the silence. "I meant what I said, Kara. You have no reason at all to feel embarrassed. Just because I'm idiot enough to sell my soul for fame and fortune is no reason you should walk around with my name engraved in your memory."

"Your name I probably would have recognized if I'd heard it," Kara offered almost apologetically. "But your face..." She hesitated, once again unable to tell him what was in her mind, that his face was gorgeous and that although the image of its rough, chiseled beauty seemed to have always existed in some deep chamber of her heart, she was certain she'd never seen him smiling that crooked, heart-stopping smile at her from the glossy pages of a magazine. "It's just that I don't get to see a whole lot of movies out here."

"Don't apologize," he ordered. "If you think it bothers me that you didn't recognize me, you're wrong. The truth is, I loved it. Why do you think I held off telling you the truth?"

Sudden irritation filled her dark blue eyes. "I'm sure I don't know. But as long as you brought it up, why didn't you tell me?"

"Because we had a deal not to pry into each other's backgrounds. Remember?"

Kara wasn't likely to forget. "Yes, but I never would have made that deal reciprocal if I'd suspected there was something this fascinating about your background. Besides, you had plenty of opportunity to tell me before then—that very first night, for instance."

"Sure. After I let myself in through your window I could have said, 'Will you please keep the noise down, and by the way did you happen to catch my last movie?' It's not the easiest thing to casually slip into a conversation."

"I see your point." Kara also suddenly saw how harmless his omission was compared to her own dark secrets.

"Can you understand why I didn't tell you right away?" he asked. "Or at least as soon as I knew you really had no idea who I was? You have to realize that at the very start I was convinced that you were putting me on, playing some sort of devious little game.''

"Yes, I can see that now. But at the time..." She shook her head, laughing. "You remember that morning I went over to ask you to quiet down?"

Max nodded.

"Well, I thought you were the one playing games then. And not especially nice ones."

Max winced at the memory. "I'm not usually that callous—even to groupies. You were just unlucky enough to catch me at an off time."

"At that point I was convinced that all you had were off times."

"And now?"

She wrinkled her nose, refusing to compliment him on cue. "Now I'm of the opinion that you have moments of sheer congeniality."

"Thanks. I suppose that's a step in the right direction. And basically that's what this was all about. Do you know what a novelty it was for me to meet a woman who had no preconceptions about me? What a relief it was just to spend time with you and not have to worry if I was living up—or down—to my reputation?"

"I think I understand. I'm sure a life such as yours can get pretty overwhelming."

"Actually, tedious would be a more apt description." He dropped his voice to so low a pitch that its gravelly cadence was almost tangible. "The past couple of days have been overwhelming."

Kara paused for a sip of her ice water, hoping it would cool the thrilled blush his words had caused before Max caught sight of it. "I've enjoyed the last couple of days, too. Although I'm still mortified over those remarks I made about your singing and guitar playing. I suppose it just goes to show how much I know about music."

"Not at all. In fact, that's what I was getting at earlier today when I said you'd never be lonesome knocking my style. Critics have been doing it for years."

"I wasn't knocking. I was teasing... sort of. Besides which, Max, I'm not such an outcast that I don't know they don't hand out Grammy Awards to critical failures."

"I didn't say *nobody* liked my stuff. Just that there are plenty who don't—and who aren't shy about saying so. Of course, nothing that's ever been said or written about my music comes close to being as contemptuous as what's been said about my acting."

Confusion shadowed Kara's eyes as she tried to reconcile the wry half-smile on his lips with the bitterness edging his tone.

"I have a feeling that's quite an exaggeration," she murmured.

"You do, huh? Well, then, I wouldn't wager any money on my intuition, if I were you." He took a sip of his beer. "One of the more kindhearted critics wrote that my first movie would have been tolerable if the director had remembered to wake me up before the cameras rolled."

"Okay, so your first movie wasn't *Casablanca*. Everyone makes mistakes when they try something new."

"His reviews of my next two films said in essence that I was hurtling steadily downhill." After another gulp of beer he added, "I didn't hang around for his review of this last one. When you hit bottom, you know it without being told."

His need for some kind of comfort or reassurance was obvious, but without knowing more about him than Jack's thumbnail sketch had provided, Kara had no idea where to begin. For once she decided she could afford to simply speak her mind.

"Max," she ventured, her tone gently skeptical, "everyone who chooses a career in the public eye is going to get their share of knocks from critics. That's how critics justify their existence. I think maybe you're taking yours a little too seriously." The look he leveled her over the rim of his mug was uncomfortably sardonic, prompting her to continue in a rush. "I can't claim to know everything about you or your work, but Jack filled me in a little bit. And judging from what he told me—not to

mention the reception you got a few minutes ago just b
strolling into this place unannounced—I'd say you're
pretty famous."

"Yeah, well, this is a strange world we live in," com
mented Max. He didn't have to lift his gaze from the bee
in front of him for Kara to know that the expression in hi
green eyes was harsh and mocking. "You can become fa
mous for the weirdest things. Things that have absolutely
nothing to do with who you are, only with an accident o
nature, like the shape of your face or the color of you
eyes. Do you know that I made more money from sales o
a poster of me wearing nothing but unsnapped jeans and
a guitar than I did from my last album—an album tha
took me fourteen months to put together."

Kara didn't doubt that at all. She had seen the man in
unsnapped jeans. Somehow, though, she sensed thi
wasn't the moment to ask what a shamefully shallow par
of her wanted to know—namely, where one might pur
chase such a poster.

"That's the way it goes sometimes, I guess. We receive
recognition for reasons we least expect." Her speech wa
slow, tenuous. Fame and recognition for any reason were
far outside Kara's realm of experience. The words she wa
dredging up came solely from some innate need to soothe
the hurt in Max. "But if you've made four movies, I'n
sure they couldn't have been as bad as a few critic
claimed. I'm not expert on movie moguls, but I do knov
they're in business to make money."

"Oh, they made money. I supplied the pound of flesh
and everybody got rich . . . or rather, richer."

"Then your films were a success!"

Max glanced at her, smiling bleakly at the relief in he
exclamation. "Blockbusters...financially. At least the firs
three were big money-makers. They all dealt with the same
character, a vigilante type, and they must have touched
something dark and violent in people, because they went
to see them in droves. Plus there were enough offbea
touches in them to attract a small cult following. But the

bottom line is that the serious critics were right: those films had about as much depth as a kiddie pool.''

Kara was almost afraid to ask the obvious. She shifted on the barstool, bit her lip and smoothed a wisp of hair back from her cheek. "And this last film you made?''

Max's short laugh could have cut glass. "That one was supposed to be a masterpiece, a chilling portrait of a man emotionally frayed, the story of how society and his family unwittingly drive him over the edge. And it might have worked, if they'd hired an actor for the leading role instead of a star. It turned out to be a classic example of the folly of believing your own press releases.''

"You sound pretty raw about this, as if it happened very recently.''

"Ellis's Folly—that's what the movie was dubbed—opened three weeks ago.''

"Is that why you came to Diamond Cay. To get away from the press?''

"Not really. I learned early on that you can't outrun the press, and you can only drive yourself crazy trying to outwit them. It was like dying a little bit more each day, but I hung around L.A. and took most of the heat.'' Resting one elbow on the bar, he twisted to face Kara with a small, self-deprecatory smile that felt as if it were directly attached to her heartstrings. "I came here because sitting in that theatre opening night I decided that if I had to make an ass of myself again, I sure as hell wasn't going to do it in technicolor. And I *was* going to do it working at something that really mattered to me, not being chased around a movie set by a makeup guy wielding a powder puff and clucking his tongue because my face sweats too much.''

Kara couldn't help laughing at the picture he painted. "Your face looks fine to me,'' she declared in massive understatement.

"I don't care what my face looks like,'' he shot back emphatically. "A while back I got so sick of seeing it everywhere I went that I started throwing a towel over the bathroom mirror when I got up in the morning.''

"So you came to Diamond Cay...''

"To write," he interjected. "Or at least to try. While
was sitting in that theatre it also suddenly occurred to m
that writing songs gave me the most pleasure and satisfac
tion I've ever had. Somehow, amidst all the publicity and
other bullshit, that got lost. I came here to find out if I ca
still do it."

"And can you?"

"I don't know," he admitted.

Kara had to fight the urge to reach out and stroke th
grim lines from his face. She watched the cords in hi
throat ripple as he swallowed hard.

"Sometimes," he mumbled into his empty mug, "
think I'm scared to find out."

Chapter Eight

Kara was spared having to come up with a response to Max's unexpected admission of vulnerability by the hand that suddenly wedged between them to land caressingly on his forearm. The hand was tanned and feminine, and Kara recognized the perfectly sculptured, blood-red nails as belonging to the blonde by the door even before she glanced at the woman's face.

"Hi again, Max," the blonde opened in a soft, breathy voice. "You said you'd like to dance later, and this is later. I read somewhere that slow-dancing is your favorite pastime."

"Next to fly-fishing," Max amended in a dry undertone.

"Really? I adore fishing," the woman purred.

Kara suppressed a snort.

The blonde tightened her claws on Max's arm. "Shall we?"

"I'd love to," he responded, at the same time disengaging her fingers with practiced efficiency. "But I've al-

ready promised this dance.'' He tugged Kara off her stool
and with one arm around her waist steered her toward the
small dance floor. Over his shoulder he winked at the
pouting blonde. "You understand . . . she's a friend of my
mother's.''

The look Kara shot him as he pulled her into his arms
was one of indignation mixed with laughter.

"Don't be mad," coaxed Max, his smile crooked and
irresistible. "I had to let her down easy."

"By all means," she concurred dryly. "After all, I'm
closer to being a friend of your mother's than that woman
is to being a fisherman."

"Ah, beautiful and insightful," he chuckled, gathering
her closer to him. "What more could a man ask for in a
woman?"

Kara had to bite her tongue to keep from blurting out
the answer that popped instantly to the front of her mind:
honesty. Irritated with her unflagging conscience, she
nudged aside thoughts of her personal shortcomings in the
honesty department. Max's question had been rhetorical
and flirtatious. He didn't expect an answer, much less a
confession. She reminded herself that there was no longer
any need to even consider the foolhardy possibility of
confessing the truth.

Things had changed dramatically since this morning
when she'd been moved to try to protect Max from whatever feelings were developing between them. It was clear
now that nothing of consequence was going to develop.
Their lives couldn't have been less compatible if they'd
hailed from different planets.

Ignoring a foolish stab of disappointment at that realization, she tried to concentrate on the positive aspects of
the situation. Now she was free to surrender to the intense
desires Max aroused, secure in the knowledge that he
would soon be returning to his own world and leaving hers
intact. As long as she kept a tight rein on her own emotions, it would be perfectly safe to indulge in the fling she'd
long ago given herself permission to have. As she'd told
Anne, all she'd been waiting for was the right man to come

along. Heeding the warm, gentle pressure of Max's body as they danced, there was no doubt in Kara's mind that he was the right man.

Earle and his three-piece band had taken a break and disappeared outside to the terrace, and it was the soft strains of a popular love song wafting from the overhead speakers that set the tempo for their lightly swaying bodies. They might have been alone on the dance floor, so utterly was Kara absorbed with Max. He held her with proper restraint, considering that she was still technically at work here. But even if he'd gathered her against his lean body in a more intimate embrace, Kara might not have been able to resist.

The light, slightly abrasive touch of his fingertips on her bare back and the teasing pressure of his thighs brushing hers all too readily filled her mind with the memory of that morning and the reckless passion he had unleashed in her. It was as if since then there had been only the thinnest veneer of restraint over that passion and now even that was rapidly dissolving.

The fact that they were surrounded by other people— many of whom were studying Max and her with veiled curiosity—only intensified the spell of sensuality that seemed to isolate them from the rest of the world. Sliding his fingers higher to weave them through the loose coil of her hair, Max tipped her face up to his. Their eyes met and clung, neither of them saying a word. Kara wished she could turn the clock back to that morning and relive those last few minutes in his arms. Or better yet, turn it ahead to see how this night would end. Anticipation was a slow, steady throbbing down low inside her.

"Kara," Max said finally, his voice pitched intimately low, for her ears only, "about this morning... I want to apologize."

"Don't." Instinctively Kara reached up and pressed her fingertips to his lips to silence him. She wasn't yet prepared for the ripple of pleasure even so mild a touch could produce, and she quickly dropped her hand back to his shoulder. "There's no need for you to apologize. I was wrong."

"It's not wrong to say no when you're not ready. A decent man accepts a no from a woman graciously, even if he doesn't like it much."

"That's just it," she began, summoning the courage to tell him as much of the truth as she was able to. "I *was* ready."

Confusion narrowed his eyes, edging them with shallow lines in a way Kara found entrancing. "Then why...?"

"For all the wrong, stupid reasons," she lamented. "I was jumping to conclusions, afraid that we would be getting involved in something that could never work. But now all that has changed."

Max stared down at her, spellbound by her simple beauty. Still, the subtle invitation in her words managed to penetrate the muddle that being close to her always made of his common sense. *But now all that has changed.* He felt something new and barely formed inside of him begin to crumble.

"You mean now that you know who I am?"

If Kara detected the brittleness underlying his question, there was no indication of it in her excited smile.

"Yes. That changes everything, Max."

Forcing a smile in return, Max pressed her head to his shoulder before she could see the look of bitter disappointment in his eyes. It wasn't Kara's fault that he was who he was. Or that she wasn't the paragon of simplicity and honesty his imagination had created. Of course the fact that he was rich and famous and rumored to be unattainable made a difference. He'd accepted the inevitability of that a long time ago and had been crazy to let himself hope otherwise where Kara was concerned.

Why she wanted him shouldn't even matter. Certainly it didn't stop this white-hot desire for her from clawing at his gut. What it did bring to a crashing end was the sense of boundless possibility he'd experienced these past few days. It had even begun to spill over into his writing. Max was still struggling to come to terms with the loss of something so intangible when the music ended.

Automatically his hand went to the small of Kara's back to turn her toward the bar. The muffled sounds of instruments being arranged as the band reclaimed the stage were familiar to Max's ears, but he drew to a startled halt when a voice as smooth as thirty-year-old scotch called to him through the microphone.

"Hey, Delta Bent."

He felt Kara hesitate beside him and he swung around to face the tall, slender black man grinning at him from center stage. Max had been doubly glad he'd ventured out tonight when he'd discovered who was performing here. Earle Biddle ranked high on his list of musical greats. Who would have guessed the man would be a fan of the Delta Bent trilogy of films? Breaking into a smile, Max acknowledged his greeting with a slight nod. It never failed to stun him into awkwardness when a man he held in such esteem recognized him.

"What do you say, Mr. Delta Bent?" Earle continued. "Do you feel like kicking out with us tonight?"

The invitation to join Earle on stage brought a grin to Max's face that reminded Kara of a new kid in school being approached by the most popular kid in class. He looked elated and anxious at the same time. He turned to her as the scattered applause and encouraging calls from the audience built to a low roar.

"Do you mind?"

"Mind? I'd love to hear you play with them. But why did he call you . . . ?"

"Delta Bent," Max filled in hurriedly, shouting to be heard over the noise. "That's the name of the character I played in those first three movies. I told you they were pretty bad."

"Well, tonight you're going to be pretty wonderful." She squeezed his arm, ending by giving him a slight push toward the stage. "You'd better hurry. It sounds like your fans are an impatient bunch."

He nodded, then bounded up onto the spotlighted stage to the excited clamor of the crowd. One member of Earle's group stepped forward to hand him a spare electric guitar, and while Max slung the strap over his shoulder and fiddled with the sound, Kara returned to her seat at the bar. A minute or so later Jack ambled over to join her.

"This should be good," he predicted.

Kara interpreted the remark to be facetious, and it touched a concern she was afraid to voice. Rankled, she whirled to face Jack. "I'm sure Max will be able to hold his own."

"I wasn't implying otherwise," he informed her, his expression blatantly amused. "Max has a reputation for being a hell of a guitar player." He leaned closer. "You know, you'd better watch out or you're going to get a reputation for being a mother hen."

Kara rolled her eyes eloquently. "Don't you have glasses to wash or something?"

"Nope. What I have is an in with the boss lady."

"Don't count on it."

Their sparring was brought to an end by Earle stepping back up to the mike and introducing Max, by his real name this time. He was lavish with his praise of Max's talent, proclaiming him to be the man who introduced rock to country music.

"Or was it vice versa?" he added, drawing more laughter and clapping from an obviously smitten crowd. "Either way, we'd like to open this set with a genuine Max Ellis masterpiece, 'Lonely Town.'

Within minutes of their first note any fear Kara had had that Max might be out of his league was banished. There was, she discovered, a monumental difference between the sound he produced when he was plucking experimentally on the back deck and what he was capable of. Also laid to rest was her suspicion that the two men's styles would clash. Their roots might be in different musical ground, but they shared a zest for what they were doing and a respect for each other's talents that enabled them to soar over any differences.

Both men played with reckless abandon, Max's roughhouse singing finding a natural counterpoint in Earle's heartfelt blues. Max's songs were far different from what Kara had expected. They touched her deeply. He wrote without pretense or artifice, presenting images that left the listener with nowhere to hide from his own feelings. Later, when the two of them joined forces on the older man's famous "Back Beat Rag," Max demonstrated that his instrumental technique was every bit as finely developed as his gift for writing lyrics.

Toward the end of the set Kara finally zeroed in on another talent the two men shared. Neither of them erected—or permitted—walls between themselves and their audience. After watching them perform, you would walk away feeling you knew them, and what's more, liking them. They were able to play together so smoothly, neither worrying where one's musical style began and the other's left off, because they were both men accustomed to ignoring barriers. In their work and, Kara suspected, in their lives. She shrugged off a niggling concern about how that might affect things between her and Max, reminding herself that once Max finished sulking over his last film and had recharged his confidence, there wouldn't be anything between them.

After the impromptu jam session finally ended, Max hung around nursing a beer as the last customers filtered out, and Kara checked to make sure everything was in order for the night. When her inability to concentrate on the figures she was tallying became embarrassingly obvious she finally accepted Jack's offer to take over and lock up for her. She didn't even pretend to object when Max announced that she should leave her bike at the club until the following day and ride home with him in the late-model sedan he'd borrowed from Victor's garage. Unfortunately, whatever confidence she had managed to talk herself into concerning their relationship evaporated as soon as she and Max were alone together.

The drive to the northern point seemed impossibly brief. Far too soon for Kara's peace of mind they were parked in

the garage behind the main house and Max was circling the
car to help her out. As they walked along the short path
between the two houses their conversation was as sporad-
ic and superficial as it had been in the car. Kara tried to
reassure herself that the tension she sensed beneath Max's
lazy stride and laconic tone was most likely due to the very
same apprehension she was feeling. She was nervous,
wondering if he would linger when it came time to say
good-night. Would he attempt to make love to her again?
No doubt he was wondering what her reaction would be if
he did. With her smile and the fleeting brush of her body
as they moved along the narrow path side by side—a subtle form of communication as old as woman—Kara tried
to make him understand that this time her answer would
be an irrevocable yes.

They reached the end of the walk. From behind, Max
grasped her arm just above the elbow, spinning her around
to face him. His eyes were dark as moss and glittering in
the moonlight. Holding her in their unwavering path, he
lowered his head slowly, giving her plenty of time to resist, and asked the question that was on both their minds
in a manner that could not be misunderstood. He kissed
her, long and deep and hard, and Kara poured every ounce
of the longing that was bubbling inside her into kissing him
back. When her breath ran out she inhaled and breathed
in the warm, moist taste of him. Her head was whirling,
and her legs were weak. Instinctively her body strained toward Max's, needing his strength to keep her from melting into a puddle of desire on the flagstones beneath their
feet.

Still without saying a word, he scooped her up in his
arms and turned toward his house. Kara vaguely registered a glimmer of relief that he didn't assume she would
prefer her own bedroom. The more she could keep Max
separate from her day-to-day life, the fewer reminders of
him she would have to deal with after he'd gone. He
opened the unlocked door and carried her through the
darkened house, relying on the glow of the moon washing
through the windows to guide his steps up the stairs and

along the long hallway. Not until he had stepped inside a room dominated by a massive four-poster bed did he stop.

Carefully he tipped her feet to the floor, reaching out to frame her face with his cupped hands.

"Are you sure, Kara?" he whispered.

She nodded, her eyes ablaze with passion. The wall of windows behind her filled the room with a hazy yellow light, yet Kara felt unable to read Max's reaction clearly. Crazy as it seemed, she almost got the impression that he was disappointed she hadn't said no again.

"I hope you know that nothing has changed," he declared roughly. "I'm still the same man I was this morning."

Suddenly she understood, and she was overcome by his sweetness. He was trying to warn her about what she'd already accepted in her heart, that there was no future in what they were about to share. That this moment of pure passion was no more than a time warp in each of their lives, disconnected from their pasts and their futures. He was trying to shield her from making an impulsive mistake. Lifting her hands, she placed them over his on her cheeks, turning to plant a kiss in his palm.

"I know exactly who you are, Max," she told him in a voice free of all doubt. "You're the man I want to make love to me." She leaned into him. "Please, Max."

She might have imagined his hesitation, it was so fleeting. Then with a groan ripped from deep in his chest, he was wrapping his arms around her to jerk her against his hard, muscled body. His mouth rained kisses on her face and neck while his hands roamed over her so quickly it felt as if he were touching her everywhere at once.

Twining her arms around his neck, Kara closed her eyes and relinquished all hold on reality. Willingly, eagerly, she let her senses take control. She parted her lips under the insistent pressure of Max's, parrying the stab of his tongue with her own, then venturing forth to explore the sleek, heated chamber of his mouth. It was far more aggression than she'd showed the last time he kissed her, and a responsive shudder shook the strong shoulders where her hands rested.

Such tactile proof of the ability of her touch to arouse him spurred Kara on. Her hands swept down to tug his shirt free of his waistband, delving beneath to caress the warm, smooth skin of his back. Following the slant of his ribs, her fingertips found their way to the edges of the soft, thick mat of hair covering his chest. Kara plucked at the curling tufts with her fingers, eager to explore all the varying textures and tastes and temperatures that were uniquely his. Pressing her palms flat to his chest, she slid them over his skin in slow spirals that inched steadily higher until his shirt bound at her wrists, halting her. Pulling one hand back with a muffled, impatient sound, she reached for his top shirt button, only to have Max's fingers close over hers like steel clamps.

"Uh-uh, baby," he breathed against her parted lips. "Ladies first."

Kara's heart was pounding like thunder as he took her hands and led her across the room, turning so he could sit at the edge of the bed with her standing a few feet in front of him. Placing his palms on the mattress behind him, he leaned back. His eyes were almost black and burning with intensity.

"Strip for me, honey," he commanded in that slow, gravelly voice that sent a tingle racing along her spine.

Kara's laugh was brief and jittery. "Wh...what?"

"Strip," he repeated. The passionate sulk left his mouth, replaced by a cajoling smile. "You want to, don't you?"

She nodded, wanting to do anything that would bring him the same pleasure he was so adept at giving to her. She was also aware enough of the limits of her seductive skills to be open to any pointers Max cared to give, even if the mere thought of taking off her clothes while he lounged on the bed watching did make her knees shake so much she was afraid she was going to collapse.

With a deep breath she averted her eyes from his expectant gaze and fumbled with the catch on her braided belt, finally managing to unclasp it and to let it drop to the floor at her feet. The unstructured lines of her blouse made it easy to pull off over her head, even with trembling fingers. Within seconds it had drifted down to join the belt, and she stood before him clad in the unintentionally erotic combination of a backless black lace bra, black slacks and high-heeled black sandals. Holding on to the night table for support, Kara dispensed with her shoes next, pulling off first one, then the other, then reaching for the tiny button at her waist. Once the button and zipper had been undone, the slacks slithered down her legs with a silky rustle, and Kara stepped out of them.

Until that moment Max had been following the movements of her hands with a steady, almost dispassionate gaze. Only the rapidly flexing muscle at the left side of his mouth gave away how affected he was by her unpracticed, slightly awkward striptease. Kara drew encouragement from that, and now from the sight of his chest heaving with breaths that were anything but normal. The look in his eyes rapidly turned hot and sultry as they traveled over every inch of her flesh, lingering on the dark circles of her nipples and the triangle between her thighs, which the sheer black lace on her lingerie barely concealed.

"Go on," he directed.

The huskiness of his voice made Kara shiver with excitement. A new sense of power infiltrated her discomfiture, shaping her movements as she slowly lifted her hands and slipped her fingers beneath the narrow straps of her bra. More slowly still she slid the straps down over the curve of her shoulders until the wisp of black silk fell away from her breasts and Max bolted upright on the bed. Some instinct she hadn't even dreamed she possessed prompted her to sway seductively as her bra floated to the floor and her thumbs hooked inside the narrow sides of her bikini panties.

"No," Max croaked. "Let me."

Still sitting on the edge of the mattress, he reached for her, pulling her hips close to his face. He kissed her through the sheer fabric, using his teeth to nibble across

her belly and then lower. Kara clutched his shoulders for
support as he opened his mouth over the quivering mound
between her thighs. His breath was hot and moist, making the fabric and the soft part of her beneath it wet and
slippery. Max shoved his hands inside the back of her
panties to cup her bare bottom, holding her still as his face
ground against her. Her eyelids lowered, shutting off the
rest of the world as he nuzzled the cradle of her femininity
until she cried his name out loud, half in joyous demand,
half in panic.

"Shh. Easy," he murmured against her, the rough words
one more caress of her ultrasensitive flesh.

Whimpering softly, Kara writhed in his hands. Without
warning he curled his fingers around the inch-wide strip of
silk at her hips and ripped the panties off her. Her gasp of
surprise faded into a string of short, breathless pants as his
tongue found her, teaching her things she never knew
about intimacy. The teasing nibbles of a moment ago gave
way to a broad, stabbing pressure that was relentless and
devastatingly skillful and which easily sent Kara slipping
over the edge of control. She stiffened, then collapsed
across Max's back. Clinging desperately to him, she hurtled through a new and endless void, sobbing with pleasure and surprise.

She was still floating on the gentle swells of receding
passion when Max lifted her onto the mattress. Through
half-closed eyes she saw him tearing off his own clothes.
Then his body was a lean, magnificently aroused shadow
moving to cover hers. She sighed as he came down half
beside her, half on top. He bent his head to kiss her
breasts, sucking just hard enough to pierce her languor-
ous afterglow. Kara smiled contentedly, thinking it would
take her ages to recover. But soon his fingers trailing over
her stomach and playing lightly between her legs had once
again aroused her senses to a quivering state of anticipation.

He rolled to cover her completely. Kara delighted in the
feel of his naked body pressed to hers. He was hard where
she was soft, rough where she was smooth, strong and ag-

gressive where she was tenderly receptive. Bracing on his elbows, he spread her thighs apart with his knee. His body hovered above hers, close enough that she could feel his heat, but he touched her only with his mouth, claiming her in a kiss that was slow and deeply erotic. Still kissing her, he began to lower his hips, brushing against her, teasing her with his arousal until she tingled with newly awakened need.

Kara instinctively arched her hips off the bed, but still he didn't complete the union she was aching for. She licked the full curve of his bottom lip, whispering between shallow breaths, "I want you, Max."

"Yes, I'm sure you do," he countered with a quick gust of laughter that threw her off balance. Then he settled himself between her thighs, pushing inside her just enough to make her thoughts slip out of focus. "Tell me *how* you want it, Kara," he crooned in a voice darkened by passion. "Hard? Fast? I aim to please."

She moaned softly, squirming against him, telling him with everything but words that she simply wanted him, any way, at any price.

"No preference, huh?" he asked, dipping his head to kiss the curve of her breast. "All right, we'll make this dealer's choice."

His words ran without meaning through Kara's head. She was lost in the pleasure-shock that shook her body as Max thrust deep inside her. He froze for a second, trembling, his fingers clenched around her upper arms. Kara knew without doubt that the fierce control he'd been exercising had just snapped. She twisted her hips, trying to draw him tighter.

Finally he began to move, his first strokes quick and unmeasured, but rapidly finding a rhythm that kept his hips pumping against hers. There was no teasing now by either of them, and no gentle courting of each other's senses. Everything was flash and fire, hunger and heat. The sounds of their labored breathing grew louder as a fine coat of sweat turned their bodies slick, making each brush of flesh against flesh erotically slippery.

A fever built inside Kara, burning her up, threatening to rage beyond all control. She felt as if she were surrounded by a sea of white-hot sensation and clutched at Max's shoulders with the desperation of a drowning woman. She clung to him, uncertain if he was a lifeline or the force pulling her under or some combination of the two, until the fever inside her exploded. This time her climax was like a long ride on a steep roller coaster, with wind rushing past and her stomach flip-flopping uncontrollably, ending at the pinnacle of bliss and satisfaction. The tense, heavy weight of Max's body anchoring her to the mattress was evidence that she hadn't made the journey alone.

She hugged him tightly, and when he rolled off her a minute later Kara rolled with him, not wanting to break the warm, reassuring contact with his body. She lay curled against his side as her breathing gradually slowed and the jackhammering of Max's heart beneath her cheek returned to normal. The regular rise and fall of his chest made her think he might even have recovered right into a sound sleep. Smiling bemusedly, she lifted her gaze to check it out.

Far from sleeping peacefully, however, she found Max staring at the ceiling. Even in the dimly lit room it was clear his expression was not the drowsy, untroubled one of a satisfied man. Tentatively she touched his arm.

"Max..."

Before she could say another word he pulled his shoulder out from under her head and sat up. Without turning on a light he rummaged in the night table drawer. Kara heard a crinkling sound and then the striking of a match. The smell of sulfur and smoke drifted her way, overlaying the sweet scent of gardenias carried through the open window on the tropical breeze.

"I thought you quit smoking," she ventured, straining to keep the sudden fear in her belly from riddling her voice.

"I did."

"Then..."

"Then why am I lighting one up?" Max finished for her when she had second thoughts about probing what might well be a sore spot. He took another deep drag, releasing it as he spoke. "Because I figured a cigarette might give me the shot of courage I needed to ask you."

He turned to her, his face showing no emotion whatsoever, and Kara knew she wasn't going to like whatever came next.

"So tell me," he drawled, "did I measure up to all your expectations?"

Chapter Nine

Kara volleyed to a sitting position beside Max as his
question reverberated through the silent room. Actually it
had been more of a taunt than a question, and heavily
laced with bitterness. Snatching the only thing within
reach—his shirt—she drew it around her shoulders, feeling suddenly cold and angry and...betrayed. Kara knew
that feeling wasn't only ridiculous, it was impossible. You
can't be betrayed by a stranger. Yet there was no other
name for the pain burning inside her, which meant that
somehow, in spite of all her best pragmatic intentions, Max
Ellis had already gotten close enough to hurt her badly.

"Would you like to explain what you mean by that?"
she asked him.

"Nothing very complicated. I'm just curious as to
whether making it with a movie star was as good as you
expected."

Numbly Kara decided it was the regal nonchalance in his
tone that made the deepest cuts in her soul.

"You're really something, you know that?" Her voice cracked from the tension within.

Only his left brow moved. "I take it that's a yes?"

"You can take it however you damn well please," Kara spat. Eyeing his stony profile, she shook her head disgustedly. "How could I possibly have let myself forget how arrogant and rude and insulting you can be? I should have known better than to let you anywhere near me. My mother was an actress, you know. Granted, she was just a local celebrity," she revealed in an impulsive burst, her voice dripping sarcasm. "Certainly not a big, important star like you. But I still learned early on how totally self-absorbed and self-centered a person has to be to live solely for the adulation of others."

Max speared her with a venomous look. The only thing that prevented Kara from fleeing before he could dish out more abuse was the fact that between her and her clothes lay his very naked, very male body.

"Are you saying I'm self-centered?" he demanded.

"It goes with the territory, doesn't it?"

He stared at her, his mouth drawn in a pensive sulk, and finally gave a reluctant nod. In amazement Kara realized that she could almost feel his anger cooling.

"I suppose it does," he agreed quietly. "Maybe that's why I never really fit in that territory."

He glanced down at the half-smoked cigarette in his hand as if not sure where it had come from, then stretched to crush it out in the ashtray. Reaching behind him, he tugged a pillow from beneath the satin bedspread, turning it sideways before leaning back. Hours seemed to pass without either of them speaking.

Part of Kara was still busy searching for a graceful way to retrieve her clothes and escape, while another part struggled to keep from reaching out and touching Max and begging him to tell her what had happened to change him so quickly. No matter how it seemed now, Kara knew she wasn't such a poor judge of character that she could be taken in by a man who got his kicks this way. Not that she

had expected words of undying love from him afterward
but she certainly hadn't expected animosity.

"Is that really what you think of me, Kara?" he finally
asked without looking at her. "That I live solely for the
adulation of others?"

"You said it yourself. How did you put it? Oh, yes, you
told me you'd sold your soul for fame and fortune."

Max's short burst of laughter sounded harsh and con-
torted. "Yeah, that's what I did all right. Only once I had
all the fame and fortune one soul can buy, I realized they
weren't what I wanted after all. Pretty clichéd, huh?"

"Very. If you're trying to garner sympathy from me,
Max, I'm afraid it won't work. Not only am I feeling
especially unsympathetic toward you at the moment,
usually find it hard to feel sorry for any man who's rich
and famous enough to go wherever he wants in this world
and do whatever he feels like doing."

Max glanced at her with wry amusement. "That's not
me, honey. Not by a long shot. Money might bring freedom, but fame sure as hell takes it away."

"Oh, please, spare me. I'm not in the mood to hear how
trying your life is because you're constantly hounded by
worshipping fans."

"It's not that," denied Max. "Fans can be . . . fright-
ening, that collective rush of emotion coming at you in the
middle of a restaurant or when you're stopped at a traffic
light. But I've finally learned to deal with all that after
years of running and hiding from them. What I'm talking
about is something different, a subtle kind of freedom that
I lost somewhere along the way. Maybe what I want back
is freedom from myself."

His eyes flickered shut briefly, opening to expose a look
of such anguish it aroused in Kara a slow uncurling of the
sympathy she had denied she could feel for him.

"Hell," he continued with a mixture of sheepishness
and resentment, "I'm not even free to take a woman to bed
without worrying whether it's me she wants or that bastard Delta Bent."

"That's a handy excuse, Max, but in this case it doesn't work, and you know it. I've never seen a Delta Bent film in my life. In fact, until a few hours ago I'd never even heard of him."

"And once you did, you promptly changed your mind about going to bed with me. See my point?"

Abruptly the pieces started clicking into place, and Kara wasn't sure whether to laugh or scream. It stunned her to think that a man of Max's renown could feel insecure in this of all areas, but why else would he have so totally misinterpreted her reason for being here? And why else would it bother him as much as it obviously did? Feeling something akin to relief spring through her, Kara directed a playful jab to his biceps.

"What I see," she scoffed, "is a supposedly successful man who borders on being paranoid." Catching his skeptical scowl, she added, "I admit you might have had cause to question my reason for changing my mind so suddenly, but you should have trusted me, or at least asked me about it, for heaven's sake."

"I did. You said that finding out who I was changed everything."

She looked at him, aghast. "But that's not what I meant."

Max rubbed his jaw, looking like a man trapped between bewilderment and violence.

"At least I didn't mean it in the way you thought," she hastened to explain.

His sardonic expression told her that she was only muddying things further.

"Listen, Max," she implored, struggling to order her thoughts before they tumbled from her mouth, "when I said that finding out who you were changed everything, I didn't mean that I wanted to go to bed with you *because* you're Max Ellis. I meant that it's because you are who you are that it's *okay* for me to make love with you."

"Would you like to run all that by me again? Real slow this time?"

"Maybe what I should have said is that knowing who you are made it safe for me to get involved. When I said no this morning it was because I was worried that if anything happened between us, you or I, or maybe both of us, might get too emotionally involved. And that's something I couldn't allow to happen."

Max took time to roll that around in his head before responding. "I see. So you only changed your mind about saying no once you were certain that nothing serious would come of this?"

"Exactly." With a half-smile she added, "I know you're going through a rough time right now, Max, but I hardly think you'd consider giving up your career to live on the edge of nowhere with any woman."

"And I suppose you'd be just as unlikely to give up living on the edge of nowhere because you fell in love with a man whose work was somewhere else?"

Her look of distress was so fleeting that Max might have missed it if he'd blinked. For some reason he was glad he hadn't.

"I would never let myself fall in love," she announced breezily. "So, now each of us knows up front how this will have to end."

Her words slammed the lid on Max's gradually lifting spirits. He hadn't liked believing that Kara was no different from the women who hung around outside the stage door after a concert, but for some reason he liked this seemingly casual dismissal even less. It was sort of like having someone give you a terrific present and then announce that they'd be taking it with them when they left. He was used to being the one who decided when something ended, and how.

Of course, she was right about the odds against this thing coming to anything. But she was also scared. He should know. He was an expert at what this particular kind of fear looked and sounded like. What—or who—he wondered, had wreaked such havoc on Kara's emotion that she was scared to death to risk having it happen again

The shadow lurking behind her smile was a clear warning not to ask. Max was reminded of the way she'd looked that morning when she'd made that wistful remark about nothing feeling better than being safe. Despite the physical closeness they'd just shared, he felt as unfit to deal with her chilling sadness now as he had then. It would take time, maybe more than he had to spare, to loosen the knots inside Kara. If only he'd kept his mouth shut a few minutes ago. Lord knows she seemed to have erected enough walls for him to scale without him throwing up any more with his... paranoia. Grimly he acknowledged that she might have had that right, too.

Bending his arms, he laced his fingers at the back of his neck and slanted her a sideways glance. "So, you still haven't answered my question."

Kara tilted her head, her eyes narrowed quizzically.

"Did I measure up or not?" Max asked her again. This time the start of a smile played at his lips.

She studied his face, looking first surprised, then slightly wary. Finally she smiled back, a slow, seductive smile that made Max as instantly hot for her as his first glimpse of her in that backless top had earlier. With one polished fingertip she reached out to trace his bottom lip, making his heart slam against his ribcage. Her soft laughter caressed him. The innocent, sexy, flowery smell of her drove him crazy.

"I'm not sure," she whispered. "Why don't you try running it past me again? Real slow this time."

Max's breath caught with excitement. Then he was bringing her down flat on her back beneath him with one mighty roll. He started out by loving her slowly, the way she'd requested, then hard and fast and every way in between. It was a long time before he fell asleep with Kara still in his arms, her body a sweet, damp pressure against his own. For the first time in years he slept through the night.

When he awoke, sunlight was a pink beam slanting through the window, and the bed beside him was empty. Panic came quickly, taking Max by surprise and making

the sound of blood pumping furiously fill his head, unt
just as he was ripping aside the sheet someone had tucke
around him, he detected a different sort of sound filterin
up from the kitchen. So she hadn't deserted him after al
he mused, settling back against the pillow with a comfor
able grin. In fact, it sounded as if she might be makin
breakfast. Max's mouth watered. Not for whatever foo
Kara was preparing, but for the morning taste of he
mouth and the delicate touch of her fingers on his skin. H
was already reaching for his pants as he rose from the bed

He found Kara in the kitchen, humming softly as sh
fiddled with the skillet on the stove. Propping his shou
der against the door, Max indulged his longing to simpl
look at her. Her dark hair was pulled back into a ponytai
giving her an air of innocence that clashed with the pr
vocative nakedness teasing him from beneath his whi
cotton shirt. Unconsciously he rubbed his fingertips t
gether, remembering how it had felt last night when she'
lain on top of him and he had pulled the pins from her hai
one by one, letting the long silken strands wash over h
face and chest. He was still savoring the memory when sh
glanced up and saw him standing there, and her fac
flushed with delight.

"Max!" she exclaimed. "You're not supposed to be u
yet. I wanted to surprise you. I planned to wake you u
with breakfast in bed."

Crossing the room, he gathered her in his arms an
brushed his lips lightly across her throat, aching to kiss he
mouth but wanting to prolong the sizzling anticipation c
it a little longer.

"Mmm. I had planned to wake up with you in my bed.
He nibbled her earlobe. "Come to think of it, you'd mal
a terrific breakfast."

She shivered as his tongue explored her ear, playful
nudging him with the spatula in her hand. "Max. In ca
you didn't notice—"

"I notice everything about you," he interjected, h
fingers circling the back of her neck to hold her still.

"I happen to be in the middle of some very serious cooking here," she concluded breathlessly. "How do you feel about...about...oh, yes...French toast?"

"Nowhere near as horny as I feel about you."

"That's too bad, because the French toast will burn, and I won't."

He drew back to look at her, the edges of his mouth lifting suggestively. "You wanna bet?"

Her head shook, and a tremulous sigh left her body as she tipped her face up to his. Her lavish black lashes fluttered against her cheeks as her lips parted slightly, the barest tip of her tongue skittering out to moisten them. Once again Max marveled at her delicate beauty as he slowly lowered his head. All languor and restraint vanished the instant their mouths joined. He kissed her the same way she was kissing him, eagerly, hungrily, with a desperation that shouldn't have been in them after last night. He dropped his hands to her hips to pull her closer, shifting his stance so one of his thighs rode high between hers.

"Max," she breathed against his lips. "Breakfast—"

"Will have to wait," he broke in, reaching behind her to turn off the stove. "I can't."

The French toast was soggy by the time they got around to finishing cooking it, the bacon cold, and the coffee a little too strong. When Kara insisted the meal was not an accurate reflection of her cooking ability, Max grudgingly offered to give her another chance the following morning. He kept carefully tucked inside him the truth of the matter, that it was without question the best breakfast of his entire life. He wasn't sure himself why he felt that way, but he had a hunch that hypothesizing about it out loud would send Kara streaking back into her shell. He couldn't understand how one woman could be so open and at the same time so mysterious, but those were only two of Kara's fascinating layers that he planned to explore before he was through. One small step at a time.

After the late breakfast they went for a swim, returning to the thickly padded chaise longues on Max's terrace to

dry off. The heat of the sun was lulling Kara into sleep with
the cozy thought that she could easily stay right there for
ever when a thread of guilt jerked her back to reality. She
glanced over at Max, who was stretched out just as lazily
on the chaise beside hers. Within easy reach rested his
guitar, a reminder of how he was supposed to be spending
his days. She sighed, telling herself that she should at least
offer to let him work.

"Max?"

He didn't lift his head. "Mmm?"

"Should you be working?"

"Mmm."

"Then should I be leaving?"

His fingers moved to close around her wrist. "Not on
your life." With obvious reluctance he adjusted his chair
to an upright position. "Actually, I think I could do my
best work looking at you."

Kara laughed.

"Don't laugh," he ordered gruffly. "You inspire me."

She laughed again.

"You think I'm kidding, don't you?"

"Either kidding or hallucinating. I've never thought of
myself as the type of woman who inspires works of art."

"Then I'm going to have to change the way you think
about yourself," he commented gravely. "Starting right
now."

Kara watched with mounting anxiety as he moved to
pick up his guitar, slinging the wide leather strap over his
head. He settled with it at the end of her chaise longue,
taking only a few seconds to tune the well-worn instrument to his satisfaction.

"I wrote this yesterday," he told her, his fingers poised
on the strings. "After I left you down there on the beach."

"Then I can believe that I inspired it," Kara countered
wryly. "I'm just not sure I want to hear it."

"I want you to hear it, though. It's called 'Reckless
Heart.'"

The melody he played was simple and slow, an undis-
tracting backdrop for his dramatic lyrics. The image pre-

sented in the title was cleverly woven through the song. There was nothing revolutionary in the story of a man who had failed so often at love, at life, that he stopped trying until he met a woman who cut through all the guilt and pain from the past to touch his heart and move him to take one final chance, on her and on himself. Yet Max's rough voice made the emotions laid bare in the song seem achingly real to Kara. Tears welled in her eyes as he delivered the final lines, which tempered reality with hope.

"...the risks are too real, the chances too few, I'll spend all that I have left on you."

"Max, that was beautiful!" she exclaimed when the last note had faded and she'd brought the lump in her throat under control.

"You really liked it?" The look in his eyes was eager and uncertain, once again not what she would have expected from a man in his position.

"Of course I liked it. It's as good, maybe even better, than any of your old songs you played last night."

It was as if she'd swept a heavy weight from his shoulders. Even the lines at the edges of his eyes seemed to ease.

"Were you worried that it wasn't as good?"

Her slightly incredulous question caused him to shrug uncomfortably. "Yeah. I was worried. The past few years everything I've written has been...less than enthusiastically received. And rightfully so," he acknowledged.

"Is that why you said you came here to find out if you could still write?"

He nodded. "It seems like when I abandoned music to make films, music abandoned me, too. Now I want it back, but God, I don't want to go back a loser."

"That's the last thing anyone could accuse you of being."

"Thanks for the vote of confidence, but I'm afraid that's exactly what people would think." His hands were still on the guitar. With their angular shape and sun-browned color his fingers almost seemed to be one with the lime-polished wood. He looked past her as he spoke. "My first films were seen by my friends and the guys in my old

band as a joke, a lark. But there's no way this last one
could be considered anything but a serious effort on my
part, and a serious failure all the way around. More than
anything I want to put that behind me and play again, but
not if it means being seen by anyone who counts as a
washed-up has-been making one last desperate grasp at
fame.''

''Who do you mean by anyone who counts?''

''Other musicians,'' he returned without hesitation.
''Serious musicians. That's why Earle Biddle's invitation
to play last night meant so much to me. It was proof that
not everyone has forgotten that I made good music long
before I started making bad movies. If I announce my decision to quit acting completely in order to concentrate on
my music and then turn in a mediocre effort, it will prove
that those who have been saying I sold out because I
burned out were right. That's why my next album, if there
ever is one, has to be the best I've ever done.''

His statement wasn't a cheap bid for reassurance or encouragement, and Kara didn't offer either. She simply
waited, giving him time to find the words to say what his
eyes told her he needed to get out.

''You may find this hard to believe,'' he ventured with
a forced edge of humor that quickly disappeared, ''but I'm
just like that guy in my song. It seems I've screwed up
everything that ever mattered to me. And lately I've been
wondering if I've got what it takes to try again.''

He paused once more, the expression on his face free of
the cynicism and the cockiness she had seen there at different times. It was very easy for Kara to think of him not
as a major sex symbol but as the man who had made love
to her with such sweetness that she had cried in his arms
afterward.

''I joined the Navy mostly just to make my old man
proud,'' he revealed abruptly. ''A hopeless task to begin
with, but I never stopped trying until the day he died. He
was a retired rear admiral, had a complete set of every
damn medal ever minted framed and hanging over the
dining room table. I grew up staring at those medals every

ingle night while I ate dinner, and it never once occurred
o me that I couldn't meet the standard he'd set until the
lay I sat shaking in the cockpit of a chopper hovering over
ome Godforsaken village in 'Nam.''

The cords in his neck were as tight as the wire strings
eneath his fingers.

"Max," Kara ventured tentatively, "if it bothers you to
alk about—"

"It doesn't bother me," he cut in harshly. "There's just
tothing about that part of my life worth talking about."

Kara remembered something Jack had said about Max
eing a war hero and had to bite her lip to keep from ask-
ng him about it.

"I did my tour of active duty," he continued in a mat-
er-of-fact monotone, "and then let my father down by
opting for a soft job teaching at Annapolis instead of another hitch overseas. You know what the very last thing he
ver said to me was? He said, 'You could have been a
tero.'"

"I'm sure he didn't mean it that way—"

"You didn't know him."

"That still doesn't mean you failed—"

"That's sure how it felt."

"It just means that his dream for you wasn't the same
is your own," she continued with conviction.

"That's true enough. My dream was writing music, and
fter he died I figured I might as well give it a shot. I sure
s hell wasn't winning any medals for what I was doing."
His expression was tense, his voice strained. "I had a wife
nd two kids..."

The words took Kara by surprise, landing like punches
o her stomach, making it hard to focus on what he was
aying for a few seconds.

"...no job, and precious little cash," Max went on,
"and I sat around home all day writing songs and spent
very night in one Nashville bar or another trying to get
omeone to listen to them. And the only thing I felt when
Connie finally packed up herself and the kids and made
ood on all her threats to walk out on me was relief. It

meant I didn't have to look at my failure reflected in he
eyes every morning when I woke up.''

"But you were right to hang on and keep trying; you fi
nally made it.''

He tilted his head with only partial agreement. "Yeah
Which meant I could afford to write Connie big check:
both of us know will never make up for what I put he
through.'' He suddenly glanced over and caught her pen
sive frown and grinned. "If you're wondering if I'm car
rying a torch for my ex-wife, the answer is no. She's a very
contented housewife in Texas now, who does her best to
forget the lapse in common sense that ever brought me into
her life in the first place.''

"Falling in love might not always be the wisest thing to
do,'' Kara ventured, feeling her own conscience prickle
"That doesn't mean it's a lapse in common sense.''

"It does if you fall in love with a uniform instead of
what's inside it,'' Max retorted. "Connie thought she wa.
getting an officer and a gentleman. Instead, all she got was
me.''

"You must have loved her, though, or was she wearing
a uniform, too?''

His eyes narrowed above a sardonic smile. "I loved
having someone love me, just me. As soon as we both
found out we hadn't gotten what we bargained for, the
party was over.''

"What about your children?''

The smile fled his face as his right hand automatically
lifted to the empty pocket of his T-shirt, where Kara sus
pected he'd once carried his cigarettes. He dropped it back
to the guitar with a sheepish glance in her direction. "Force
of habit.'' Clearing his throat, he continued, "My kids are
great. Lenore is twelve and Nicole almost ten.''

"Do you see them?'' The question had been prompted
by the trace of wistfulness in his reply.

"I used to. I still would, if they'd see me. Or rather, if
Connie would let them see me. She says my life-style is a
bad influence on them now that the girls are old enough to

know better." He slanted her a crooked grin. "See why Connie and I never got along?"

Somehow Kara found a smile to offer him in spite of all the painful memories from her own childhood that he had disturbed. "But don't you miss them?" she asked softly.

Max looked away, the muscles in his shoulders bunching with tension. "Yes, I miss them. That's another reason I want what I'm working on to turn out right. I want to be more than a dollar sign in their lives, and more than some larger-than-life image toting an automatic weapon and whipping off snappy one-liners. I want them to be proud of me. Which sort of brings me right back to where I started, doesn't it? Turning myself inside out to make someone else proud of me?"

"Not if you want them to be proud of you for something you're proud of yourself," Kara pointed out.

"Yeah, I guess that would be a switch." His gaze was sober as it swung back to meet hers. "I sure wasn't very proud of myself yesterday morning."

"Max, we already—"

"I know," he continued over her protest. "I've already apologized, and you've already said you understand, but this is something different, something important to me. The reason I wasn't proud of myself was because I suddenly realized that it's been so long since I've had to take no for an answer that I've forgotten how. I've come to expect that everything and everybody around me will bend to my will, and when you wouldn't, it didn't only infuriate me, it shocked me. You forced me to take a look at a side of myself that isn't very pretty.

"Once I started thinking about it, I realized it's been the same with my writing. I want it, and therefore," he said, snapping his fingers, "voilà, I expect it to happen. I'd forgotten that life doesn't work like that, that sometimes it takes more than desire and hard work to make something happen. It takes luck and timing and..."

He paused, and some instinct for self-defense prompted Kara to drop her gaze from his eyes to his lean, graceful fingers.

"Sometimes it takes something more," he went on. "Something intangible that gives you the courage or drive or whatever you want to call it to keep trying even when you know the deck is stacked against you. That's what I was talking about in 'Reckless Heart.'"

For some reason his words left Kara feeling dangerously exposed. She shifted in her seat. Even with her eyes averted his gaze wielded power over her senses, heating every cell of her body to an unfortunate degree.

"And that's what I feel like I've found," Max concluded simply. "Crazy, huh?"

She swallowed hard and finally looked up at him with as composed an expression as she could manage. "I... Not if it works, I suppose."

Max's smile struck Kara as disturbingly confident as he nodded, then turned his attention to the guitar cradled in his lap, murmuring a cryptic, "I guess we'll have to wait and see about that."

He began playing, steadily being drawn further into the sound he was creating until his expression of concentration told Kara she was as good as alone with her thoughts. Though the music he played was totally different, the lyrics of 'Reckless Heart' echoed persistently in her head, demanding that she confront a question she'd shied away from earlier. How serious had Max been when he'd said that she was the inspiration for the song?

Of course, it might well have been nothing more than meaningless flattery, a standard songwriter's line he had used so often he'd honed it to a perfect sham of sincerity, but something told Kara that was wishful thinking on her part. Then there was his announcement of a moment ago to consider. He hadn't actually come out and said that she was this mystical source of inspiration he'd discovered, but he'd sure left that impression hanging in the air between them. Kara's earlier vague feelings of anxiety started to crystallize into something more foreboding. Maybe what was really wishful thinking was her utter confidence about the outcome of their affair.

Kara caught her frantically spinning thoughts short with silent laugh. Who was she kidding? If there was any wishful thinking at all going on here, it had to be this recurring fantasy that Max could possibly fall so hard for her that he wouldn't be able to tear himself away when the time came. What did she have to offer that could possibly compete with the glamour and excitement that a man of Max Ellis's past experiences and future possibilities was accustomed to?

Nothing, she concluded, wondering why the obvious answer didn't bring her more joy. Where Max was concerned, she had no need to worry about sticky complications developing, and that was, after all, what she wanted. This was supposed to be a fling, a carefree, spontaneous, self-indulgent break from her day-to-day reality. All she had to do was to stop second-guessing herself and enjoy it. And if her own feelings weren't as guaranteed not to get sticky as Max's...well, she'd already faced that possibility sometime around dawn.

She had lain there watching Max asleep beside her, his dark hair tousled around a face that looked much younger than it did when he was awake, and she had seen very clearly the limitations of her life. Just as clearly she had seen her options: she could choose to go on living a little for a lifetime or to live recklessly for one glorious moment. It wasn't a hard decision. Then, as now, she'd known in her heart that, regardless of the risks, she wanted this moment with Max.

Very consciously Kara barred from her mind thoughts of how long the time they shared would be. The days together passed, and she collected memories like souvenirs of a special trip, never permitting herself to consider that each might be the last. The very lack of definition gave their relationship an exciting air of fantasy. Routine was nonexistent. Their days were shaped only by their seemingly insatiable desire to be near each other and by the whim of the moment. They ate Max's special turkey and avocado sandwiches for breakfast one morning and

strawberries for dinner more than once. They made love i
Max's bed and, in spite of Kara's secret fears for the fu
ture, in hers. And when even the short trek back to th
house outdistanced their self-control they took each othe
on their own private stretch of pink sand. They made lov
on the beach when it was warmed by sunlight and when i
was silvered by the moon and once when a sudden hot rai
turned the air around them to steam.

Max adapted his schedule to hers, writing nights whil
she worked and showing up at the club just before closin
to bring her home. Kara loved the songs he was writing
and, more important, so did Max. He even felt confiden
enough to contact his record company with the news tha
'Reckless Heart' would be the cornerstone for a new a
bum, the theme of which would be lives rebuilt. As wit
everything they discussed, Max didn't speak about th
planned album in terms of when or how soon, and Kar
didn't ask. During long walks on the beach she listened t
Max talk about his life, discovering that while he was jade
in some ways, in others he was much younger and mor
trusting than his years and his experiences should have le
him. About herself she said as little as she could grace
fully get away with. Max never pressed, yet in subtle way
she sensed him testing her defenses.

About a week after the first time they made love, h
played for her a song he'd been working on with hi
daughters in mind. It was simple and unaffected, offerin
no excuses for the past, only the promise of a parent's un
conditional love and the hope that he could get to knov
them again as well as he once had, back in the days whe
they used to laugh down at him from the giddy heights o
a toddler's swing he was pushing. This time the tears hi
words brought to her eyes spilled over, and in the warr
cocoon of Max's embrace Kara found herself speakin
more freely about the barren landscape of her own child
hood than she ever had to anyone except Jack. Max's sof
chambray shirt muffled the words that told of a little girl'
pain and absorbed the long overdue flood of tears Kar

hadn't permitted herself to shed at the time of her father's death.

Only when he gently questioned her about the last time she'd seen her mother did Kara's armor of reticence slam back into place. She had shrugged off the question with a vague reference to the truth, that they hadn't been in touch in more years than she liked to count, and Max had obligingly backed away from the subject, pulling her back into his arms and soothing her with his skillful hands and mouth. But as she had on several other occasions, Kara sensed that in Max's mind the discussion wasn't closed, only postponed.

She told herself that it was inevitable that as they spent more and more time together, growing so close physically that she knew Max's body as intimately as she did her own, that emotional borders would blur as well. Sometimes he seemed so integral a part of her existence that it was an effort to remember what her life had been like before he came. And sometimes it felt as if he had put his brand on so many small parts of her soul that there would be nothing left behind for her to rebuild on once he was gone.

Careful, careful, she cautioned herself each morning when she awoke to the soft, snuffly snoring of one of the world's foremost sex symbols. Then Max would stir beside her, waking to caress her with eyes that were green and shone with words and promises neither of them ever spoke out loud. He would touch her, the scrape of his fingertips on her soft skin as familiar and as wondrous as a brand-new morning, inciting such a rush of feeling that there was no room left inside Kara for caution.

If there had been, if even a single thread of the tapestry of self-control and caution she had woven of her life during the past thirteen years had survived the sensual onslaught of Max intact, Kara never would have made the mistake of agreeing when he suggested a day-trip to nearby Harbour Island.

Chapter Ten

It wasn't that Kara never dared to venture off Diamond Cay. At one time or another she'd visited all the other islands in the area, including Harbour Island. She had also vacationed as far away as South America and Europe. But that was alone, as a nondescript female tourist, certainly not as the companion of a man whose face was as familiar to moviegoers as buttered popcorn.

Unfortunately, Kara would rationalize later, it was easy to forget how big a star Max was when you had never seen one of his movies but *had* watched him chewing the eraser on his pencil and chugging milk straight from the carton and scowling at the first hint of gray in his beard just like any other man crowding forty.

Anne gleefully consented to let them use one of Westwind's sleek sailboats for their trip to Harbour Island When Kara stopped by her office to ask about it, Anne had reacted as she had almost every other time the two women had seen each other during the past week or so, beaming and shaking her head and exclaiming ''I still don't believe

it!'' as if Kara had been awarded the Pulitzer prize for romantic achievement. The boat's crew was accustomed to
having celebrities on board and adept at staying out of the
way unless needed. The trip took a little over an hour, and
the privacy she and Max enjoyed en route lulled Kara into
a false sense of security that was shattered almost as soon
as they set foot ashore.

Dressed in anything but what she considered movie-star
fashion, she had naïvely assumed that they would blend in
with the crowd at the island's most popular tourist spot,
Dunmore Town, a tiny village where historic mansions and
brightly painted clapboard houses stood side by side, all
owing their origins to the Loyalists who had fled the
American Revolution. However, as she and Max strolled
along the narrow, flower-bedecked streets and wandered
through the small shops, a wave of tentative whispers
rolled along behind. Max remained at ease, seemingly oblivious to the speculative stares directed his way, but Kara
felt as if she'd suddenly been cast in the starring role in
''The Emperor's New Clothes.'' The sunglasses and
leather-banded white hat Max was wearing with his jeans
and T-shirt were a flimsy disguise, and eventually a heavy-
set woman in a flowered sundress cornered them in a jew-
elry boutique and issued a loud ''Aren't you Max Ellis?''

Max handled the woman, and the others who stopped
him outside to ask for his autograph or just to reassure
themselves that it really was he, with friendly expediency.
Most passersby concentrated their attention on Max,
sparing only a fleeting, curious glance at her. Still, Kara,
who'd spent a large part of her life trying not to call attention to herself, grew more tense by the second. Except
when he was scribbling his autograph Max held on to her
hand tightly, and she worried whether he noticed how
clammy it had become. Each click of a camera shutter
sounded in her ears like a gunshot. How many hands
would these prized photos pass through once the proud
picture-taker had returned home? How many pairs of eyes
would peruse them at leisure, studying the plain-looking,

unidentified woman with Max Ellis? And how long could she hope to remain unidentified?

Although he chatted briefly and intermittently with those who spoke to him, Max devoted most of his attention to her. Kara nodded and responded, but it was as if a heavy fog surrounded her, isolating her from Max and the rest of the world. She felt the way she once had when she'd suffered an allergic reaction to some medicine, hot and cold at the same time and slightly disoriented. Sweat trickled along her spine, dampening the yellow cotton fabric of her sundress. Her temples throbbed, and panic simmered in her veins, making her feel as if she might explode at any second. Finally Max led her to a relatively private spot near a stone wall overlooking the ocean and stood so that his broad shoulders shielded her from the crowd of passersby a short distance away.

Purely an illusion, Kara reminded herself, refusing to be tricked into feeling relieved. She'd played enough tricks on herself lately. The truth was that the crowd behind him was more important to Max than she could ever hope to be, although despite his rough-around-the-edges image he was far too much of a gentleman to say so. Stares and attention and cameras snapping were a crucial part of his business. If her life with its shaky foundation was reminiscent of a house of cards, his was a constant string of explosions. There was no way the two could peacefully coexist.

Numbly Kara was forced to acknowledge that all this time, in some small secret corner of her heart, she had been clinging to the hope that somehow she would find a way to go on seeing Max. The past half hour had put a chilling end to that foolishness and brought her to a wrenching awareness. Not only was it possible for her to fall in love with Max Ellis, she already had.

Max's hands rose to rest lightly on her shoulders, his thumbs tipping her face up to his. It took every bit of self-control Kara possessed not to bury her head against his chest.

"I think coming here was a bad idea," he said with quiet regret.

"No, really—" Kara stopped. Really what? She couldn't deny that she was miserable, and she couldn't tell him why.

"I had no idea the attention would bother you so much."

"I guess I'm just not used to it."

"It didn't affect you this way when people asked for my autograph at the Shady Lady."

There it was again. His subtle way of questioning without asking any questions. Kara shrugged, unable to tell him that only on Diamond Cay did she feel safe and in control. "There were fewer people there. Here I feel as if I'm surrounded. It's like I can't breathe."

"I know, honey." His fingers kneaded the rigid muscles at the base of her neck. "But I can tell you from experience that you'll get used to it."

"No." She shook her head in a sudden spurt of panic. "No, I'll never get used to it. There's no need for me to."

"There is a need, Kara. My need. Look, I've been wanting to talk to you about this for days, but I've been afraid you'd turn away, afraid you'd say no. The fact is, I can't stay down here much longer. I have commitments—"

"Fine. I understand. I told you at the start—"

"I know what you told me, damn it, but things have changed. I've changed."

"Well, I haven't," she countered, wrenching away only to find herself corralled between his body and the stone wall behind her. "What I said then stands. I don't want to get involved."

"We're already involved, and I intend to keep it that way. I want you in my life, Kara."

"Why? Because I'm the first woman you ever met who doesn't want to be there?"

His eyes clouded. "I don't think I deserve that."

"No," Kara agreed tersely, "you don't. You don't deserve any of this. And I really don't want to talk about it."

Max's eyes narrowed in concern as he took in the desperation in hers, but his voice remained low and calm. "We have to talk about it. Maybe that's the real reason I wanted to come here today, to try to force everything out in the open between us. Kara, I don't know why, but I do know that you're hiding on Diamond Cay. I've known almost from the beginning. I can help, honey, but first you have to trust me. You have to—''

"No, you can't help.'' Only the years of ingrained control kept her from crying out loud. "No one can help. Now, if you don't mind, all I really want is to go home.''

This time when his hand rose to touch her face Kara levered out of reach. She felt like one of the porcelain vases on display in the window of an antique shop they had passed, the kind with thousands of fine lines crisscrossing the polished surface. But unlike those vases there was nothing beneath her surface to hold her together anymore. If he touched her now, she would shatter.

As if sensing how close to the edge she was, Max gave a frustrated nod, his fingers clenched into tight fists at his sides. "All right. Let's go. We can talk later.''

Kara didn't argue. Later was soon enough to tell him there was nothing left to say. She had just started to step around him when a middle-aged man wearing khaki shorts and a plaid sports shirt blocked her path. He had a cigar clamped between the fingers of one hand, but that didn't stop him from clicking away with the 35mm camera he was holding.

"Gotcha,'' he cried jovially. Extending his right hand to Max, he introduced himself. "Sam Wasserman. I put out a little paper called *Island Highlights*—some ads, lots of pictures.'' He patted his camera. "Got some real beauties of you two. Maybe do a full-page spread. Not everyday we get a genuine celebrity passing through. How about introducing me to the lady, Max, so I can put her name in the captions? I know I've got a pencil here somewhere.'' He began to rummage in his pockets as he spoke. "Yes, sir, my little paper's available at the front desk of all the hotels on all the islands. I could have sworn I had one... Why, sometimes our photos are even picked up by the wire services. I wouldn't be a bit surprised if these are, to tell you the truth. Unless I left it in the car...''

The fact that he was promising to brandish her picture from one end of the Bahamas to the other—maybe even around the world—was slow to penetrate the anguished tangle of Kara's thoughts. As soon as it did she whirled to Max with fresh desperation.

"Max, do something."

"I don't have a pencil."

"I don't want you to help him," she cried impatiently. "I want you to stop him."

Both men stared at her in surprise and started to speak at once.

"Now, ma'am..."

"Kara, I..."

She interrupted. "He has no right to just take our picture and print it without even asking."

"Honey, it happens all the time," Max soothed. "It's no big deal."

"It's a big deal to me. I don't want my picture in his paper."

"Ma'am, the last thing I want to do is offend anyone," the portly photographer insisted. "No, sir. If you want me to ask your permission, then I certainly—"

"No. I don't want you to ask for permission. I want..." Her mind was spinning frantically. "I want the film."

"Out of the question," Sam Wasserman shot back without hesitation. There was suddenly a firmer set to his double chin. "Freedom of the press aside, I have other shots that are important to me on this roll."

Her fingers gripped Max's forearm. "You can't let him get away with this."

"Kara, it's not really a question of letting him get away with anything."

"I don't believe it. You mean you're not going to stop him? Where are all your highly touted heroic instincts now?"

"I guess I don't have any," he replied, his smile a little strained at the edges. "Maybe you've got me confused with my alter ego. Are you sure you've never seen a Delta Bent film?"

Kara recognized the remark as an effort to defuse the situation with lightness, but the taste of disaster had risen too high in her throat for her to even attempt to smile back. All she cared about was keeping those photos out of Sam Wasserman's paper. Her gaze locked on the camera hanging at his side. If the pictures appeared and someone recognized her, she wasn't the only one who would suffer. Jack would also pay a stiff price, and most likely Victor as well. The rippling effects would even spread to touch people like Anne, people who had trusted her as a friend. If the truth about her past had to come out, and maybe it was time that it did, Kara didn't want it to happen this way.

Panic was like a strong wind at her back, pushing her ahead without time to think. If she had thought, or given Wasserman time to react, there was no way she could have wrestled the camera from his grasp. Instead her sudden lunge for it took all of them, including her, by surprise. The camera was only in her hands for a matter of seconds, barely long enough for her to register the feel of it. Solid. Expensive. Then it was over the wall, hurtling fifteen feet to the water below, as Sam Wasserman bellowed something obscene about her.

Max watched without moving, half expecting to hear a director shout "Cut!" as soon as the camera broke the waterline. But there was no shout, only Kara's stricken expression and Sam Wasserman's red mottled face and the collective gasp of surprise from the circle of curious spectators who had gathered nearby. Guilt sliced through him. It was true that he'd hoped something would happen here today to shed some light on the secrets he knew Kara was keeping from him, but he hadn't wanted to push her anywhere near this far.

"You idiot!" Wasserman screamed at Kara. "Do you have any idea what a Nikon F3 costs? That's it. I'm suing you. And you too, Ellis. Yes, sir. Cost of equipment, plus business interruption, not to mention pain and suffering. And humiliation. Look, look around you!" He made a sweeping gesture toward the rapidly growing crowd, ending by waving his fist close to Kara's face. "And all because Miss Snooty here doesn't like to have her picture taken. Well, let me tell you, sister—"

"No, Mr. Wasserman, let me tell you something." Max's move to put himself between the man and Kara had been swift and instinctive. "I'll pay you for the loss of your camera and your film, and I'll settle for full damages if you'll contact my business manager. But I won't let you abuse this lady, verbally or otherwise."

"Some la—" Wasserman broke off at the warning glitter in Max's eyes. "Yeah, all right. Where do I reach this business manager?"

Wasserman finally located his pencil and a scrap of paper, and Max gave him Louie's name and address. He also gave him enough cash to replace the camera without delay, then grimly shouldered his way through the crowd, one arm securely around a silent Kara. As they hurried back to the boat he spoke intermittently, saying whatever he thought might reassure her that everything was okay. Max finally realized that she either wasn't listening or wasn't hearing when she turned to him and asked, "Are you very angry with me?"

Amazingly he wasn't, although he sensed she didn't believe him when he told her that. He wasn't angry or embarrassed or concerned about how outrageously the incident would no doubt be magnified in next week's supermarket tabloids. Overriding any and all other emotion he might feel was his need to protect Kara, even from herself, if necessary.

He sat close to her on board the sailboat, surreptitiously watching her watch the glassy swells that lifted the bow, then gently fell away. The desire to know what she was thinking, to understand why she had reacted so desperately to having her picture taken, roiled inside him, but Max was determined not to ask until Kara made it clear she was ready to talk. His only glimmer of satisfaction came from knowing that at least he no longer had to dance around the fact that she was hiding something.

The crew of the boat obligingly detoured to drop them off at home. Kara immediately went into her own house,

leaving Max wondering if he was going to be able to wait
her out after all. He sat on the terrace for what felt like
hours, his guitar in hand, unable to concentrate. Finally he
heard Kara's footsteps behind him. She ignored the arms
he opened to her, selecting instead a chair a safe distance
out of his reach and perching carefully on the very edge,
the way a bird lights on one branch while eyeing the next.
It gave Max an unwelcome feeling of foreboding. She had
changed into cutoff jeans and a loose-fitting white cotton
blouse. Her hair was wet, her face paler than Max had ever
seen it. The only trace of color was the pink rimming her
eyes. His heart clenched as he remembered that she had
once told him the only place she ever cried was in the
shower.

"Kara," he began, having no idea of the right thing to
say. He breathed a sigh of relief when she intervened.

"No, please, Max. I think it's my turn to talk. In fact, I
think my turn is long overdue." She folded her hands in
her lap, then unfolded them and curled her fingers around
the wrought-iron arms of her chair. "I guess it's fitting that
you should be the first person in fourteen years I've ever
told any of this to. If it weren't for you, I might have gone
on as I am for another fourteen years, wasting more time,
and ending up hurting more people. Max, I—"

She broke off, glancing down at the ground, then lifting her gaze back to his with her chin set at a determined
angle. "There is no easy way for me to tell you this, so I'm
just going to say it straight out. You were right when you
accused me of hiding here on Diamond Cay. I am. The
reason I'm hiding, and the reason I told you there is no
future for us, is because I'm wanted by the police."

Max felt his jaw drop. Quickly he masked the shock he
was feeling before seeing it added to Kara's anguish. He
had convinced himself that it was a bad family situation
she had run from. He'd figured that maybe, at the very
worst, there was still a legal husband somewhere that
would have to be dealt with. He hadn't even considered the
possibility that she was running from the police.

"Wanted for what?" he asked, thankful that nothing of the distress he was suffering sounded in his tone.

She waved her hands. "Who knows? Trespassing. Destruction of private property. Accessory to murder."

Max shot from his chair. "Well, which is it, Kara? There's a hell of a big difference between trespassing and murder."

"Accessory to murder."

"Sorry. You'll have to excuse me. I get a little out of sorts when I learn that the woman I love might be wanted for murder. Accessory to murder," he amended.

"What did you say?" Her eyes were a stormy blue battlefield where hope warred with dismay.

"I said I love you," Max replied. It was the first time he'd admitted it even to himself, yet the words felt as comfortable rolling off his tongue as his name did. "I don't care if you're wanted for every crime committed in the last century. I love you, baby."

"Oh, Max, I love you, too."

With a sob she rushed into his arms, clinging to him as if he were the last solid object in her universe. Max smoothed his hands over her hair, whispering whatever words he thought might comfort her. Inside him the urge to rescue her from whatever demons were out there was transformed from a vague desire into granite. When her shoulders finally stilled and her breathing was no longer choppy, he pulled away enough to smile down at her tear-streaked face.

"I thought you never cried outside the shower?" he teased gently.

"I thought so, too."

He rested his arms on her shoulders. "Don't you know you're supposed to be clutching your cheeks and telling me how awful you look when you cry?"

"Why? By now you already know that without my telling you."

Max shook his head, love for her flowing through him like a fast-moving river. "No. You're always beautiful to me. And you always will be." He slid his hand down to catch hers. "Come on. We're going to take a long walk on the beach, and you're going to tell me everything."

Kara didn't begin talking until they had reached the hard-packed sand near the water's edge and started walking west.

"It happened fourteen years ago," she began in a carefully controlled monotone. "I was a freshman in college. My brother John had just finished spending two years in the Peace Corps and was enrolled in the graduate school at the same university. The war in Vietnam had been over for a while, but there was still a lot of lingering activist sentiment on campus." She shrugged bleakly. "You know, kids in search of a cause."

"No, I don't know. I flew med-evac missions in 'Nam, remember? I never saw the war in terms of placards and slogans."

"Neither did I," Kara countered defensively; then her shoulders sagged. "Oh, maybe I did. I don't know. I was only a kid. All the time I was in high school I was looking ahead. I envied my brother and other kids in college. I couldn't wait to get there, couldn't wait for my chance to be involved in something that mattered."

"Is that what happened? Did you get involved in something that mattered?"

"I thought so at the time. Now? Now I'd give anything to be able to go back and undo what happened that afternoon . . . or at the very least be somewhere far away when it happened."

Max put his arm around her shoulders, fitting her close to the side of his body in the spot that seemed to have been carved with her in mind. "Tell me about that afternoon."

Kara spoke slowly, giving herself time to bring into focus events that she'd tried so hard for so long to blot out. "My brother had joined this group, a chapter of Students for a Democratic Society, and I started dropping by their campus office. John was really opposed to my hanging around, but I made some friends there and started doing little things to help out, typing, posting leaflets on telephone poles, that sort of thing."

"What kind of leaflets?"

"Mostly calling for local prison reforms. That was the cause of the moment, and I really got reeled into believing I was helping with something noble and important."

"Against your brother's wishes?"

"Right. Back then I was convinced John was just playing the heavy-handed big brother because he didn't want me seeing this other guy in the group, a guy I had sort of a crush on." Kara folded her arms tightly across her chest as the memory of that time started unspooling faster and faster. "It turned out he had good reason not to want me to get involved with Dwight, but . . ."

"Dwight?" Max prodded mildly when she fell into preoccupied silence.

Kara shook herself back to the present. "Dwight Billings. He was more or less the leader of the group. At least he was until John came along." She smiled affectionately. 'John has a way of sort of surging to the lead wherever he happens to be, which didn't sit well with Dwight. They hated each other from the start."

"I take it you didn't automatically side with your brother in this war of personalities?"

The trace of wry disapproval in his question caused Kara to frown. "I certainly didn't side against him. But Dwight made it impossible for me to side against him, too. He was charming in his own way, intelligent, ambitious for something beyond his own personal success. Something that made him the antithesis of both of my parents and therefore a saint in my eyes," she observed cynically. "When I was eighteen years old Dwight Billings seemed to be everything I could ever want in a man. He was intense and passionate—" her mouth crooked "—and he wore cowboy boots and straight-leg cords."

Max told himself it was crazy to feel jealous over anything that might have happened between two kids fourteen years ago. But he still wanted to know. "How passionate?"

"Are you asking if I slept with him?"

"Yeah. I guess I am."

"That's not exactly what I was implying by the word *passionate*."

"I'm still asking."

Kara sighed. "Yes. Once. At the time I had nothing to compare him with, but once I did I realized that he was a much better activist than he was a lover." She slanted a small smile up at Max. "You, on the other hand, would make a rotten activist."

He brushed the top of her head with his lips before breaking into a grin. "Thanks."

As if they both remembered at once that this wasn't a moment for smiles, theirs faded in unison. Warm water foamed at their bare feet as they walked along in silence for a few minutes. Max didn't pressure her to speak, and Kara slowly drew confidence from the warmth of his closeness.

"Dwight convinced everyone that a sit-in was the fastest, surest way to force the university's board to publicly support some controversial legislation calling for prison reform," she continued finally. "I wasn't even supposed to be there. My brother had made me promise to stay away, but the night before, Dwight stopped by my room and . . . and that was the night we made love." She chewed the inside of her bottom lip. "Afterward I wondered if he'd come by just to make sure I went the next day. He'd known for weeks how I felt about him—it was obvious, but nothing ever happened. Then all of a sudden . . . I think maybe Dwight decided I might come in handy to use as leverage against John if the need arose. The next afternoon was warm and sunny. I remember wishing I could be outside and thinking how occupying the dean's office wasn't nearly as exciting as it used to look on the six o'clock news."

"Kara, are you trying to tell me that's why you're wanted by the police? For taking part in some ridiculous sit-in years ago?"

Kara shook her head quickly, not wanting to encourage the relief she heard hovering just behind his slightly incredulous tone. "I'm afraid there's more to it than that. The sit-in dragged on for hours. Everyone got tired and hungry—everyone except Dwight, that is. He seemed to be on some kind of emotional high. Eventually we sent out for sandwiches, as if it were a damn picnic.'' She shook her head, remembering. ''Dwight had set himself up in the dean's private office while most of the rest of us stayed in a couple of rooms down the hall. I went to bring him some food and...and...'' Bile rose into her throat as she relived the seconds of violence that had changed her life forever.

''What is it, baby?'' Max implored in a voice rough with compassion. ''Tell me what happened. Please, Kara.''

They had come to a sudden halt. Kara let Max gather her against his broad chest and pull her down to sit beside him in the sand.

''Did that bastard hurt you?'' he demanded suddenly. ''Is that why—?''

He broke off as Kara shook her head frantically. Her words poured out in clipped spurts. ''No, not me. He didn't hurt me. I thought Dwight was alone in the office. I pushed open the door, and then I don't know what happened next. I saw a man—just this old man, a security guard who'd come up on his own to try to talk us into leaving—and I heard an explosion. I think there was a flash, and then the man fell. There was blood, so much blood, on his uniform and the rug—everywhere. Oh, God, Max.'' She was crying and clutching his shirtfront. ''Have you ever seen a man die? Do you know what it's like to watch and not be able to do anything?''

His arms tightened almost painfully around her. His face was wet, and Kara didn't know if it was from the tears he was crying or from his own. ''Yeah. Yeah, I've seen men die.''

''I got sick, and when I finally pulled myself together and looked at Dwight, he was wiping his fingerprints off the gun. And the blood on the floor had spread so it was touching his shoe. And he just stood there wiping the gun. He said I startled him when I pushed open the door, that the gun went off accidentally.'' She turned her head to look out over the ocean. "John said he killed the guard in cold blood."

"What do you think?"

"For a long time I didn't want to believe John was right. I blamed myself for opening the door without knocking, I blamed the security guard for being foolhardy enough to confront Dwight alone, I blamed everyone else who was there for not knowing that Dwight had a gun and that something bad might happen. During the next year or so my brother and I moved from safe-house to safe-house throughout New England. Occasionally our path crossed Dwight's, and I finally had to accept the fact that John had been right about him all along. What I thought was intensity and concern for others was something different, something dangerous and fanatical."

"You mean you ran away after the shooting and hid someplace for a year?"

Kara turned to meet his thunderstruck expression. "Max, I've been hiding ever since."

"Holy—" He broke off, shaking his head as if having trouble comprehending what her life had been like. "But why? God knows, you didn't do anything wrong."

Her laugh was bitter. "God might have, but at the time I wasn't so sure. The police had already gathered outside the building, and when they heard gunshots they started tossing in tear gas. Somehow John found me in all the confusion and got me away from there. For the next week I could hardly think straight. Then I was just plain scared to go back."

"That's crazy. There was no evidence you did anything besides be in the wrong place at the wrong time. All you had to do was tell the truth."

"I was afraid no one would believe the truth. If you remember, at that time the country was about fed up to the teeth with protests by spoiled college kids. Dwight and I were the only ones who really knew what had happened, but there were plenty of witnesses who said I was in the room when the shooting took place."

"Your brother should have made you go back," insisted Max with stubbornness that bordered on anger. "He was old enough to think clearly."

"I don't think John knew quite what to do with me. He made it clear that he planned to remain underground, and gradually I came to realize that he had no alternative, that he was much more deeply involved in antigovernment activity than I had ever dreamed. For weeks he wouldn't even talk about any of it with me, just went around slamming doors all the time. In fact, that whole period when we were on the move had a sort of unsettled quality. I mean," she added with a sardonic smile, "even more unsettled than moving every few weeks already is. It was as if he were constantly searching for someplace out of the way to stick me. Then he finally remembered Victor and sent me to Chicago to see him, complete with my brand-new identity. Victor helped me finish college and gave me a job, and here I am."

"Victor Hazard did all this as a favor to your brother?"

Kara nodded, not at all surprised by his narrow-eyed expression of disbelief.

"Kara, no offense, but how the hell does someone like your brother, a fugitive for God's sake, get so buddy-buddy with one of the richest men in America?"

Briefly she told him all she knew of the two men's friendship, ending with a mystified shrug. "I find it hard to believe myself."

"Yeah, me, too. None of it makes sense. I mean, why didn't your brother ask Hazard to pull some strings with the law and give you back your life instead of sending you off to school under an assumed name? Didn't you even ask Victor to use his influence to try to help?"

"I thought about it," Kara admitted. "I thought about it a lot. Deep down I was willing to take my chances that my story would hold up—"

"Good," Max interjected. "Because you're finally going to get your chance to tell it. I have to fly back to Los Angeles tomorrow, and you're coming with me. I'm going to find the best lawyer there is for this kind of case—believe me, you're not the first radical from the sixties or seventies to surface—and we're going to let him tell us what the next step should be."

Kara was slowly shaking her head while he talked. Now she stopped and asked, "Don't you think I've considered consulting a lawyer? Don't you think I've lain awake nights, looking at this mess from every possible angle? I could have hired a lawyer years ago, Max, but I was always afraid that my brother might not be as—as innocent and deserving of understanding as I am. I'm afraid that they would make any leniency toward me contingent on his surrender."

"Then let him surrender!" Max roared, clearly enraged. He lunged to his feet. "It's about time he started answering for himself instead of hiding behind you."

"It's not like that," Kara protested, standing to face him squarely. "He loves me, and he's always taken care of me. I'm not exactly living in a hellhole," she declared, indicating the beauty all around with a sweep of her arm "Besides, he's really the only family I have. I don't want to see him in prison any more than I want to go there myself. It's been my choice not to turn myself in, and he's respected that."

Max's eyes glittered like shards of green ice. "Your choice? Your *choice*? You were a scared kid, for God' sake. What kind of choice were you capable of making To hide for the rest of your life? To live here in some kin of gilded tropical cage? No, Kara, if your brother real gave a damn about you fourteen years ago, he never woul have let you get involved in this mess. And if he gave damn about you now, he'd be standing here trying to tal some sense into you instead of me."

"He is here," Kara announced quietly. "Jack Hogan real name is John Haggerty. He's my brother."

Chapter Eleven

At Kara's insistence Max flew to L.A. the next day to keep his scheduled appointments. He was reluctant to leave her alone, but she convinced him that she needed some time by herself to think, and that so did he.

They had sat on the beach talking for hours. Max was steadfast in his belief that they would find a way to solve the problem and be together. Confidence and optimism clung to him as if by long habit. Kara, on the other hand, was well-versed in bowing to hard, cold reality. It wasn't until the sun started to set and their growling stomachs reminded them they hadn't eaten since breakfast that she allowed herself to be persuaded that there might possibly be a solution that wouldn't hurt someone involved more than it would help.

She had agreed to give it some time on the condition that Max not try to handle matters on his own by hiring a high-priced California lawyer and telling him the whole story. She had also elicited his grudging promise not to go to see Jack behind her back. Max might not be willing to believe that her brother always had her best interests at heart, but Kara knew otherwise. If Jack so much as surmised that he was standing in the way of her happiness, she had no doubt he would do something rash and self-sacrificing. Max hadn't liked hearing it, but Kara had meant every word when she told him that she didn't want any part of a new life with him if it had to be built on the ruins of her brother's.

At least she was spared having to face Jack while her feelings on the whole matter were still so raw and unsettled. Max had talked her into arranging to take the night off in anticipation of their big excursion to Harbour Island, although neither of them had known beforehand just how draining an experience it would turn out to be. After a solemn dinner of tuna salad sandwiches, they went straight to bed.

Despite all his professions of confidence in their future Max undressed her with painstaking care, kissing each part of her body he uncovered as if the memory of her that he carried away with him in the morning would have to last him a lifetime. Kara cried out softly, writhing against him as his mouth explored her daringly. Her fingers kneaded his shoulders and wound through his thick hair. Releasing a deep groan of desire, he rolled with her across the bed until she was stretched out beside him. He rubbed her neck with his mouth.

"God, I don't want to leave you," he whispered hoarsely. "Not for a day, not even for a minute."

"Shh." She closed her suddenly misty eyes and found his lips with her fingertips. "Don't talk. Just kiss me. Please kiss me."

Max kissed her as if he would never stop, twisting her head for a better vantage point, his hands sweeping over her breasts and thighs in slow, heating caresses. Kara burned to feel him inside her, but she forced herself to go slowly, touching him in all the places she'd learned that he loved to be touched, stroked, licked. Her nipples hardened against his chest, then ached with pleasure when

bent to pay them tribute with his lips and tongue and the
playfully rough edge of his teeth.

When her desire to be joined with him as intimately as
possible grew frantic, she wound her arms around him,
silently urging him on top of her, begging him to fill the
void he had created. Max obliged, but not at once. First,
holding himself poised close above her, he let her know the
strength and power of his desire. He was full and throbbing with need. Kara's fingers glided down between their
bodies, coasting over his ribs and his flat belly and into the
thick nest of dark hair at the juncture of his thighs. Lovingly she circled him, rubbing him against her velvety
softness, letting him feel that she was as ready and eager
as he was.

Max surged forward as she arched to meet him. Their
bodies moved as one, with a harmony that was echoed in
the pounding of their hearts and the broken rasp of their
breathing. Kara chanted his name and gathered to the very
core of her heart the disjointed words of love he whispered against her skin. In one way, now that there were no
shadows between them, their lovemaking was sweeter than
ever before. But it was also underscored with pain and
desperation. Long after their bodies had soared to com-
pletion she clung to him, afraid to let go, unable to quell
the feeling that this night might be their last together.

Max left early in the morning by chartered plane from
the island's small airstrip, and Kara soon discovered that
her little corner of the island wasn't the same without him.
She had lived there alone for years and loved it, yet suddenly the solitude was unbearable. Perversely, being with
other people was almost worse. Kara came to the sad conclusion that she wasn't lonely in general, simply lonely for
Max.

On the second day he was gone she biked to Westwind
to see if Anne wanted to play tennis on her lunch hour.
They played two sets, with Anne's superior skill keeping
Kara on the run almost nonstop. Still, when they finally sat
down at one of the courtside tables afterward, she was
bubbling with restless energy. It wasn't fair, she mused,

that you could work your arms and legs until they felt
ready to drop off, but the part of you in charge of worrying never even slowed down.

A warm breeze stirred the fringe on the yellow-and-white
striped umbrella overhead so it created a dancing shadow
on the glossy white tabletop. Idly Kara traced it with the tip
of her index finger.

"You really miss him, don't you?"

She glanced up to find Anne regarding her with a sym-
pathetic smile. Sheepishly she fiddled with the straw in her
iced tea. "Is it that obvious?"

"I could say no, that only a close friend such as myself
would notice, but the truth is that it's that obvious. You
look absolutely forlorn. And I couldn't be happier."

"What a pal."

"You know what I mean. Max Ellis is the best thing that
ever happened to you. Of course," Anne amended with a
sly inflection, "Max Ellis would probably qualify as the
best thing that could happen to any woman. I'm not only
happy, I'm green with envy."

Kara shook her head at her friend's teasing. "I'm not
sure I'm to be envied. In fact, I'm not sure if Max is the
best thing that ever happened to me or the worst."

Anne responded with a scoff of disbelief. "You're just
feeling morose because he's not around. How long did you
say he'll be away?"

"Another day or so. And you're right about my missing him, but what's really bothering me is the thought of
how much I'm going to miss him when he leaves for
good."

"Who says he's going to?"

"Common sense. The man is a certified star, Anne.
There's no way he's going to give all that up to be close to
me."

"Then maybe if you want to be close to him," her friend
advised in a firm, pointed tone, "you'll have to be the one
to do some bending for a change."

Kara shifted uneasily in her chair, feeling guilty that
she'd scratched the surface of this with Anne when the

were so many layers underneath that she wasn't free to discuss.

"It sounds as if you're trying to get rid of me," she teased in an effort to keep things light.

"Not at all. You know I'd miss you if you ever left Diamond Cay. And for all you know, Max would love to relocate here, someplace far away from the hustle of show business. He could always fly back and forth for concerts and whatever else it is that certified stars spend their time doing. But even if it means you have to live somewhere else, Kara, I think you owe it to yourself to give what you've found with Max every possible chance."

"Moving back to L.A. with Max wouldn't be giving it a chance. It would be signing a death sentence."

"I'm glad to see you're approaching this with an open mind," Anne observed dryly.

"I mean it, Anne. Max's life is completely different from mine. I got a little taste of it yesterday, more than enough to know it's not for me." Kara rattled on, surprised by just how desperate she was to talk to someone about this and at the same time frantically censoring the thoughts that rushed through her head. "Publicity and signing autographs and shaking hands—that's all crucial to his success. Sure he's enjoyed this break from the pressure, but if he'd wanted to live a simple, private life he would have been a sculptor or an accountant, not a performing musician. Deep down Max knows all this is true. He once told me that his public image is like a sponge, soaking up more and more of him until sometimes he thinks that's all there is."

"Then it must be true that opposites attract," countered Anne with quiet certitude, "because I've often thought that you have everything locked up so tightly inside that all anybody ever sees is a pretty shell. Maybe Max needs you to help him see inside himself as much as you need him to reach out."

Kara stared across the table at Anne with wide eyes, stunned by her observation.

"I'm sorry if I hurt your feelings," Anne went on in a gentle but thoroughly unapologetic manner, "but it's the way I feel. The way I've felt for a long time. I mean, we're friends and all—we joke and play tennis, and occasionally when I invite you to a party you even show up—but it's like there's this steel door between you and everybody else, and most of you is on the other side of it. For a while I had hoped that you and Jack Hogan might . . ." She dismissed the rest of the thought with a wave of her hand. "Obviously, the magic just wasn't there the way it is with Max. In all these years Max is the only one I've ever seen you with who seems to be able to unlock that steel door. Heck, when you two look at each other even I get goose bumps." Her sudden grin eased into an affectionate smile as she took in Kara's slightly bewildered expression. "If you're honest with yourself, you'll admit that what you feel for Max is worth more than any job and any beach house on any island in the world. And it's worth fighting for, Kara. Even if it's yourself you have to fight."

Anne's words stuck in Kara's mind as she rode home, no matter how hard she tried to rationalize them away. *Even if it's yourself you have to fight,* Anne had said, probably never dreaming of how painful a nerve those words would touch inside Kara. They raised a question she would have preferred to keep carefully at bay, telling herself the answer really didn't matter. But with Max in her life, everything was turned upside down. Things that had seemed so important before paled in comparison to her love for him. And answers that she'd convinced herself didn't really matter now threatened to shape the rest of her life.

Why *had* she spent the last fourteen years hiding? Was it to protect Jack, as she'd told Max, as she'd told herself every time the prospect of ending her self-imposed exile reared up inside her? Or was she simply afraid? Not afraid of whatever punishment might await for her part in the botched sit-in. Through the years she'd read enough accounts of similar cases to conclude that any sentence a court handed down would be lighter than this one she had assumed for herself. As for Jack, no matter how secretive he was about his activities, Kara knew in her heart that he wasn't capable of the kind of cruelty or senseless violence that would justify an unmerciful punishment. She also knew that if there was a price to be paid for his political beliefs, he wasn't the kind of man who would want his sister to spend the rest of her life paying that price for him.

She wasn't nearly so certain that she hadn't chosen to live this way because it was the easy way out. Here she was in control of her life. No one came too close. No one, that is, until fate had seen fit to complicate her existence with Max. There were no preoccupied parents to hurt or disappoint her here, no Dwight Billings to whisper words that he knew she desperately wanted to hear just to get what he wanted to get. There was no pressure to be witty or popular or wise, no pressure to be anything more than she was. It was safe and serene, but if she was honest with herself, she would have to admit that it wasn't really life. Maybe it was time she started being honest. No longer could she avoid confronting the fact that life, with all its unpredictable facets and potential for pain, was what she was really hiding from.

By the time she reached home Kara's mind was as weary as her body. She was hot and sticky and thirsty for the iced tea she'd hardly touched back at the courts. As she walked along the path to her front door it felt as if she were dragging lead weights, inside as well as out. She unlocked the door and headed straight for the refrigerator. When you live alone you grow accustomed to having things remain exactly as you leave them, and you develop little idiosyncrasies, such as always placing a glass upside down on the left side of the sink after you rinse it out. Kara noted that there was less orange juice than there should have been in the pitcher a split second before she noticed the glass right side up in the sink.

Her first thought was that Max had returned a day early, and the lead weights fell away from her heart. Even her legs felt bouncy again. Then the realization that Max never, ever would have rinsed out his glass and probably wouldn't even have remembered to return the juice to the refrigerator caught up with her excitement. Her blood chilled. Instinctively she whirled to look behind her and released a high-pitched gasp at the sight of Dwight Billings sprawled in the white wicker rocker fifteen feet away, his feet propped up on the coffee table.

He was dressed in a black nylon bathing suit skimpy enough to leave no doubt in Kara's mind that his body was as wiry as it had been when he was twenty-two. His dark hair was cut much shorter than it used to be, and he'd grown a mustache that gave his smile a sinister cast. But the biggest change she noticed was in his eyes. Or maybe the change was in her, she thought in panic. Maybe his eyes had always been that hard and cold and glittering with unpredictability.

He let her stand a minute in frozen silence before swinging his legs off the table and getting to his feet. As soon as he took the first step in her direction Kara forced words from her painfully dry throat.

"What . . . what do you want?"

Dwight made a clucking sound. "Is that any way to greet an old friend, Carolyn?"

Her split second of confusion was proof of how far behind she had left Carolyn Haggerty.

"An old and very close friend," he continued. "Especially one who's gone to as much trouble as I have to see you. It was a long swim from my friend's boat to your beach. I tried to be as discreet as possible so no one would try to toss me off the island for being an undesirable. That would be pretty ironic, wouldn't it, considering some of the fat cats they roll out the red carpet for around here?"

His smile was disconcertingly conspiratorial as he moved in close enough to lay his fingers on her cheek. They felt cold against her skin. Recoiling from his touch, Kara lifted both hands to keep him from coming any nearer.

Dwight chuckled softly. "You didn't use to push me away, Carolyn. Remember?"

"My name isn't Carolyn," she told him, willing herself to think logically even as dozens of alarming possibilities for his being there assaulted her concentration. "It's Kara

That and a lot of other things have changed since the last time we saw each other.''

"I'll say." He glanced around consideringly. "This place is a long way from a cellar in Portland, Maine, isn't it?"

She shuddered at the reference to one of the less appealing places where she and John had spent time on their long-ago trek through New England. "Yes, a very long way. This is my home now, Dwight, and I'd like to know how you managed to get in?"

"I broke the lock on the bedroom window," he replied without compunction. "I figured you wouldn't want me hanging around outside on your doorstep in case any of your fancy new friends happened by . . . like, for instance, your famous movie-star boyfriend."

It was very obvious that he was carefully monitoring her reactions, so Kara did her best to appear composed. "How do you know about Max?"

"Same way I knew how to find you. You take a great picture, Carolyn—I mean, Kara."

Her tenuous composure cracked wide open. "Picture? You don't mean . . ."

"The *Island Highlights*," Dwight supplied when she lapsed into horrified silence.

Swiftly he moved to retrieve from the table a plastic bag he must have carried ashore with him and extracted from it a copy of the small newspaper dated the day before. He shoved it at her, and Kara snatched at it with trembling fingers.

"You and old Max got front-page coverage," he taunted. "Good thing, too. Otherwise we might never have had this little impromptu reunion. Fancy that."

Kara stared at the photos of Max and her splashed across the paper's front page, hardly listening. So Wasserman had managed to publish pictures of them after all. Not his own certainly. Which one of Max's fans, wondered Kara, had been so quick to sell his or her film to Sam Wasserman? The lady in the flowered sundress? The parents of the little boy who had so solemnly gone about comparing his flexed muscle to that of his hero, Delta Brent?

"Of course, you weren't really smiling too convincingly in any of these shots," Dwight observed, glancing at the paper over her shoulder. "As a matter of fact, it looks to me like you were trying to hide behind your boyfriend in most of them. Any particular reason for that, Kara?"

Kara carefully refolded the paper and tossed it onto the table, determined not to let him see how thoroughly he had succeeded in rattling her. "None that I'm sure you don't already know about," she retorted. "Now, if you don't mind, you were only half right a minute ago. I don't want you hanging around *inside* my house, either."

"Afraid your new lover might walk in and find your old one here?"

"We were hardly lovers, Dwight," Kara parried, managing a tone of smug amusement. "But, yes, Max will be back any moment, and I'd find it...awkward trying to explain your being here."

"Is that so? Well, I'll bet you'd find it considerably more than awkward trying to explain to him why you changed your name and ran away from a murder investigation. Which is exactly what you're going to find yourself doing if you don't cooperate with me every step of the way."

"Sorry to disappoint you, Dwight, but it so happens I've already explained the whole thing to Max."

He didn't so much as blink with surprise. If he was suffering any of the stomach-twisting, sweaty-palmed tension she was, he was much better at hiding it. "Good. Then you should be well-practiced for when you tell your story to the feds."

Unbelievably, he started to walk out. No matter how badly she longed to be rid of him, Kara couldn't risk letting him leave with that threat hanging in the air. "Wait."

He stopped, turning back to her with a quizzical smirk.

Kara licked her lips nervously. "What did you mean when you said I'd have to cooperate with you every step of the way?"

"Just that I need your help securing a little information—information you are in a unique position to provide."

"Dwight, if you want to know where my brother is, I can't help you. I haven't seen him in years."

She held her head high as Dwight eyed her skeptically, determined not to give the slightest sign that she was lying. Of course, that had to be the reason he'd come here, to try to locate Jack. Why now? Kara lamented. Why, just when it was so important to her that Jack be amenable to straightening his life out—and when it looked as if he might be moving in that direction all on his own—did this sleazeball have to show up looking for him?

Then again, maybe it was precisely because Jack had dropped out of sight that Dwight was here. Maybe the two of them had been more closely associated through the years than she'd realized. And maybe Dwight and whoever else belonged to the loose-knit group of activists Jack was part of had decided they couldn't afford to let him just walk away. At that moment she was more afraid for Jack than she had ever been for herself.

"No, Kara, I didn't come here looking for information about your precious brother," Dwight announced finally. "I came here only to see you. You, my sweet, are the key to a very important project I've undertaken."

"What sort of project?"

His mouth twisted. "Ever read any James Bond novels?"

"No."

"Too bad. Because you're about to get a chance to live one."

She swallowed a gust of hysterical laughter, afraid it might provoke him. In the last couple of minutes his eyes had become unnaturally bright, his manner more agitated. It reminded her of that afternoon a long time ago, and of the sudden violence of which she knew Dwight was capable.

"I have no idea what you're talking about," she told him, "but believe me, I'm not involved in anything like that anymore. I never was, really. My being at the demonstration that day was all a mistake. And now I just manage a small club here and—"

"And pal around with Anne Hazard."

"But Anne's not involved in anything like this, either," she protested.

"But she is involved with a group of men who are planning some important changes for little old Diamond Cay."

She glanced at him in confusion. "You mean the architects working on the expansion plans for Westwind?"

"I mean the government architects working on something a whole lot more sinister than a few new hot tubs. What Hazard's planning to allow the government to build here is a tracking station to monitor the launching of test missiles. Of course, that's not what they'll call it, but that's sure as hell what it will be. One more step in the development of their suicidal star wars defense system."

"That's ridiculous!" Kara exclaimed. "Victor is dead set against development of any sort on the island. He didn't even want to build bicycle paths, for heaven's sake."

"Victor Hazard is a puppet," Dwight declared with an ugly sneer. "He'll make whatever concessions are necessary to protect his big tax breaks and his corporate write-offs. He's not about to bite the hand that's keeping him rich."

Kara shook her head, thinking of the legal risks Victor had taken for her sake and for Jack's. "No, you're wrong about Victor. And the idea of missiles and tracking stations . . ." She waved her hand in the air. "It's crazy."

"Maybe," Dwight conceded with deceptive mildness "In which case, by helping me you'll be doing nothing more dangerous than humoring a madman."

"Dwight, I'm not going to do anything to help you, period. I don't want to get involved in anything like that ever again."

"Fine. As long as you understand that I'll have to make a phone call letting our friends at the FBI know where they can find that dangerous fugitive Carolyn Haggerty. I'm sure they'll have questions about her dear brother John

too. But first," he drawled, coming toward her with a
nasty smile twitching about his lips, "first I'll have to make
you pay the price for not cooperating with me."

A wave of panic broke over Kara, a wave so strong it left
a brassy taste in her mouth and a sickening pressure in her
throat. She backed away from him until the kitchen wall
stopped her. He really was a madman, she thought wildly,
capable of anything.

"Of course, this isn't the way I want it to be," he told
her with mock regret. "What I want is for two old friends
to work together. You know, for old times' sake. You get
me the information I want, and then I walk out of your
nice, neat life just as discreetly as I walked in. For good
this time."

Kara took a deep breath, not believing him for a moment but deciding that her best hope might be to buy herself some time to think by agreeing to whatever he
suggested. Of course he was too cunning to be duped by
any sudden capitulation. She would have to appear to
brazen it out before agreeing.

"How do I know I can trust you?" she demanded.
"How do I know that you won't ask me for another favor
a week or a year from now?"

"I'll give you my word of honor."

Miraculously she managed not to laugh in his face.

As she pretended to think it over, he added, "Bear in
mind, Kara, that if you don't do it, I'll simply send someone here who will. That was the original plan. Seeing your
picture in that rag was simply a stroke of good fortune."

Send who? she wondered anxiously. Someone who was
bound to recognize Jack? She cleared her throat. "All
right, I'll do it. If I can, that is. Assuming you're right and
that those men are working for the government, they're
hardly going to answer questions from some woman they
don't even know."

"I don't want you to ask questions. I want you to *take*
me pictures for a change."

'Pictures of what?"

"Charts, documents, whatever you find that pertains to this project. I'm sure a woman as creative as you will manage to turn up what I need. Mostly I want to know when and exactly where they're planning to build the tracking station."

"Why?"

"So I can decide what my next move should be. Any monitoring of the skies around here is going to be a major obstacle to my...shipping business. Which is precisely what I suspect the feds intend."

Kara knew instantly what he was in the business of shipping. Everyone who lived in the Bahamas knew that running drugs by small planes capable of flying low enough to avoid traditional radar was common. Most people also knew that a portion of that drug-smuggling was done to bankroll terrorist groups around the world. She could imagine what havoc the installation of sophisticated tracking equipment on Diamond Cay would wreak on local drug-running operations.

With a pang of dread she again wondered how closely Jack was tied in with Dwight and his "business." Somehow she'd always imagined that her brother's was a noble brand of activism, if a slightly unpatriotic one. She pictured him helping to plant crops or to build one-room schools in poor, undeveloped Marxist countries. It had never occurred to her that he might be capable of anything as sordid as drug-smuggling, not to mention the violent terrorist acts it financed. One thing was certain, she couldn't afford to agonize over it now, not when she needed all her wits and more bravado than she possessed to deal with Dwight.

"I think I'd have more luck asking questions than trying to take pictures of top-secret charts and documents," she pointed out with seeming annoyance. "They're not about to leave that sort of thing lying around."

"Exactly. It's probably locked up safe and secure in Anne Hazard's private office. Which is why you're the perfect choice to handle this. You're in and out of there all the time."

"How do you know so much about me?"

He laughed. "I've asked around."

"That's a lot of asking, considering that you only saw my picture yesterday."

"When I want to know something, I don't waste any time. And I don't take no for an answer."

There was no mistaking the last for anything but a warning. "Well, I may be a friend of Anne's," snapped Kara, "but I'm definitely not in and out of her office all the time. At least not by myself. And certainly not lugging a camera."

"The camera won't be a problem. I told you this was your chance to play spy." From the plastic bag that had held the newspaper he pulled a miniature black camera that could easily be concealed in the palm of his hand. He tapped it on the edge of the counter. "Sturdy, waterproof. The latest in covert technology."

"How did you—" She broke off, disgust replacing her wide-eyed amazement as she considered how much technology the profits from just one drug shipment could probably buy. "So I have a camera. I still can't whip it out and ask Anne for permission to photograph her private files. I'd have to get in there alone to do that."

"Exactly."

"Exactly how?" she shot back.

"That, my sweet, is your problem." He tossed the plastic bag onto the table beside her and turned away, pausing at the door. "In that bag you'll find a telephone number and instructions on how to reach me. Check in within two days, Kara, or I'll make you wish you had."

Kara clutched the table for support as the door closed shut behind him with an inappropriate little click. It ought to have been a resounding slam, something violent enough to bring her whole world crashing around her, because that's exactly what was happening.

Shakily she pulled out a chair and lowered herself into it. Her legs felt rubbery, and her whole body trembled with the panic she had fought so hard to conceal while he was watching her. Feeding that panic was the realization that she hadn't solved her problem by stringing Dwight along, and she might even have made it worse. How enraged would he be when he discovered that she never had the slightest intention of cooperating with him? Clenching handfuls of her hair so tightly it hurt, Kara tried not to think about the answer to that question.

What a mess. She couldn't stand to contemplate the consequences of not helping him, and she hadn't the faintest idea of how to go about doing what she'd promised him she would do. Not that she would consider deceiving Anne and betraying her own country under any circumstances. Not even if she trusted Dwight to do as he said and stay out of her life permanently if she did. As far as she was concerned, Dwight Billings's word wasn't worth as much as a bag lady's wardrobe. She had no choice but to do what should have been done years ago—turn herself in to the FBI before Dwight stole even the last shred of dignity from her.

Her thoughts shifted to Max, and achingly Kara considered how, once the news stories about her broke, his reputation would be sullied by his mere association with her. And Jack. What would happen to Jack? Before Dwight's visit she had been willing to believe that any crimes her brother may have committed were not so horrendous that he would spend the rest of his life in prison. Now she wasn't sure of anything, except that the matter had been catapulted beyond her control. The outcome was inevitable. She only wished there were some way to present their case in the best possible light, some way to convince the authorities that they regretted their mistakes and would make any sacrifice, do anything in their power to make amends.

Kara's mind latched on to a wisp of an idea that she was almost afraid to allow to develop. She stood, crossing to the sink to get a drink of water. The sight of the glass Dwight had used made her anger flare, but it didn't push the idea from her mind. On the contrary, it strengthened it, giving it substance and direction, the way a bully's taunts might give substance and direction to a child's d sire to strike back. The idea became something more, a plan, the pieces sliding into place without any conscious effort on Kara's part. She bit her lip, her fingers tapping out a jittery beat on the countertop as she contemplated the end result of her inspiration.

It was outrageous, she told herself, too farfetched to even consider. It was crazy and dangerous and reckless. She knew firsthand how disastrous it could be to indulge reckless impulses. But just maybe this was what Max had been talking about when he told her that some things are worth going after even when the deck is stacked against you. The odds would definitely be against her in this. But if by some miracle it worked, it just might mean a happy ending for Jack as well as for her and Max. And it would mean that Dwight Billings would finally get what he deserved, too.

She'd been wrong to think she had no choice, Kara realized. She did. And this was once she was going to choose to live recklessly.

Chapter Twelve

Kara recognized the telephone number Dwight had given her as another island exchange. She wanted to call him as soon as possible to put her plan in motion, but instinctively she knew it was wiser to let him wait. All his talk about their being old friends aside, common sense told her Dwight didn't trust her any more than she trusted him. He would expect her to have second thoughts about this, and the last thing she wanted was to invite his suspicion by doing the unexpected.

From the moment she decided to challenge Dwight head on she devoted herself to playing to perfection her role in their little game of cat-and-mouse. Having no idea whether he already had someone on Diamond Cay monitoring her movements, she was careful not to be drawn into lengthy conversations with anyone, lest he think she was revealing his blackmail attempt. She was equally careful to appear as preoccupied and on edge as he would expect her to be.

That part was easy. Whether she was chatting with customers at the Shady Lady or alone in her office ostensibl going over the weekly order sheets, her mind was constantly whirring, fine-tuning each minute detail of the events that would soon begin to unfold. Timing was going to be crucial. Some aspects of her plan she was able to schedule down to the last second; others were in the hands of fate.

When she checked the club's schedule she discovered that by a stroke of luck Jack was scheduled to be off that night and on the following one. Vaguely she remembered his saying something about an overnight sailing expedition with a friend. At the time she'd been too preoccupied with missing Max to applaud anyone else's romantic escapades, but now she was thrilled. This was perfect. Not only did it mean she didn't have to worry about being seen with Jack, just in case she was being watched by someone who would recognize him, but also that he would be safely occupied behind the bar at the time she planned to meet with Dwight. Maybe at last fate was on her side.

Unfortunately, Max's schedule was more difficult to pinpoint than her brother's. He had phoned twice from L.A. to let her know that matters there were taking longer to resolve than anticipated. He told her how much he missed her, describing what he planned to do as soon as he got back in such erotic detail it made her blush.

Kara missed him, too. His leaving stole the color from her life and created holes in corners of it that she hadn't even been aware he had touched. But no matter how badly Kara longed to be with him, she prayed that his business would drag on until hers with Dwight had been resolved, one way or the other.

The day after Dwight's surprise visit she left for work early, busying herself at the club until she was certain that both Anne and Ben would have left the office for the day. Then, playing to the unseen audience that might or might not be watching, she borrowed a passkey from the unsuspecting cleaning woman hard at work in an office farther down the veranda and let herself into the reception area of the administrative offices. Of course the key wouldn't open the door to Anne's private office, and even if it had, it

certainly wouldn't unlock the file cabinets inside. That
didn't matter. Kara had no intention of taking any pictures of anything, only of creating the impression that she
had. She stood well back from the windows across from
Ben's desk, nervously lingering long enough to convince
anyone observing that she had done Dwight's bidding. On
her way out she kept one hand thrust deep in the pocket of
her jacket, as if holding the camera he'd given her.

Returning the key to the cleaning woman, she hurried
directly to the club, locking her own office door behind
her. Her palms were damp as she lifted the receiver from
the phone and carefully dialed Dwight's number.

"Hello."

The urge to hang up, to bail out while there was still
time, rose up inside Kara. Trembling, she reminded herself that this was her only shot at any hope of a future with
Max. She licked her lips as Dwight's voice curtly repeated, "Hello?"

"It's me," she said quietly. "I—I have what you want."

There was a brief silence. Kara could sense him deliber-
ating on the other end and bit back the impulse to reassure him that she was telling the truth. She had to
remember that if she really had pictures to turn over, she
would be operating from a position of strength, not uncertainty. Every word she said, even her tone of voice, had
to reflect that.

"So soon?" he asked finally.

"I want to get this over with as quickly as possible."

"You're sure you have what I need?"

"See for yourself. When can you come and get it?"

"I can't. I want you to bring it to me."

Kara's heart lurched. "Why can't we just meet at my
place the way we did the last time?"

"Because that's the way we did it the last time," he retorted cryptically.

Anxiously Kara considered how this would affect her
plans. She knew how cunning Dwight was. Why hadn't she
anticipated that he would throw her a curve? "All right,"

she conceded because she couldn't afford not to. "Where do you want me to bring it?"

"To my friend's boat. She's a thirty-foot sloop, the *Crazy Eye*. I'll drop anchor a couple of miles north of Diamond Cay, where we won't be seen from shore."

It was the worst, most risky location he could possibly have suggested. And it wasn't merely a suggestion. Kara knew that if she protested the terms he dictated, Dwight would become suspicious and everything would be ruined. She would just have to go along with it. Taking a wild chance, she announced, "I'll come out to the boat, but it has to be tonight."

"Sorry, I'm tied up tonight. Tomorrow night. Eight-thirty."

"I'm supposed to work tomorrow night," she protested, striving to sound irritated instead of relieved. Chalk one up for reverse psychology.

"Tough. And, Kara?"

"Yes?"

"Make sure you're alone."

"I will be. Believe me, I want this to go smoothly as much as you do," she assured him in a massive understatement. "But there's one more thing."

She held her breath, rehearsing the words of her demand yet again. Not only would it make her participation in this more believable, but also, if he agreed, it would provide her with additional evidence against him later.

"What's that?" he asked, his tone guarded.

"I want more than your word that you won't pull anything like this again. I want to be paid for my trouble, paid enough to leave here and start over somewhere where you'll never find me."

"You think there's that much money in the world?" he retorted, his chuckle affecting her like fingernails dragged along a chalkboard. "Never mind. How much did you have in mind?"

"Ten thousand dollars."

"All right."

He hadn't hesitated, which told Kara that either his drug dealing had rendered money no object or that he had no intention of ever letting her walk off the *Crazy Eye* alive. Lord, what was she getting herself into?

"I'll have your money waiting," she surfaced from her worrying to hear Dwight assuring her. "You make damn sure you've got what I'm paying for."

"I will. I mean, I do. I have it right here."

"And remember, come alone."

As soon as she heard the line go dead she dumped the receiver back in the cradle and dropped her head to her hands, her thoughts racing as wildly as her pulse. All right, his demand that they meet at sea changed things a little. Kara winced. All right, so it changed things a lot. But it didn't make them impossible. Sure, the risks were great, but so were the stakes. Straightening her spine, she opened her top drawer and took out the piece of paper on which she'd written the telephone number the operator had given her earlier. She was still breathing as heavily as if she'd run a marathon but determined to go on with the next step while the adrenaline was fresh in her system. With icy finger she again reached for the phone. It seemed forever until the island operator responded.

"Operator. May I help you?"

Kara cleared her throat. "Yes, I'd like to place a long distance call to Washington, D.C."

Slowly she repeated the number in front of her, then listened with mounting tension to the clicks and buzzes a some computer somewhere worked to link her with a place miles and light-years away. Would anyone even be there a this hour? she fretted. Finally she heard ringing. I sounded crisp and unfriendly, and so did the distant fe male voice that came on a moment later.

"Federal Bureau of Investigation."

"I need to talk with someone," blurted Kara, all he carefully formulated statements and requests fleeing he mind in a storm of trepidation. "I need to talk with some one about something that happened a long time ago."

"I'll put you through to Inspector Cassidy," the impersonal voice responded without missing a beat, as if fielding phone calls from frantic-sounding women was routine.

Maybe it was, thought Kara, grasping for confidence. Maybe fugitives called Inspector Cassidy every day with insane, off-the-wall ideas. Maybe he would welcome her proposal, and even go so far as to assure her that her brilliant insight and brave participation were so crucial to its success that he personally could guarantee her and Jack full immunity from prosecution.

Unfortunately, Inspector Vince Cassidy didn't turn out to be a miracle worker of that magnitude. But he did prove to be a man who was very easy to talk to, and during the next few hours Kara found herself doing a whole lot of talking. Sometimes he put her on hold while he checked out what she was telling him, other times they hung up and she waited nervously for him to get back to her. Always Kara sensed that he was willing to trust her and that she could in turn trust him.

"Don't cry," he ordered at one critical point in their discussion. "I'm not saying that you've got an easy road ahead, but I can tell you that I've helped people out of worse jams than this. If you're sure, absolutely sure, that you're up to handling your part in this crazy scheme, then I can promise you I'll get clearance on this end to back you up. And I promise I'll do everything in my power to help you and your brother afterward."

From that moment on Kara relinquished control of the plan to him. By the next afternoon they had gone over and over every last detail and contingency. Inspector Cassidy agreed with Kara that sending someone to meet personally with her on an island as small as Diamond Cay would only serve to alert anyone watching. He also took seriously her hunch that Dwight might have a well-placed government contact to have found out about the tracking station in the first place and assured her that besides himself, only his immediate superior and those field personnel directly involved in the action would know of their plans in advance.

Cassidy ended their final phone conversation with such a casual "See you in a while, Kara," it gave her a feeling of near normalcy that lingered for hours, helping her to survive the time until she was to meet Dwight without going berserk.

Late in the afternoon she contacted Don Medeiros, the man in charge of Westwind's fleet of boats, and arranged to borrow a small motorlaunch. She crossed her fingers as she lied about needing to pick it up that evening in order to get an early start the next day. She was ready with a line about how she planned to give scuba diving another try in case he asked what she wanted it for. He didn't ask. Kara chose to interpret that as another favorable omen.

Not until that evening when the hands on the clock behind the bar inched close to seven-thirty and Jack still hadn't shown up for work did the stress she had been living with for days threaten to erupt into hysteria. Maybe he wasn't going to show up, tonight or any other night. Maybe he had been lying about the sailing trip. Maybe in a few days she would get a letter from him saying that he'd left without telling her just so he wouldn't have to face the disappointment in her eyes.

Kara jabbed a long-stemmed rose into the final vase and wiped her hands on her jeans. She was definitely becoming paranoid. If there was one person in this world she could trust as much as she did Max, it was Jack. She'd even been trusting Jack longer. There had to be a good, perfectly ordinary reason why he was late getting back. Unfortunately, she wouldn't be able to wait around to hear it. Her superstitious craving to see him here safe and sound before she set out to meet Dwight would simply have to go unsatisfied. She was just about to ask the most experienced waitress working that night to handle bar duty until Jack arrived when he walked in.

"Where have you been?" she demanded as he ambled up to the bar looking relaxed and freshly sunburned and wonderful.

"Philandering," he retorted cheerfully.

"Very funny."

"Then why aren't you laughing?"

"Because you're late."

"Dock me."

"Maybe I will."

"Could I charm you out of it by saying that you look absolutely ravishing this evening?"

She followed his amused gaze as it touched on the faded jeans and bright yellow tank top she'd had on since early morning and laughed out loud for what felt like the first time in years. "Consider me charmed."

"You laughed. You actually laughed," observed Jack. "That must mean Max is back."

"No. Not yet."

"Soon, though?"

She nodded curtly, her smile frozen in place. "Soon."

"Good. It's about time you found a man who makes you smile." His expression grew solemn. "Kara, I did a lot of thinking out there on the boat, and there's something I need to talk over with you."

Kara's gaze strayed to the clock even before he'd finished speaking. Seven fifty-two. "Fine, Jack, but this isn't a good time for me. I have to run home and change before anyone walks in and sees me this way."

"Since when do you have to run home and change? You've got enough clothes in your office to dress the Rockettes."

She shrugged airily. "Since I have to take a shower. Do my nails. Water my cactus."

"And maybe check to see if Max is back?"

Why hadn't she thought of that? If Jack believed she was with Max, he wouldn't question how long she was gone. Flashing an enigmatic smile, she drawled, "Maybe. Will you hold the fort until I get back?"

"Sure." She turned to go as he placed one hand flat on the bar and swung himself over it. Grinning, he called after her, "Have a ball!"

Kara kept her pace sedate until she was safely out the door; then she dashed to the marina. The young man who led her to the boat set aside by Don was wearing a Los

Angeles Dodgers baseball cap. What were the odds of seeing that around here? Kara mused, a smile struggling to break through her tension as she thought of Max. Maybe she was grasping at straws, but it seemed there were little signs everywhere that this was going to work.

"Don said it's been a while since you handled one of these," the young man reported. "Think you need a quick refresher course?"

"No," Kara lied, climbing in. "I'm sure it's like riding a bicycle."

He grinned as he untied the rope and tossed it into the back of the boat. "Close. Just don't try pedaling backward when you want to stop."

Forcing a smile, she started the engine and held her breath until she'd successfully maneuvered past the several million dollars' worth of yachts ringing the harbor basin. Once safely in open water she headed due north, sticking close to the shore all the way to the beach behind her house. She wished now that she'd taken the canvas tote bag containing the camera with her earlier. She hadn't expected to be running this late and had decided it was safer to stop for it on the way out to meet Dwight than to risk piquing Jack's curiosity about what might be in the bag.

Leaving the boat securely anchored on the sand, she dashed to the house and grabbed the bag from her closet. Not sparing time to bother with locks, she tore back down the path and was only a few steps from the boat when arms as strong as steel cables closed around her from behind, forcing all the air from her lungs in a terrified scream that drowned out whatever her assailant was saying.

The agonizing realization that Dwight had outsmarted her paralyzed Kara's brain. Gut-level instincts took over. She was flailing wildly with her elbows and gearing up to scream again when she finally recognized the gravelly voice of the man struggling to pin her arms to her sides.

"Max," she moaned, sagging against him with relief.

"Of course it's me, baby. I'm sorry I scared you. I didn' mean to." Gently he turned her in his arms, pressing he close to his hard chest. His voice was gruff with self-recrimination. "God, I'm sorry. I meant to surprise you, not scare the hell out of you. I'm an idiot."

"No, no. It's me. I've been on edge all day."

"Why?"

"Same reason as when you left," she replied vaguely.

Max rubbed her back in slow, soothing circles. "I take it that means you haven't spoken to your brother yet?"

"No, not yet. I can't, Max. Not until I have everything straight in my own head."

"What's to get straight?" She could tell he was straining to conceal his impatience. "We love each other, and we want to be together. And that's not going to happen until we get your past straightened out. If that affects your brother, then he's just going to have to be man enough to deal with it."

"He is!" she snapped, her frayed nerves sabotaging her own patience. "You're not being fair to him."

"I'm willing to be fair. You won't even let me near him."

"I told you why. I want to talk with him myself first."

"Then do it."

"I need time, Max." Inside, her heart was pounding, ticking off each precious second she was squandering. She curbed the temptation to check her watch.

"I gave you time," insisted Max. "Four days' worth. I was going crazy there without you, but I forced myself to stay away, to give you the time you said you needed. Now I'm back, and we're still where we were when I left. You're still afraid to break the news to your brother. And worrying about it has got you so tense that you're still trembling just because I tried to surprise you."

"I'd hardly call sneaking up behind me and grabbing me on a deserted beach trying to surprise me."

"Well, that's all I intended. I didn't expect to see you until after work. When I heard the motor I came to check it out and saw you running back from the house. Why the boat?" he asked abruptly.

"What? Oh, I borrowed it to run some errands." Before he could ask for details she added, "Why didn't you stop by the club and let me know you were back?"

"Because the way I've been missing you, I knew we'd need lots of privacy and lots of time for this reunion."

His mouth swooped to claim hers in a kiss that was rough with pent-up desire. Kara's resistance was as instinctive as the melting sensation his kiss always caused inside her. The resistance was inspired by the knowledge that she had no time to waste, even on something she'd been craving for days. But it was a flimsy brand of resistance, almost doomed to failure. With Max it would always be that way. His lips were so soft, his tongue so hot and hard, thrusting into her with wild, unleashed hunger. With one strong hand he held her head still while the other swept low to fit her pelvis intimately to his. There, too, he was hot and hard, primed with passion. Kara forced herself to wrench away before things flared totally beyond her control.

"What's the matter?" Max demanded, his voice hoarse and bewildered.

"N—nothing." As subtly as possible she put more space between them. Frantically she searched for some way to get out of there in a hurry without adding to the anxiety she saw reflected in his eyes. "I just don't want us to get carried away. I mean, I've missed you so much. I want lots of time to be with you, not a few quick moments when all that's on my mind is the fact that I have to be getting to work soon."

"*All* that's on your mind?" he challenged. Then, with a reluctant sigh, he dropped his hands to his sides. "You're right. I want this night to be perfect. I've got champagne chilling and the best linguini and clam sauce you ever tasted for a late supper. A very late supper," he stressed, his gaze darkening.

"You made linguini in clam sauce?"

"Not exactly. I just sort of ordered it to go from my favorite restaurant and carried it back on the plane. I can heat it, though," he boasted.

"Sounds great. I'd love to have a late supper with you." She smiled tightly as she took a businesslike step toward the boat. Max's hand shot out to jerk her to a halt.

"I changed my mind," he drawled. "Now that I've got you here I want an early supper instead." His arms encircled her again, confirming that supper alone was not what he had in mind.

"How early?"

He nuzzled her throat, his hands stroking her back and hips as he spoke. "What time is it right now?"

"Max, I can't."

"Why not?"

"I told you, I have to work."

"Quit."

"That's not fair."

"Okay, call in sick."

"I just left there. Everyone knows I'm not sick."

"Then call in late. We'll have a quickie now and hours later."

"Max, stop it!"

Kara was horrified at how loud and angry the command sounded and by how forcefully her hands shoved at his shoulders, but at least it got him to stop. Jerking his head up, he stepped away. For a second his expression was cold, a replica of the angry and resentful one he'd worn the day she called a halt on the beach. Then abruptly his mouth stretched in a crooked, unmistakably sheepish grin. He kicked the sand with the toe of his sneaker and uttered something cheerfully vile that seemed to clear his head.

"You're right, I wasn't being fair. It's just that I've been missing you like hell. I want you so badly that it brings out all the most selfish, greedy parts of me. But that's okay, because you bring out the best in me, too."

"I've missed you every bit as much, Max," she countered miserably. "But this just isn't a good time. I really do have to go."

"All right. But first let me at least tell you my good news."

"Your old band loved your new songs?" Kara guessed, hoping to cut through his very transparent stalling tactics.

"They did, but this is something else. Something even better."

"I give up."

He grinned. "I called Connie while I was home. It took some talking to even begin to convince her I could be trusted, but she finally agreed to let the girls spend some time with me. Only this time, instead of dragging them through Disneyland and every other glitzy place I can think of, I've decided to bring them here. I want to be with them someplace where I'll have plenty of time to talk with them. And to listen."

Kara's eyes opened wide with shock. "Your daughters are here? Now?"

Max shook his head. "They'll be in school for another couple of months yet. I told Connie we'd talk again soon and make plans for early summer. I figured by then everything will have been straightened out with us."

"Yes," she agreed tersely. "By then everything should be straightened out. Max, I really have to go."

He followed close behind as she hurried to the boat. "Do you mind if I come along?" he asked without warning. "I promise I won't force the issue with Jack. If you want, I'll even sit at a table off in a corner somewhere, as far from the bar as I can get." He waited for her to respond, and when she didn't he added, "Kara, you trust me, don't you?"

"Of course I trust you. It's just that I'm not going straight to the club," she explained, her brain turning out the lies only a split second before her tongue delivered them. "I've been so preoccupied I forgot to get next week's order forms ready in time, which will mean lots of thirsty grumpy customers unless I deliver them to the distributor by tonight." She waved the tote bag she was clutching as if it contained the phantom order forms, then hastily slipped it under the front seat of the boat, out of sight.

"Where's the distributor?"

"They have a branch office on an island not far from here. That's why I borrowed the boat. It will only take me about an hour or so to drop the order off and make it back to the club."

"Then I'm definitely coming with you," Max announced. "It will be dark in an hour or so. There's no way I want you out in a boat alone after dark."

"That's silly," Kara retorted, trying not to sound alarmed. "I'm perfectly capable of handling this on my own."

"I'm sure you are. But one of the best things about being loved is that you don't always have to handle something on your own just because you're capable of it." He scrutinized her expression, frowning. "Is there some reason you don't want me along?"

"Of course not."

"Good. Then it's settled."

He waited until she had stepped into the boat and sat down, then leaned over to push it free of the sand.

"Max, wait!" Kara exclaimed before he had a chance to climb in beside her. "I meant to bring a sweatshirt along in case it's cold out on the water. I put it on the table while I looked for the order forms and must have walked out without it. Would you mind getting it for me?"

"Glad to. Just don't take off without me."

His smile was quick and unquestioning, his remark obviously made in jest. Kara hated herself for tricking him this way. She kept her hands clenched on the steering wheel until he was well out of sight, then started the engine.

Max was pushing open the door to Kara's house when he heard the engine catch. He paused, half-glancing over his shoulder, listening. Unbelievably, the smooth roar changed in texture, as if moving. His stomach knotted, accepting before his brain was able to the fact that it couldn't possibly be another boat pulling away instead of Kara's. Still not wanting to accept it, he hustled to a spot where a gap in the foliage provided a clear view of the ocean in both directions in time to see the small boat cresting the final breaker before hitting smooth water. All he could make out of Kara was her shirt, a defiant speck of yellow that blazed in the distance even after the wind and the surf had drowned out the sound of the boat's powerful engine.

In a rapid-fire metamorphosis Max went from confusion and disbelief to a white-hot anger that blotted out everything else. Anger was a sour taste at the back of his throat and a pounding, painful pressure in his chest and in his head. He didn't have to look to know there was no sweatshirt lying forgotten on Kara's kitchen table. It had been a lie. A trick. Born entirely of her desperation to get away from him. And he knew why. She was afraid, and she was handling her fear in the same old way, by running and hiding.

Remembering her violent reaction to seeing him here, it occurred to Max that she probably hadn't expected him to return at all. Life sure hadn't dealt her many reasons to believe that anyone would stick by her if they didn't have to. He knew all about her insecurities, and yet he was still furious with her for pulling a stunt like this. Furious and determined.

He'd been pulling back, biding his time, taking things slow with Kara right from the start. First because he hadn't wanted to press her to reveal any painful secrets; then, once she had, he hadn't wanted to rush her into making decisions that he knew had to be made. But no longer. Maybe he was selfish and spoiled and too used to getting what he wanted when he wanted it, but in this case he knew that what he wanted was best for Kara, too. He could see now that even if he gave her all the time he had left in the world, she would still be too soft to handle this matter on her own.

No matter how much she loved him, she loved her screwed up of a brother, too, and she would go on protecting him at the price of her own happiness unless someone put a stop to it. Someone like him. He might not be able to get his hands on Kara right this minute the way he longed to, but he knew where to find an even more appropriate target for the fury simmering inside him. Thrusting aside the

thought that he had promised Kara he wouldn't talk to
Jack behind her back, he stomped across the flower bed,
which had the misfortune to be growing between him and
the garage. If she didn't have any qualms about playing
deceptive little games, why should he?

The instant he walked into the Shady Lady Max's gaze
homed in on Jack, who was leaning across the bar to light
a cigarette for a lady. He wanted a smoke so bad he could
taste it, and that made him feel even meaner as he crossed
the room with the speed and accuracy of a torpedo approaching its target. As he drew close Jack glanced up and
smiled at him over the woman's shoulder.

"Hey, Max. Welcome back. Get you a beer?"

"Screw you."

Jack had already started moving to get a mug, and
Max's words brought him to a stunned halt. He swung
back to face him. "Do you have a problem?"

"Yeah. And I'm looking at it."

For a full minute they eyed each other across the bar in
a scenario so obviously and ridiculously macho that Max
would have found it amusing as hell if he weren't involved.

"Why don't you come on down here where we can talk
privately?" Jack suggested finally, indicating the far end
of the bar.

Max nodded.

"Want to change your mind about that beer?" asked
Jack when he joined Max a few minutes later after quickly
seeing to it that everyone else at the bar was taken care of.

"I don't want a beer," Max shot back, struggling to
keep in mind that grabbing the other man by the shirtfront and smashing his fist into his face wasn't going to
solve anything. "What I want is to know when you're
going to find the balls to stop hiding behind your sister?"

He had wanted to see shock appear on Jack's face, and
panic, and a little bit of guilt. But there was nothing. His
face was a blank mask. Maybe his eyes blinked a little
faster than ordinary, but Max wasn't even sure about that.

He simply stood there stroking his jaw in a slow, thoughtful way that made Max want to smash it all the more.

"Which sister is that?" he eventually got around to asking.

"Do you have one besides Kara?"

"Kara told you that she's my sister?"

"She told me everything, you bastard," Max growled. "So you can stop trying to protect your own ass for a change and help me save hers."

"And just how do you plan to do that?"

"By doing what you should have had the guts to do a long time ago—making her turn herself in to the police. It's the only chance she has for a normal life."

"With you?"

"That's right. That's what Kara wants, too. The only thing standing in her way is you."

"How do you figure that?"

"Because she's willing to take her chances with the law. And with good reason—she never did anything wrong. What she isn't willing to do is risk having them use her as bait to lure you in. Although why the hell she thinks you'd be that self-sacrificing for her sake is beyond me."

Jack seemed oblivious to Max's scorn. His expression was vaguely bewildered as he asked, "Did Kara actually tell you that? That she thought she'd been protecting me all this time?"

"That and a whole lot more. I know that your parents did a pretty good job of convincing her she wasn't important to start with, and she's had her share of refresher courses since then. The only scraps of attention she ever did get evidently came from you, although I'm a lot more suspicious of your motives than she would ever be. It's no wonder she's spent the past fourteen years of her life doing what she thought she had to do to hang on to the closest thing to family she's ever had. Sorry as it is."

Finally he had succeeded in producing a reaction in Jack, only Max wasn't sure exactly what that reaction was. Grabbing the towel tucked into his belt, Jack flung it across the bar, then raked his hair in frustration.

"What a mess," he muttered, staring at the ceiling.

"At least we agree on something," Max said coolly. "The question is, what are we going to do about it?"

"I'll take care of it."

"The hell you will. I'm not going to stand by and watch you make things worse. I happen to love your sister."

"So do I."

"I'd never have guessed. She's been a bundle of nerves for days now. Have you even bothered to ask her why?"

"I thought I knew why," snapped Jack. "I thought it was because you were gone. Look, this isn't going to get us anywhere. I need to talk with Kara myself. Where is she now?"

Max laughed harshly. "Good question. She's off somewhere dropping off order forms."

"Order forms for what?"

"This joint," Max returned impatiently. "I wanted to go with her, but she sent me running back to the house on a wild goose chase and then took off by herself in the boat. Maybe it's my fault for pressing her so hard that she just wanted to get away, but it's your fault for causing all this to begin with. I just hope nothing happens to her out there all alone, especially in the state she was in when she left."

"What are you talking about?"

Max hadn't even noticed the strange way Jack was looking at him. Now he did, and he suddenly felt cold, even though the club was crowded and warm. "I'm talking about Kara worrying about getting to some other island on time in order to drop off some damned forms."

"What island?"

"Don't you know? She said something about her distributor's branch office. You must have some—" He broke off at the way Jack was shaking his head. It felt as if someone were tightening wires around his chest.

"All the ordering for the club is done by computer," Jack explained in a distracted manner. "There are no forms, no branch offices."

"Then why would Kara tell me there were? Why would she take off by herself in a boat?" Max lashed out, his concern for her exploding into more anger directed at Jack.

"I'm not sure. And I pray that what I'm thinking isn't true. Give me a minute to—"

"Take all the time you want," Max interrupted, snapping the paralysis that had briefly kept him frozen in place and lunging off the bar stool. "I'm going to find her."

"Not without me, you're not."

Max whirled around in time to see Jack signal a waitress to take over for him at the bar. The urge to tell him that it was a little too late for him to start playing the concerned big brother burned his tongue.

"I know what you're thinking," Jack ground out, coming around the bar to stand shoulder to shoulder with him. "But you're wrong. At least give me a chance to try to explain it to you. Besides, we'll find her a lot faster if we work together. For Kara's sake," he pleaded in the face of Max's stony silence.

For Kara's sake. That had become tantamount to a golden rule in Max's life. He would give all that he had, make any sacrifice, for Kara's sake. So how could he refuse to let his anger and distaste for her brother get in the way of finding her?

He nodded curtly. "All right, but let's move. It's getting darker out there all the time."

Chapter Thirteen

Kara had little trouble locating the ship belonging to Dwight's friend. It was the only one in the vicinity with its anchor lowered. Breathing a sigh of relief that he had waited even though she was over thirty minutes late, she approached with much trepidation. From a distance the ship had been only a long, sleek silhouette against the darkening sky, but as she drew closer the details of its structure and trim came into sharp focus, and so did the risks of what she was about to undertake. Emblazoned below the name *Crazy Eye* on the ship's stern was precisely that, a rendering of a bloodshot eyeball that only a lunatic could have created. Looking at it sent shivers crawling along her spine.

Standing by the top rail watching her arrival was Dwight. He was flanked by two men she had never seen before, and Kara recalled with disgust how adamant he had been about her coming alone. Pulling alongside, she cut the engine and waited for one of his two cohorts to grab the rope she tossed him. He secured it around a metal hook on the deck, then lowered a short rope ladder. With fear like a ball of fire in her belly, Kara started to climb. She reminded herself with each stiff step that even though it looked and sounded and felt as if she were facing these three all alone, she wasn't.

Somewhere out there Inspector Cassidy's men were watching and waiting. They would give her enough time to complete her transaction with Dwight, then swoop in to apprehend him in the act. At the very least, Cassidy had assured her, the blackmail charges resulting from this would be enough to hold Dwight until the government had organized its evidence on a string of other charges into a rock-solid case against him.

Somehow she managed to make her way to the deck on rubbery legs, still holding on to the bag for dear life, only to discover that Dwight had disappeared. She turned to the man who had lowered the ladder and now stood by eyeing her speculatively. He was younger than Dwight, a burly man with curly red hair and a bushy beard the color of rusty metal. He didn't look very open to questions.

"I'm sorry I'm late," she stammered. "I was held—"

"This way," he said, cutting her off.

Hitching his head to indicate she should follow, he started toward the companionway door. Obediently Kara trotted along behind. She'd anticipated that Dwight wouldn't risk making the exchange in full view of anyone who happened to be passing by, but thinking about going below decks with him and actually descending the narrow companionway stairs were two different things. For all its obvious newness and immaculate condition, the ship itself gave her the creeps.

"Down there," the man ordered, stepping to the side of the open door at the top of the steps.

Kara hesitated, feeling as if she were being prodded to walk the plank instead of keeping an appointment she herself had arranged with a man she knew. A man she knew was capable of killing for no reason other than that the victim was an inconvenience, she reminded herself, in stinctively glancing at the horizon. Just how far away were Cassidy's men waiting?

"Let's go, lady," the bearded man urged. "We ain't got all night."

He lifted his hand to give her an impatient shove. As he did, the plaid shirt he was wearing unbuttoned over a grimy white T-shirt fell aside, and Kara saw the gun shoved into the waistband of his jeans. Immediately she started down the steps.

"About time," Dwight commented as she entered the small, windowless cabin at the foot of the stairs. He was sitting at a compact table against one wall, arms folded negligently behind his head. For effect, Kara was sure. Along the wall opposite the table were built-in appliances and a sink; directly in front of her was a door, which Kara assumed led to the sleeping quarters. It was closed.

"I'm sorry," she told him, speaking slowly in the hopes she wouldn't stutter nervously. "I ran into some problems at work and—"

"Where's the film?" he interrupted.

She lifted the bag. "In here."

"Well, let's have it."

Automatically she started to hand it over, then pulled back. "Where's the money?"

"In here." He tapped the top of the table, calling her attention to the drawers built into the base.

"I think I should see it."

"I think you should shut up and give me the film before I forget what old friends we are and take if off you. Would you like that, Kara?" he taunted when she continued to hesitate. "Would you like me to force you to give it up? Would you like me to wrestle you to the floor right here and now and make you do what I want? As I recall, you don't put up much of a struggle."

Heat flashed to her cheeks. Angry and embarrassed, she flung the bag onto the table. "Here. Take it."

His laughter was cool, insinuating. Removing from the bag the small camera with film still inside, he examined it closely. Kara was thankful she'd remembered to advance

the film, gleefully snapping a full roll of shots of magazine pages.

"You have what you wanted," she pointed out as a
triumphant grin twisted Dwight's thin lips. "Now give me
the money."

"Not so fast. My old man told me always to make sure
I get what I'm paying for." He stood up, sweeping his arm
toward the empty bench with exaggerated formality.
"Please, have a seat."

Panic started clawing at the inside of Kara's chest.
"Why?"

"Like I said, I want to be sure I'm getting what I bargained for."

"But how can you be sure until you—"

"Develop the film," he finished when she broke off in
stricken silence. Expertly he flipped the back of the camera open and dumped the tiny roll of film into his cupped
palm. The smile he shot her was perverted by the narrow
mustache stretching down both sides of his chin. "I must
have forgotten to mention that my friend is something of
a photography nut. He's even set up a darkroom here on
board. But don't worry, I work real fast. I'll have these
developed in no time, and you'll be on your way, ten
thousand dollars richer. That is, if what you claim is on
this film is really there."

Sweat beaded on Kara's upper lip while the inside of her
mouth and throat turned so dry that each word she spoke
felt like the slash of a razor blade. "I said I *thought* it was
the information you wanted. How could I be sure what
you were looking for? I don't know anything about any of
this. It was just a bunch of papers to me. I shot what I
thought—"

"Shh. Shh." Dwight's soothing tone urged her to silence. "There's no need to get all upset. In a few minutes
we'll know exactly what you're trying to sell me." His gaze
suddenly chilled. "Now sit. Or else I'll have to call Barry
down to keep you company. Barry would love that. He
doesn't ordinarily get to spend much time alone with a
woman," he added pointedly.

Kara quickly moved to the seat he'd vacated. "Do you have any idea how long this will take? I have to get back to work."

"What for? I thought you planned to take the money and run?"

"I do. I just—I just really don't like being here, and I want to get it over with."

"In that case, I'll hurry."

Kara could have kicked herself as he disappeared behind the closed door, still wearing that snide smile. The last thing she wanted was for him to rush and discover that she'd brought him two dozen photos of health-food recipes and diet suggestions before the police arrived. *If* they arrived. Sitting there all alone, there was no way she could avoid worrying about all the things that could possibly go wrong. Maybe they wouldn't find the boat. Or maybe signals got crossed somewhere along the line. A simple error in time or place could cost her her life.

After compiling a mental list of so many things that could go wrong that it seemed inevitable that one would, she started thinking about Max and was swept by a wave of sorrow so strong that tears stung the back of her eyelids. She thought of his smile and the power it had to light up her whole day. And she thought of how his smile could suddenly melt into that sensuous sulk that made her dizzy as his head slowly, slowly bent to hers. She thought of the feel of his mouth on hers, the taste of him, and of his hands, hard and loving on her body. God, why hadn't she let him make love to her tonight? Why couldn't that have been the last thing that passed between them instead of a lie? If for no other reason than to erase that, she had to come out of this alive.

Lifting her hands, she pressed the heels of them into her eye sockets until the tears subsided. Her situation was precarious enough without having to explain to Dwight or one of his henchmen why she was crying. Quietly she got to her feet and paced across the cramped cabin, then back again. Why didn't the police get here? Fear had pushed her to a point where she no longer cared if they succeeded in

catching Dwight. All she cared about was getting safely
back to Diamond Cay and to Max. If she thought she had
even a sliver of a chance of making it past the two mon-
sters standing guard above, she would make a run for it on
her own.

She continued pacing, her gaze skittering restlessly
around the cabin before snagging on the drawer beneath
the tabletop. Suddenly it seemed very important to know
if Dwight had brought the money along, intending to pay
her, or if... Not wanting to consider what it meant if he
hadn't brought the money, she bent to examine the drawer.
There was no handle, only a small circular lock on its face.
Kara hooked her fingertips under the wooden lip and
pulled, not the least bit surprised to discover the drawer
was locked. Dwight, as she'd told Inspector Cassidy, was
no fool.

Still taking pains to move quietly, she stepped to the
door and put her ear against it. She couldn't hear a sound.
Maybe Dwight had been bluffing about it being a darkroom, hoping to scare her into giving herself away if she
was lying. Had she? Or had she managed to convince him
that her anxiety was only due to the fact that she wanted
to get this over with? A sudden noise on the other side of
the door sent her scurrying back to her seat. She was no
sooner in it than the door opened and Dwight emerged,
carefully closing it behind him. His expression was un-
readable.

"You," he announced, "are amazing. Truly amazing."

What on earth did that mean? Was he still trying to bluff
a reaction out of her? Kara shifted uneasily. "I tried."

"Don't be so modest. You did more than try." He
sauntered over to stand beside her, so close Kara could
smell the chemicals he'd been using. It didn't smell as if he
was bluffing. Pulling a key from his pocket, he reached to
unlock the drawer in front of her. "And now it's time I
paid you off. Or vice versa."

Kara no longer expected the ten thousand dollars to be
there when he opened the drawer. But the sight of the knife
lying there, its blade a seven-inch flash of hammered steel,

was such a shock she gasped out loud, frantically jerking backward. Instantly Dwight's hand clamped around the back of her neck, holding her in place as he slowly lifted the knife and held it only inches away from her face.

"No matter how you look at it, Kara, one of us owes the other something. And I say it's you who owes me."

She was trembling so violently that her voice quavered. "I was afraid to tell you the truth—that I couldn't get into Anne's office, afraid you'd make me keep trying and I would eventually get caught. I tried, I really did. And then I thought—"

"Then," Dwight broke in, sliding the tip of the blade inside her shirt and pressing it sideways against the soft swell of her breast. It was deadly cold. "Then you thought, why should you worry about telling me the truth when you could get paid ten thousand dollars for a recipe for carrot cake. Right?"

"No, that wasn't it."

"No?" The knife traveled lower, pressed harder. Kara was afraid to look down. "Then why don't you tell me what you were trying to pull here tonight?"

"I . . . you . . . you're hurting me."

"Not nearly as much as I'm going to hurt you if you don't start talking."

"What difference does it make?" she cried. "You obviously know I don't have the information you want. What possible difference can anything I say make now?"

"Let's say it will make a difference in how I decide to extract payment for this double cross. Fast. Or slow. I want to hear you admit that you tried to cheat me out of ten thousand dollars. And that you thought you were smarter than I am, just the way your brother thought he was smarter than I was. But I showed him who had more guts, just the way I'm going to show you."

With a sudden, violent motion he jerked the knife free of her shirt, leaving a four-inch slash in it in the process. An oppressive wave of heat washed over Kara. She felt weak, as if she might ooze right off the seat onto the floor if she didn't grab on to something for support. Before she

could move or say a word, though, there was a loud crash
somewhere above. Dwight stiffened beside her, tightening
his hold so that his fingernails gouged the side of her neck.
The sudden pain cut through her wooziness so that she was
once again fully alert.

"Barry?" hollered Dwight. "Barry, what the hell is
going on up there?"

There was more noise over their heads, now unmistakably the sounds of a fight. Swearing viciously, Dwight
grabbed a handful of her hair and used it to drag her to the
bottom of the stairs. This time he pressed the knife to her
throat, causing a sharp, stinging sensation that told Kara
he'd pierced her flesh. She forced herself to stand absolutely still.

"Answer me, Barry!" he yelled. "I want to know what
the hell is going on up there."

Obviously Barry was too busy to respond. It had to be
Cassidy's men, Kara thought desperately. She was biting
her bottom lip so hard that she tasted blood. Any second
now they would overpower the two men on deck and come
searching for her. As if on cue the scuffling sounds moved
closer to the top of the stairs, and then legs appeared, long,
masculine legs. Kara's view of them was interrupted briefly
as Dwight yanked her head back, pulling her with him
across the cabin. He backed into a corner, positioning
himself behind her, the knife still an all too real threat at
her neck. By the time she refocused, the men were already
in the cabin, less than six feet away from her, and Kara
wondered for a moment if she was hallucinating.

Standing behind Barry and his sidekick, staring at the
knife in Dwight's hand with a look of stark outrage, was
Max. Jack had halted several feet away. Both of them were
holding guns aimed at the heads of Dwight's accomplices
who had entered with hands bound and faces battered.
Kara swung her gaze from Max's grim expression to her
brother's, for the moment too glad to see them to worry
about how their appearance was going to affect her
plan.

"Well, well, well," intoned Dwight, breaking the thick silence in the small room now packed with sweating bodies. "I couldn't have planned this better myself."

"Let her go, Billings," Max ordered through clenched teeth.

Dwight snorted, a sound of such raw amusement that Kara forgot the knife long enough to twist her head around to see his face. Far from looking threatened, he seemed to be thoroughly enjoying this unexpected turn of events. A grin twisted his lips, and his eyes were alive with that strange overbright glitter.

"Let her go?" he echoed mockingly. "Not a chance, Mr. Ellis. Or should I call you Mr. Bent when you're holding a gun?" Dwight laughed unhurriedly. "If you gentlemen are in the mood for playing a little game of chicken, I'm more than willing. But my sense of fair play demands I warn you that I care a whole lot less about seeing you blow those idiots' brains out than either of you do about watching me carve up this lady's pretty face."

Max went white beneath his tan, prompting another snicker from Dwight. Jack's reaction was less obvious, but Kara sensed that he, too, was very close to losing control.

"All right, Billings," Jack said, his tone level but tight, "it's clear you're holding the trump card this round. What is it you want?"

"You, for starters," retorted Dwight. "I should have guessed that you were behind this scheme of hers. Think you're really clever, don't you? Well, you're nothing, and it's time I'm going to prove that once and for all."

"Fine. As long as we agree that this is between the two of us, why don't we let everyone else leave and settle it ourselves, once and for all?"

Kara strained against Dwight's hold. "Jack, no. I'll—"

"Shut up."

The harsh command came at her from three directions at once. Her chin lifted in indignation. "I beg your pardon," she snapped, glaring at Max and Jack in turn.

"Not now, Kara," Max growled.

"Yes, now. I told you I could handle this, but oh, no, you two have to come plowing in here with guns drawn and make everything worse."

"I don't think it can get much worse than having a man hold a knife to your throat," Max countered.

The sardonic slant to his mouth was achingly familiar, touching a chord deep inside Kara that threatened to be her final undoing. She'd thought nothing could be more horrendous than wondering if Dwight was really going to kill her, but she was wrong. It was far more heart-wrenching to think of someone she loved being hurt because of her.

"This isn't a damn movie," she muttered. "Why couldn't you have just minded your own business?"

"You are my business," Max informed her tersely. "And as soon as this is over I'm going to make it crystal clear to you what I'll do if you ever pull a crazy, lamebrained stunt like this again."

With a completely spurious show of calm, Kara lifted her chin a defiant notch higher. "I'll have you know that until a few minutes ago I had the situation here completely under control."

Even Dwight stared at her. She didn't have to turn her head to know that he was looking at her the same way the other four men were, as if she'd taken total leave of her senses. If only Cassidy's men would come charging to the rescue now, proving how right she was.

"Well, I did," she insisted.

"This little lovers' spat is charming," Dwight interjected suddenly, "but I have other things planned for the evening. Both of you put your guns on the floor. Now," he barked when neither Jack nor Max made a move to comply. Not until he slowly twisted the knife against her neck did they both lower their guns. Their jaws were rigid as they bent and placed the weapons on the wooden floor at their feet.

"Now, you, Ellis, kick them over here to me. Nice and easy."

Max obeyed, but the look of barely leashed fury in his eyes was fearsome. The fact that he'd once told her didn't have any heroic instincts offscreen didn't stop Kara from worrying that he would do something dangerous if this didn't end soon.

"Good," Dwight drawled. "In a second I'll give you another chance to please me by untying my friends."

First, forcing her down with him, he leaned over and picked up one gun, jamming it into his waistband, then the other. At last he let the knife fall away from her neck. As he stretched to place it on the counter to his left, Kara noticed the blade was stained with blood, her blood, and a high-pitched whimper escaped her.

Max's raspy voice wrapped around her from across the room. "Don't worry, honey, it's going to be all right. I promise."

The nasty grin was back on Dwight's face. Just as he opened his mouth to make some acerbic comment on Max's concern for her, there was a muffled thud outside, and the boat lurched as if rammed.

"Billings," called a voice amplified by a bullhorn, "this is Inspector Cassidy of the FBI. We have your craft surrounded, Billings. You have no choice but to give yourself up."

Dwight's gaze moved around the room frantically. Uttering a string of obscenities, he edged over to the stairs, pulling Kara along by an arm twisted painfully behind her neck. Once there he hissed at Max and Jack to move to the other side of the cabin.

"You're wrong, Cassidy," he shouted up the stairs. "In fact, I have something much better than a choice. I have hostages, three of them. One's even a hotshot movie star. How much bad press do you think you guys will get if you force me to kill Max Ellis, huh, Inspector?"

There was a brief silence. Kara held her breath until her lungs ached. She could imagine the scene above as the FBI team hurriedly tried to figure out what had gone wrong, and when he finally spoke again Inspector Cassidy's voice was as smooth and unruffled as it had been on the telephone.

"Billings, believe me, no one out here wants to force you to kill anyone," he insisted. "We want everyone to leave that boat unharmed."

"Well, everyone's not going to leave this boat unharmed!" Dwight roared back. "In fact, I'm not leaving it at all. It's up to you who—"

His belligerent words exploded into a yelp of pain as Max's foot connected with his wrist. Kara had been so intent on the exchange between Dwight and Inspector Cassidy that she hadn't noticed Max stealthily inching to within striking distance. Obviously, neither had Dwight. Max's kick was forceful enough to send the gun flying across the room, discharging harmlessly at the ceiling and setting off a flurry of activity overhead. It sounded as if the entire U.S. Army had just landed on deck.

The cabin itself had exploded into action. Kara pressed her back to the wall as Max followed up on the kick by lunging at Dwight, knocking him to the floor and holding him there with a well-positioned knee. As Max was delivering a rapid-fire battery of blows to his face, Kara saw Dwight pull the second gun from his pants.

"Max, no, he has a gun!" she screamed at the same instant that Jack's foot came down hard on Dwight's wrist, breaking it, if the scream that ripped from Dwight was any indication.

Within seconds it was over. Heavily armed men piled into the cabin from above, those who couldn't fit jamming the stairwell. There were men dressed in dark business suits and in the familiar uniforms of the Bahamian police force. Kara surmised that the United States government wasn't taking any chances on Dwight getting off on a technicality of jurisdiction. With an unsmiling efficiency that Elliott Ness would have envied, one of the men wearing a suit jerked Dwight to his feet and handcuffed him roughly enough to draw a pained protest. Immediately Dwight started ranting about his rights and his lawyer and how he wanted to speak with whoever was in charge of this half-assed setup. Giddily Kara longed to tell him it was she. Then the calm that had been slowly

turning to her fizzled as she realized exactly what he
wanted to talk with someone about.

"I'm being framed," he insisted to the room at large.
"And I can prove it. Who do you think these people are,
anyway? Innocent tourists? Well, I'll tell you who they are,
and it's going to make this your lucky day. Commenda-
tions all around, boys, because this here is John Haggerty
and his sister, and there are arrest warrants for them that
are at least as old as mine. I can tell you all about Haggerty's involvement with drugs in this area. These guys will
bear me out, right?" He thrust his chin at Barry and the
man beside him, both of whom had stayed well out of the
recent fight.

"Sorry," Barry retorted with an icy glare at Dwight.
"Us idiots don't know nothing about any of this."

Dwight's eyes glittered like cartoon lasers. "Who needs
you?" he snapped, turning from them to the armed men
surrounding him. "I got enough to tell on my own. And
if you guys really make it worth my while, I'll talk about a
murder that happened a long time ago—a murder that
only I witnessed."

"No...no!" Kara shook her head wildly, feeling sick to
her stomach. "He's twisting everything around. He's
lying."

He had to be lying about Jack, she told herself, the same
way he was lying about witnessing a murder that he had
committed. From the corner of her eye she saw a police-
man block Max's attempt to reach her by slapping his ri-
fle across his chest.

She looked at him pleadingly. "Max, please, you have
to believe me. Please..."

She tore her gaze from his anguished face as if relin-
quishing a lifeline and anxiously scanned the sea of others, all stern and unsmiling. Which one was Cassidy? she
wondered. Would even he believe her now? Or would it
become a case of Dwight's glib word against her own? Her
eyes lit on a man who looked to be in his late fifties, his
gray hairline receding above a round face and a pair of pale
blue eyes richly framed by laugh lines. Kara knew he was

Inspector Cassidy even before he nodded, stepping forward.

"Relax, Kara," he said, his soft, authoritative tone restoring some order to her thoughts. "You've been through quite enough for the moment. This will all be straightened out later." Before she could argue that she wanted it all straightened out that very moment, he turned, glancing briefly at Max before addressing Jack.

"So you're John Haggerty?" he queried in a voice not nearly as easygoing as the one he'd used with Kara. Her fists clenched so tightly that her nails pricked her palms. "I've got quite a bit I'd like to discuss with you. You can take those other three away," he instructed over his shoulder.

Within minutes the room had cleared except for Jack, Max, the inspector and her. She heard the sounds of the three prisoners being transferred to another boat and of it pulling away. Finally Cassidy turned to Max.

"I think you should leave, too, Mr. Ellis," he said. "And you, Kara. This won't take too long. You can make yourself comfortable upstairs, and as soon as we're through I'll arrange for you to be escorted safely back to Diamond Cay."

Kara would have taken that promise as a very encouraging sign if he had included Jack in it. "Look, Inspector Cassidy," she began, but Jack interrupted.

"It's all right, Inspector," he said. "Max already knows about me, and it's time my sister did, too. Past time, actually." His rueful manner was as confusing to Kara as what he said. "I expect you've been in touch with the special operations office?" he asked Cassidy.

The older man nodded. "Finally. Late this afternoon. Until then we had gone on the assumption that what Kara told us was true, that both of you were wanted for your part in that demonstration fourteen years ago. The warrants are real."

"Of course," Jack said wearily. "They had to be. It had to look absolutely real for it to work."

"Oh, it all looks real, all right," confirmed Cassidy. He sounded almost impressed. "Why, if some sharp assistant over at special operations hadn't caught a whiff of what we were planning here and put two and two together, we would right this minute be hauling you off to a federal prison."

"You mean Kara knew about this ahead of time?" Jack asked in amazement.

Cassidy grinned. "Knew about it? Who do you think orchestrated it?"

"Well, I'll be a—" Jack shook his head, clearly stunned. "It looks like the government has got the wrong person on their payroll."

Kara, who herself had been listening to the exchange with no small amount of amazement and growing suspicion, couldn't stand it any longer. She looked from Inspector Cassidy's jovial expression to Max's very concerned one and finally to her brother, who for the first time since the start of this bizarre conversation was looking directly into her eyes.

"Would someone mind filling me in on what's going on here?" she inquired more politely than she felt like being.

There was a general shifting of gazes and shuffling of feet on the part of the three men in the room. Finally the inspector cleared his throat.

"I think I was wrong a minute ago, Mr. Ellis," he said, "I believe it's you and I who should be waiting aboveboard."

Max nodded and moved toward the stairs, his gaze on Kara every step of the way.

"Incidentally," Inspector Cassidy said to him, "I caught the tail end of your fight with Billings. Do all your own stunt work, do you?"

"No. Not until today," Max replied distractedly, still staring at Kara with undisguised love and solicitude. He bent his head to kiss the top of hers, squeezing her shoulders as he did. "I'll be right up on deck if you need me," he promised.

"This room suddenly has the feeling of a wake," Kara remarked once she and Jack were alone. "Why is that, Johnny?"

Her use of his old nickname was unconscious, but for some reason that Kara didn't quite understand, it felt appropriate. Just the sound of it seemed to saturate the air with a sense of loss.

"It shouldn't feel like a wake, Kara. We're not going to bury any more secrets. We're finally going to bring them out in the open."

"What secrets?" Her voice was a ragged whisper.

"Mine." He made a tortured sound as he threw his head back to stare at the ceiling, then finally looked back at her, his eyes filled with determination and regret. "Kara, a lot of things you've believed for a long time—that I've had to let you believe—aren't true. I'm no more of a fugitive from the law than you are, Kara. The truth is, you're an innocent victim, and I'm an agent for a small government security agency known as the Special Operations Task Force."

Kara gripped the edge of the counter for support. She couldn't have felt more shocked if he had told her he wasn't really her brother. In fact, in a way that's what it felt as if he had told her. If what he'd said was true, then for fourteen years—maybe longer, for all she knew—she had been loving and trusting and protecting a virtual stranger.

"Are you all right?" Jack asked, bolting to her side as she bent at the waist, wrapping her arms tightly around herself to ward off the chill already creeping into her bones. Kara couldn't even find words to tell him that no, she wasn't all right. That for the past four days she'd been in one long emotional nose dive, that she'd been threatened and bullied and blackmailed, and that now she had just had fourteen years of her life ripped out from under her.

"Here, sit down," he ordered, grasping her by the shoulders and leading her to the bench by the table. He settled himself across from her. "I know this is a shock a big one,'' he admitted on the heels of her harsh gust of laughter. "It's a story that's long and complicated, and it's going to take you a while to accept it, but at least give me a chance to explain.''

Kara didn't nod, didn't argue, just stared across the table at him. Fragments of scenes from their past pierced her thoughts: the day he'd left her alone in the bus station in New Hampshire, the time he'd shown up with a bullet wound in his shoulder claiming it was the result of some antirevolutionary backlash in Nicaragua, all the birthdays and Christmases they couldn't spend together because it was too risky. How could any of those things—and so many others—be explained?

"I guess the only place to start is the beginning,'' he said. "I was never in the Peace Corps. During my senior year in college I met with government recruiters and was tapped for a position in this special unit. The years you thought I spent in Africa I actually spent in a training school in the Midwest. My letters to you were always routed through Africa so the postmarks wouldn't give anything away.''

Kara didn't know why any of that should shock her after what she'd already heard, but it did. "But what about Victor?'' she demanded, finally finding her voice. "I thought you two met at some fund-raiser and—''

"No. I had never met Victor Hazard before I sent you to see him in Chicago. He was just a name given to me by my contact in Washington, a man they assured me was able and willing to provide you with protection when I was no longer sure I could. Victor and I did become friends through the years, and I'll always be grateful to him for helping you. But at the time all I knew about Victor Hazard was that he had strong government ties and that he had the facilities to get you safely out of circulation.''

"By that I assume you mean setting me up with a job on Diamond Cay?''

Jack nodded. "You're not the first, or last, person he's given sanctuary to.''

"But who... I mean, I never had any idea...''

"It wouldn't be very safe for anybody if you did. They had no idea who you were, either, or why you were there."

"And just why was I there? If I was an innocent victim like you just said, why have I had to spend the last fourteen years looking over my shoulder, wondering when someone was going to come and arrest me? And you."

Jack winced. "Believe me, honey, I never dreamed it would take me anywhere near fourteen years to catch up with Billings. But until I did, I was afraid to just let you walk around freely, afraid that he would decide he had to dispose of the one person who could nail him for killing that guard. You."

"But you told me the police might not even believe my version of what happened," she cried.

"I told you that right afterward only to get you to come with me without asking a bunch of questions. I couldn't stick around to take care of you. My only reason for being enrolled in graduate school in the first place was to penetrate the underground network in New England. Billings's screwing up that sit-in provided me with the perfect opportunity to do that. I figured they'd have him in custody soon enough, and I could send you back to school with a clear conscience." His mouth quirked mirthlessly "Then the months dragged on, with Billings always managing to stay one step out of reach."

"Not out of your reach!" exclaimed Kara. "At least twice that I remember we stayed in the same house with him overnight. If you're a—a special whatever agent, why didn't you arrest him?"

"I wasn't authorized to. It would have blown my cover and destroyed an investigation that took almost two years to set up."

"You weren't authorized to?" she echoed with bitter disbelief. "Were you authorized to destroy my life?"

The tendons in Jack's neck stood out in bold relief. "I wasn't convinced that's what I was doing. It's true that I never should have let you get involved with Billings or his crazy group to start with, but once you were involved, right up to your neck, I had to make a decision. Should I let you go back to living your life normally, hoping he wasn't crazy enough to kill you or that if he was, the local police were sharp enough not to let him? Or should I do what had to be done to make sure you were safe? I made what I thought was the right decision, and I've lived with that decision every day and night since then.''

"So have I. But at least you knew about it. When I think of how I worried about you, about what you were off doing..."

Jack's face was ravaged by pain. "I never knew. When Max told me that the main reason you wouldn't turn yourself in was because you were afraid of what might happen to me, I...I felt like the son of a bitch that I am.''

"I won't argue with that. For God's sake, Jack, how could you not know how much I worried about you?''

"I always knew you didn't like the idea of what I was involved in, or rather what you thought I was involved in, but I guess because I knew I could take care of myself, I assumed you knew it, too.''

"It looks as if neither one of us really knew the other.''

"Don't say that.''

"Why? Does the truth hurt? Face it, Jack. I have to. The fact is that the relationship that until a short while ago I thought was the most solid in my life, a relationship I was willing to give up the man I love to protect, was actually the biggest sham of all.''

"My love for you was never a sham. And there wasn't a day that went by when I didn't want to tell you the truth.''

"Then why didn't you?''

"At first I literally couldn't. I couldn't tell anyone, because—''

"You weren't authorized to?'' she interjected caustically.

"Exactly. That's the kind of job this is, Kara. Sometimes I don't like the orders, but I still have to follow them.''

"Well, I think your job sucks.''

"There was a time when I would have argued violently with that estimation. Now that this thing with Billings is finally over..." He shrugged. "That's another story. Like I said, I never expected it to go on this long. After a while, right around the time you finished school in Chicago, I thought about going to the director and insisting that I be allowed to tell you everything that related to you, to at least give you the opportunity to decide what you wanted to do from there."

"But obviously you didn't." It was an accusation, cold and uncompromising.

"No, I didn't. We had just gotten another lead on Billings, and I figured that this time we were bound to get him. And then Victor offered you the job here. You accepted it, and you seemed to have adjusted to your life."

"What choice did I have?"

"Maybe not the same choice as most people, but more than some. This isn't such a bad place, Kara, or a bad life. Millions of people would trade places with you in a second."

"No, it isn't a bad place. What did Max call it? Oh, yes, a gilded tropical cage. Catchy, huh? The real joke is that I never knew that the man I thought was my fellow captive was actually the one holding the key."

"You're wrong, Kara. In a way I've been as much a prisoner of all this as you. This has been my life, my whole life, for the past fourteen years. I've spent vacations and holidays tracking Billings. It hasn't only been my job, it's been my hobby, my obsession. No matter how many other cases I handled successfully, this was the only one I really cared about. Even when I was assigned to something totally different, I always made sure to read any report that might mention Billings, to follow every lead on every person that's ever been associated with him. I begged and threatened to get this assignment when we learned he was operating close to the Bahamas."

"So that's even your reason for coming to Diamond Cay," Kara mused, her small smile totally at odds with her distant tone and her shuttered expression. "Because of him, not me."

"Because of him *and* you," Jack insisted. "You have always been my biggest reason for wanting him caught. I expected to feel ecstatic when it finally happened, instead I feel...lost."

"Join the club."

"I did my best, Kara. You have to believe that. And you have to admit I was always checking on you. I did my best to see that you were happy. Maybe if you hadn't been, I would have handled things differently. I told myself that a new name wasn't such a big deal if it meant staying alive. Can you understand that at all?"

Kara stared at him incredulously, furious that he would dare to try to sum up everything that had happened to her as simply donning a new name. She got to her feet, leaning toward him with palms flat on the table.

"No, I can't understand it at all. I'll never understand t—any of it. And I will never, ever forgive you."

She sprinted up the stairs and hurled herself at Max, who stood waiting anxiously by the railing.

"Kara," he began tentatively as he gathered her close to his chest. He felt warm and solid. "Did Jack—"

"Yes. He told me everything. Now all I want to do is go home. Please," she beseeched, miraculously feeling as if he were already there.

Chapter Fourteen

Are you ready to talk about it now?'' Max inquired gently.

With an exasperated sigh Kara lifted her head off he beach towel spread next to his on the hot sand and ad justed her sunglasses. "Max, it's not a question of bein ready or not ready to talk about it. I simply don't hav anything to say. Really, it's not that big a deal."

"So you've told me."

"I wish you'd believe me."

"I wish I could, too."

She lay back down beside him, close enough for him t reach out and touch, yet isolated behind a wall of pain sh wouldn't even acknowledge. Rolling to his side, Ma propped his head on his hand and watched her pretend t bask in the noonday sun unconcerned. He was plent concerned.

"Did I tell you that Jack's plane is taking off from t airstrip at three?"

"Several times."

"And?"

"And nothing." Behind the dark lenses her eyes had fluttered open, but Max still couldn't see the expression in them clearly. "Max, I'm not going to discuss him, period."

"Him who? Jack? Your brother?"

"You know that's who I mean."

"Then say it, say *Jack*, say *my brother*."

"Jack. My brother. The former bartender at the Shady Lady and illustrious secret agent. I am not going to discuss any and all of the above, and if you are, I'm leaving."

Flipping her hair off her shoulders with a breezy toss of her head, she moved to make good on her threat.

Max grabbed her arm. "No, don't go. If you don't want to talk about Jack, we don't have to."

"Good. Because I definitely don't want to."

Max clenched his teeth as she settled herself back down and once more tipped her serene face up to the sun. How the hell was he supposed to keep from talking about the only thing that had been on his mind since last night?

Their escorted trip back to Diamond Cay from the boat hadn't been quite as prompt as Inspector Cassidy had initially suggested. It turned out there was the little matter of preliminary questioning to attend to first, a major matter actually, entailing several hours of detailed statement given aboard the government vessel that had carried Cassidy and his men to the scene. Jack had sat in as each of them was asked literally hundreds of questions about what had transpired, but for all the reaction Kara exhibited to his presence, he might have been any government clone. She wasn't tearful in responding to him, or accusatory, or the least bit resentful. She was cordial to the end, coolly promising to do whatever she could to assist with Bilges's prosecution. And that's what worried Max. She had more reason to collapse in self-pity than anyone he'd ever known. So why didn't she, damn it?

Last night, as now, she had dismissed his efforts to discuss the subject in a seemingly relaxed, somewhat amused,

manner. And then, like now, he hadn't bought it for a
minute. He had pulled her against him when they went to
bed, stroking her silky hair and waiting for the crying jag
he knew had to come sooner or later. In the sort of touchy-
feely sensitive language that didn't come easily to him, he
had struggled to assure her that although he loved and de-
sired her he understood that after all that had happened
that day, the time wasn't right for them to express their
love physically.

Kara had laughed. Then she had assured him in much
less sensitive style that she wanted him, physically and immediately, above her, below her, inside her. It was, she had
insisted, exactly the right time to celebrate life. A new one,
hers. They had made love until he was exhausted. Max
wouldn't go so far as to say his heart hadn't been in it, but
even in the mindless throes of release he'd been haunted by
the knowledge that everything wasn't all right. Afterward
he'd held Kara in his arms, wondering if her regular
breathing signified that she was asleep or her attempt to
make him think she was. He'd drifted off on the inspired
thought that she must have been running on pure adrenaline, that in the morning she would finally stop and face
the truth. Then together they would begin to deal with it.

It hadn't happened. He had woken first, his emotions in
turmoil, and gone downstairs to make coffee. Carrying his
cup back to the bedroom so Kara wouldn't wake up alone,
he had sat and watched her sleep, wishing she would never
have to confront anything that would eradicate that untroubled, innocent expression from her face. Unfortunately, she did have to. He might be able to wave the magic
wand of wealth and influence and see to it that her future
was as happy and fulfilled as humanly possible, but not
even he could do a damn thing to change her past. All he
could do was help her pick up the pieces and go on with her
life. And he couldn't even do that until she broke down
and talked to him. She had finally stirred beneath the pale
yellow sheet, then bolted fully awake, smiling a dazzling
smile and announcing that she was famished. Since the

the day had been one bouncy display of good cheer. And Max had had it.

Leaning closer to her towel, he lightly trailed his fingertips along her arm, caressing and at the same time ready to pin her there and force her to listen if he had to.

"Kara?"

"Mmm?"

"I know you don't want to discuss it—" his fingers curled over her upper arm as she heaved a sigh of disgust "—but I think we need to. At least I need to."

"Then go see a therapist. *I* don't need to discuss it. I've already settled the matter in my own mind. I'm at peace, maybe for the first time ever."

"Peace, my ass," he growled. "You haven't settled the matter; you've retreated from it. And it won't work, Kara. Believe me, I've tried solving my own problems that way."

"It's settled," she insisted, still without a trace of the raw emotion he longed to hear in her voice. "I thought it over very carefully—"

"When?" he interjected. "In the thirty seconds it took you to tear up the stairs into my arms?"

"Very carefully," she reiterated, ignoring his challenge, "and I've reached a decision. I don't ever want to see, or discuss, my brother John-Jack again. Now," she continued, at last lifting her sunglasses so Max could see her eyes. They sparkled like blue ice. "Want to hear about what I would like to see?"

His heart aching for her, he forced a smile to match the one she was flashing him. "Sure."

"You," Kara drawled, sliding her hand up his chest, burrowing through the thick cloud of black hair. "And lots of you. Interested?"

"Not if it means getting sunburn on my most delicate parts," he parried evasively. Max wasn't sure he could stand to hold her in her arms again and make love to the bright, beautiful facade she was determined to keep propped between them.

Laughing, she rose gracefully to her feet, her hand tugging at his. "No problem. I'll race you. My bed or yours?"

"Yours," he replied on impulse. There sure hadn't been anything in his to melt her resolve.

Unlike the day they had raced for the float, this time Max didn't let her win. He stayed a half step behind all the way up the path, brushing against her several times to let her know he could overtake her any time he chose, but not doing it until they reached the door of her house. Scooping her up in his arms he shouldered open the door to the excited lilt of her laughter and strode to her bedroom. All the way there he held her gaze captive, determined not to look away until he burned past the sparkle and the passion he feared was fueled by desperation, until she was forced to unlock the door to her heart and take him back inside. If Kara had turned her face away, he would have wrenched it back, but she didn't even try, and by the time he lowered her to the bed beneath him, she was no longer laughing.

He'd been wrong to think his concern for Kara would interfere with his passion. The two were inextricably linked, both part of his love for her. There was no way he could compartmentalize such a profound and overwhelming emotion as this love he felt, and no reason he should try. He had been trying to talk and reason away barriers that weren't rooted in reason. They had sprung from a part of Kara so deep inside her even she didn't know how to reach it. And neither had he until this moment. He was going to break down those barriers from the inside out until all she had left to cling to was the love he knew she felt for him. He wanted her helpless, defenseless, coming apart in the safety of his arms. Only then could she start putting herself back together.

They were both wearing only bathing suits, which his eager hands quickly dispensed with. He pulled away to look at her naked body the way he longed to look at her, slowly, taking ample time to watch his hands move on her silken skin and to chart her uncontrolled responses to his slightest touch. He saw the soft, pale tips of her breasts turn a deep shade of rose as they pebbled beneath his callused fingertips. He framed the fragile span of her rib caressed her belly lovingly, noting how it flattened when he moved lower as she sucked in a quick breath of anticipation.

He traced the curve of her hip with his open palm, found he sensitive hollows at the back of her knees and teased hem with his tongue. He kissed her ankles and toes, tasting sun-dried salt from the ocean, his head filled with the cent of flowers that clung to her always. Rising to his knees he parted her legs and looked at her there, too. Kara hifted uneasily until his gentle touch soothed her to stillness. Lying quietly, she permitted him to worship her with is eyes as intimately as he had with his hands and mouth. Max was well aware of the excitement simmering beneath er lassitude. Her skin seemed to sizzle when he stroked he inside of her thighs, coming close but never quite ouching that very softest spot on her whole body. He virled his fingers through the curls of dark hair that were lky even there, and she trembled. When he finally aimed her fully, touching her the way he'd learned eased her best, she cried out loud, her rush of passion ouring over him like liquid fire.

He slid on top of her, absorbing the spasms that rocked r body while he struggled to control the desire still hammering away at his. Sunlight splashed through the windows behind him, illuminating Kara's slow journey back him from someplace beyond ecstasy. But sunlight didn't the mood in the room, Max did, and it wasn't bright or hthearted. It was a mood deeper and darker than any rds they yet knew to say to each other. For long moments he lay still, skin to skin with her, letting her heart t slow. Perspiration misted her flushed face and tened in the shadowy space between her breasts. Max ced there with his tongue. Then he loved her again, and in, demanding from her more than she'd known she to give, before finally letting go of his steel restraint joining her in a final explosion of such pure pleasure as almost pain.

Determined not to give her enough recovery time to bar the gates against him, he had barely caught his breath when he rolled off her.

"I thought you'd gotten past the point where you reached for a cigarette afterward," Kara commented sleepily as he instinctively turned to check the small clock on the bedside table.

2:10. Not much time to work a miracle, Max thought.

"I wasn't reaching for a cigarette. I was just getting comfortable."

Unleashing a lazy smile, he brushed the tousled hair from her face. She purred, her eyes fluttering shut.

"Don't you dare go to sleep on me," he ordered in what he hoped was a playful manner. "Come here."

Quickly arranging the pillows so they were half sitting, he tugged her into the warm cove beneath his arm.

"I was already comfortable," Kara groused. She glanced up at his face. "Oh, no, don't tell me, you want me awake because you feel like talking. Max, how can you possibly want to talk now? Aren't you worn out?"

"No," he lied. "Actually, I feel exhilarated. You were right last night. I feel as if we're both celebrating a brand new life, a fresh start. And I know you're as eager for that as I am, Kara McFarland." He paused just as he was about to plant a kiss on the tip of her nose. "Or is it Carol? Haggerty now?" The suspicion that had already clouded her blue eyes grew thicker. He shrugged. "Never mind your name will soon be Ellis, and that will solve everything."

"Are you proposing?"

"I thought I already had. Days ago."

"Not really. Not formally."

"I think this is about as formal as I get. Are you accepting?"

"Yes. Oh, yes, Max. I love you."

"I love you, too, baby."

She hugged him tight, pressing her cheek against his chest. Max could actually feel tension start to leave his body. Part of him longed to let her drain every drop of and contentment she could from this moment, but a much bigger part of him knew that she deserved more happiness than this one moment could hold. What he was about to do was calculated and cruel, but it was necessary.

"I think we ought to get married before the music awards ceremony next week," he announced.

Kara stiffened. "What awards ceremony?"

"I'm not sure exactly—there's a dozen of them, you know. But I promised my manager I'd be at this one to present the award for best something or other. And now I won't have to worry about a date." He grinned crookedly. "I'll be going with my wife. My wife. I like the sound of that."

"Me, too," Kara echoed softly, grateful that Max didn't seem to notice that her smile was a little weak.

"Lou thinks it's important that I start to be seen in music circles again before the album is released," he continued. "Of course, once it's out there on the stands, I'll be tied up with personal appearances and talk shows. I should say *we'll* be tied up. I'll need you right there beside me, Kara, for everything." Lifting her hand, he planted a loving kiss in the palm and sealed it there. "Then there'll be the tour, naturally."

Absolutely nothing that he was saying sounded the least natural to Kara. It was as if he were talking about someone else's future. Not his. Certainly not hers. Was this the man she loved, the man she had thought she knew right down to the color of his underwear? How could she have conveniently forgotten the fact that Max had an entire life back in California that she couldn't even imagine? Probably because she'd been so preoccupied with other concerns of late. But she wasn't preoccupied now.

Grimly she brought into focus the truth, that Max lived in a house she'd never seen, ate in restaurants she'd never even heard of, entertained friends she'd never met. The enormity of all that she didn't know about his life started to unfolding inside her like the branches of a shade tree, gradually blocking out any trace of light or warmth.

"Tour?" she queried tightly.

"Always to back up a new album. Usually something insane like twenty-seven cities in twenty-seven days." He squeezed her shoulders. "But don't worry. There'll be plenty of interviews and special performances before that."

Kara opened her mouth to tell him that was all part of what she was worried about, when he continued.

"I have faith in you, baby. I know that by the time the tour rolls around you'll be an old hand at living out of a suitcase and dealing with crowds. You'll see. You just have to relax."

She wondered if she would ever relax again. Suddenly she felt disloyal for dreading the life Max described, as if she were letting him down somehow.

"What we do have to worry about is getting back to L.A. in time for you to find something to wear to that awards thing."

"I have plenty of things to wear," she returned distractedly.

Max's laughter harbored a trace of condescension Kara had never heard in it before. "Your clothes are great honey, but not exactly what you wear to one of these shows."

"Exactly what do you wear to one of these shows?"

He shrugged, apparently oblivious to the edge in her voice, not to mention the way he was making her feel panicked.

"Something that catches the light will probably show best on TV. Don't worry. You can ask around and find a designer you like and then put yourself in his hands." Kara started to lower her head to his shoulder, mulling over what it was going to be like to have someone else choose her clothes, when he added, "Your designer can probably even recommend someone who will be able to do something with your hair."

Unconsciously Kara smoothed her hair away from her face. "What's wrong with my hair as it is?"

"Nothing, nothing. I love your hair." As if to prove it, he scooped up a handful and rubbed it against his face.

"It's just not exactly the hairstyle people wear to one of hese shows?" she said.

This time she hadn't bothered to veil her irritation, and Max looked vaguely uncomfortable.

"Well, it's not exactly the height of fashion," he edged. "But, heck, that's not your fault. Once you're ack in the swing of things you'll probably find your tastes hange completely. Don't worry about it."

Kara swung her legs off the bed and moved to get a robe om her closet. If she had to lie there and listen to him tell er not to worry one more time, the knot of tension inside er was going to explode.

"Kara? Is something the matter?"

"No, not at all." Fastening her robe, she crossed to the esser and began to run a brush through her long—un-shionably long—hair. "I was just thinking," she began fhandedly, "maybe I shouldn't go back to L.A. with you ht away."

"Why not?"

"Oh, it just sounds as if you have a lot of commitments take care of. You won't want me hanging around, slow-you down."

"Hanging around is exactly where I want you." He got the bed and came to stand behind her. "And you won't w me down for long. Like I said, I have faith in you."

er fingers clenched around the wooden handle of the sh. "I know, but maybe I won't be as quick to adapt as a assume. The next few months will be very important our career. I don't want to distract you or do anything nterfere."

Months? You're talking about not coming with me for nths?"

It's not what I want," she insisted, forcing the words t the tightness in her chest. "But now that I think it r, we might have no choice but to wait awhile. I can lly leave Anne without anyone to manage the club."

Honey, the Hazards have enough money to lure the ager away from any club in the world," he said, laughing. "It's sweet of you to be thinking of Anne, but it's time you started thinking of me."

"I am." She lowered the brush. "Max, I'm not sure I'm ready for award shows and interviews—for any of it. I mean, I'm not used to crowds, or strangers. I'm..."

"Scared?" he offered, his voice a gentle rasp close to her ear.

"No!" Kara exclaimed too quickly, too loudly.

"Admit it, Kara," Max urged, forcing her to turn to him. "You're scared to death to face the new life that's waiting for you back in L.A. That's why you're making excuses about my career and the club. You're scared."

"All right, I admit it. I'm scared. Is there anything wrong with that?"

"No. It's natural to fear the unknown a little bit. But maybe there's something wrong with the way you handle that fear. Instead of trying to deal with it, your first reaction was to pull away from me."

Even as he said it Kara instinctively struggled to break free of his hold, but Max refused to let her go.

"Hold it, Kara. This is one time you're not going to run and hide—the way you've been hiding here for fourteen years."

She froze, stricken by his accusation. "What are you talking about?"

"I'm talking about the real reason you've stayed here these years."

"I told you—"

"I know what you told me, and I know that you believe that's true. But I also know that concern for your brother wasn't the only thing that kept you on this island."

"No, of course not," she agreed with a harsh, mirthless laugh. "I just happened to love living like a fugitive, wondering if any minute someone might knock on the door and arrest me—arrest me for something that everybody but me knew I wasn't even wanted for."

She tried to cover her face with her hands, but Max wouldn't permit her even that small bit of refuge.

"I know, baby, I know," he whispered soothingly. "I know that Jack or his superiors or maybe all of them played God with your life when they had no right to. Jack made a mistake. He admits that. Why can't you admit that at least part of the reason you never forced the issue with him or went to the authorities on your own was because it was easier to live here than to risk being hurt and making mistakes and failing out there in the real world?"

Kara stared at his feet, experiencing a crazy variety of déjà vu as his words were echoed by doubts and suspicions that had been inside her since her conversation with Anne a few days ago.

"Someone, somewhere along the way, shook the confidence right out of you. I'm going to put it all back," Max promised. "But first we have to lay the past to rest."

"You want me to forgive Jack," she said, sniffing back the tears she knew were inevitable.

"No. I want you to handle it however you think is right. Forgive him or scream at him or whack him over the head with a baseball bat—whatever pleases you pleases me. But don't hide from it. Jack is your brother, Kara, not some stranger you can walk away from and forget."

"I wanted to forget him," she sobbed.

His hands rested warmly on her shoulders. "I know. But you never will. You're not that kind of woman. Right or wrong, Jack did what he thought was best at the time. And in a way he's as much a victim in this as you are. But you don't have to go on being a victim. You don't have to spend the rest of your life punishing him, and ending up punishing yourself at the same time."

"I don't know what else to do." Her shoulders were shaking despite the steadying pressure of his hands.

"Just face up to it, Kara. And then let it go. I'll help."

The tears she had refused to cry the night before came in heated torrents that drenched Max's bare chest and dripped onto her bare feet. When they ended Kara's face felt hot and swollen, but her head was finally clear enough for her to know what she had to do, what she *wanted* to do.

Brushing the moisture from her cheeks with steady hands, she looked up at Max and smiled. "Do you think you can get me to the airstrip by three?"

Max drove at a speed far too fast for the island's narrow, winding road, and they managed to make it just as Jack was striding across the pavement to the waiting Cessna. Kara jumped from the car before it had completely stopped, shouting his name and knowing he couldn't possibly hear her over the roar of the plane's engine. She caught up with him about fifteen feet from the tip of the wing, grabbing the back of his shirt. He spun around with a look of surprise that deepened when he saw it was she who had stopped him. If there had been more time, or if they had been able to speak normally, Kara might have attempted to say some of the things she had rehearsed driving over. Instead, with a broken cry she threw herself into his arms, arms that opened wide the instant she leaned toward him.

"Oh, Johnny, I do understand!" she cried, moving back enough for him to read her lips even if he couldn't hear her perfectly. "And I forgive you. And I thank you."

"Thank me?" His eyes opened in amazement above a broad grin.

Kara nodded. "For Max. If you hadn't messed up my whole life the way you did, I wouldn't have been living here, and where else would I have ever met someone like him?"

"Where else indeed?" Jack countered, then threw his head back and roared. "Who'd have guessed we'd come out of this one with you owing me— Okay, okay," he quickly amended, catching her indignant look. "Let's say we call it even."

Laughing, Kara shook her head. "Let's say we discuss it further...at the wedding," she added impulsively.

Jack's brows lifted. "Wedding?"

She felt Max come up behind her.

"Ours," he said before she could think of words to tell Jack how absolutely perfect her life was going to be from that moment on.

"I can't say I'm the least bit surprised," Jack shouted over the noise. "Or sorry."

"Does that mean you'll come, no matter where you happen to be at the time?" she demanded.

"He has to come," Max interjected. "He's my best man."

Kara craned her neck to look up at him. "You didn't tell me that."

"That's okay," Jack added. "He didn't tell me, either. But I'd be honored to be the best man at your wedding. Just tell me where and when." He motioned to the pilot to wait one more minute. "I'll call you as soon as I have a number where I can be reached. I'll be in Washington for a while, tying up loose ends on this case. Then I have some decisions of my own to make about the future." He grinned. "I hear they may be looking for a manager at the Shady Lady. I just might apply."

"I haven't even quit yet," protested Kara.

"Maybe we could share it."

"Each take six months a year?"

"We'll talk about it at the wedding," Jack said, laughing and bending to kiss her quickly on the cheek. Then he was gone.

She and Max stood arm in arm, watching until the plane disappeared in the clear blue distance, neither one saying a word.

"What are you thinking about?" he asked her finally.

Kara looked up at him, smiling quickly to ease the uncertainty she'd detected in his deep voice. "I was thinking about another time Jack and I said goodbye. It was a long time ago, in a bus station a long way from here. And I was thinking that while I might change some of the things that have happened since then, I wouldn't change where I ended up."

Max closed his eyes and wrapped his arms around her, and Kara knew he understood exactly the way she felt, and that he always would.

"Come on," he said, steering her toward the car. "Now I'm ready to sleep."

"First we have to talk."

"About what?"

"That awards show."

"Oh, that. We can forget about that."

"But aren't you supposed to present an award?"

"I lied. I wouldn't even attend one of those things to pick up an award."

"What about the talk shows? The tour? My hair?"

"Anyone who ever touches one beautiful hair on your head will answer to me."

"You tricked me!" Kara wailed.

"Clever of me, huh?"

Coming to a sudden halt, she glared at him in exasperation. "Why do I love you anyway?"

"Beats me. I only know why I love you. Because you're beautiful and sensitive and intelligent. And mostly because you fell in love with *me*, not with a picture in a magazine or some celluloid fantasy."

"Why not? I saw you kick that gun out of Dwight's hand. Delta Bent doesn't have anything on my man."

"Actually, he does," Max admitted ruefully.

"Like what?"

"That guy has done some pretty amazing things with the women in his movies. Once he took this rope and—" He broke off, a not-so-subtle invitation sparkling in his eyes. "I could show you, if you like."

Kara's laugh was sultry. "I think I'd like that very much."

"Then what are we waiting for?"

"Nothing," she murmured, smiling as his arm came around her and they moved together toward the car. "Nothing at all."

It was true. She wasn't waiting for a thing. She and Max already had it all.

* * * * *

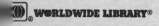

ATTRACTIVE, SPACE SAVING BOOK RACK

Display your most prized novels on this handsome and sturdy book rack. The hand-rubbed walnut finish will blend into your library decor with quiet elegance, providing a practical organizer for your favorite hard-or soft-covered books.

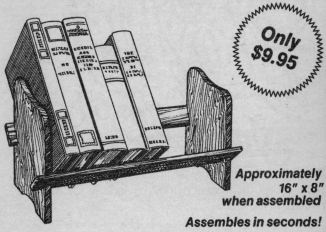

Only $9.95

Approximately 16" x 8" when assembled

Assembles in seconds!

To order, rush your name, address and zip code, along with a check or money order for $10.70* ($9.95 plus 75¢ postage and handling) payable to *Silhouette Books.*

Silhouette Books
Book Rack Offer
901 Fuhrmann Blvd.
P.O. Box 1396
Buffalo, NY 14269-1396

Offer not available in Canada.

BKR-2A

*New York and Iowa residents add appropriate sales tax.

Silhouette Romance™
Legendary Lovers Trilogy

BY DEBBIE MACOMBER....

ONCE UPON A TIME, in a land not so far away, there lived a girl, Debbie Macomber, who grew up dreaming of castles, white knights and princes on fiery steeds. Her family was an ordinary one with a mother and father and one wicked brother, who sold copies of her diary to all the boys in her junior high class.

One day, when Debbie was only nineteen, a handsome electrician drove by in a shiny black convertible. Now Debbie knew a prince when she saw one, and before long they lived in a two-bedroom cottage surrounded by a white picket fence.

As often happens when a damsel fair meets her prince charming, children followed, and soon the two-bedroom cottage became a four-bedroom castle. The kingdom flourished and prospered, and between soccer games and car pools, ballet classes and clarinet lessons, Debbie thought about love and enchantment and the magic of romance.

One day Debbie said, "What this country needs is a good fairy tale." She remembered how well her diary had sold and she dreamed again of castles, white knights and princes on fiery steeds. And so the stories of Cinderella, Beauty and the Beast, and Snow White were reborn....

Look for Debbie Macomber's *Legendary Lovers* trilogy from Silhouette Romance: *Cindy and the Prince* (January, 1988); *Some Kind of Wonderful* (March, 1988); *Almost Paradise* (May, 1988). Don't miss them!

SRT-

SECRETS SPORTS PSYCHOLOGY REVEALED

PROVEN TECHNIQUES TO ELEVATE YOUR PERFORMANCE

RICK WOLFF

Skyhorse Publishing

Skyhorse Publishing books may be purchased in bulk at special discounts for sales promotion, corporate gifts, fund-raising, or educational purposes. Special editions can also be created to specifications. For details, contact the Special Sales Department, Skyhorse Publishing, 307 West 36th Street, 11th Floor, New York, NY 10018 or info@skyhorsepublishing.com.

Skyhorse® and Skyhorse Publishing® are registered trademarks of Skyhorse Publishing, Inc.®, a Delaware corporation.

Visit our website at www.skyhorsepublishing.com.

10 9 8 7 6 5 4 3 2 1

Library of Congress Cataloging-in-Publication Data is available on file.

Cover design by Tom Lau
Cover illustration: iStockphoto

Print ISBN: 978-1-5107-1637-7
Ebook ISBN: 978-1-5107-1638-4

Printed in the United States of America

"So what are you going to do about it?"

—Harvey Dorfman, when confronting a struggling athlete

"We in baseball face a daunting task of trying to discern which player has that little 'extra' that will propel him to the major-league level ahead of others of the same skill sets. There are many aspiring athletes out there who want nothing more than to ascend to that next stratum. Rick Wolff in his new book can help you achieve that goal with his use of mental cue cards, muscle memory and visualization techniques to augment your physical skills. He breaks down problem areas—believing in oneself, dealing with nervousness, and working through adversity and turns them into positives. Any coach or aspiring player needs to read this book to learn the secrets of being ahead of the competition before the game even begins. If you're interested in elevating your game and leaving behind some of those stumbling blocks of the past, then this book can only expedite the accomplishment of your goals. Physical ability takes you so far, but the mental and psychological sides of your persona shape your destiny. Read it and you'll be ahead of the competition."

—JOE McILVAINE, Senior Advisor, Baltimore Orioles

"The difference between success and failure between the lines is in your head—remember, most hitters enshrined in Cooperstown failed in 7 of every 10 at-bats in their Hall-of-Fame careers. Rick ventured early into the world of sports psychology, and his approach to performance has helped athletes in all sports achieve from the little to the big leagues. This is a valuable read for athletes and coaches alike."

—GEORGE C. PAPPAS, International and Minor League Operations, Tampa Bay Rays, and author of *A Tribe Reborn: How the Cleveland Indians of the '90s Went from Cellar Dwellers to Playoff Contenders*

CONTENTS